Helen Palmer is a writer from Blackpool. She is the author of *Deleuze and Futurism: A Manifesto for Nonsense* (Bloomsbury, 2014) and *Queer Defamiliarisation: Writing, Mattering, Making Strange* (Edinburgh University Press, 2020). She is a 2023 Interdisciplinary Resident at the Oak Spring Garden Foundation, Virginia, USA. She currently lives in Vienna. *Pleasure Beach* is her first novel.

Pleasure Beach

Helen Palmer

Pleasure Beach

Chapter 1

VOICE	Olga, Rachel, Treesa
SCENE	The Roads
HOUR	8 a.m., 16 June 1999
PLEASURE BEACH RIDE	Alpine Rallye
SUBSTANCE	Chips, Cigarettes
ORGAN	Kidneys
SYMBOL	Triangle
COLOUR	Lichen
FORMULA	P = *3a*
ART / TECHNIC	Remembering, Forgetting
HORMONE	Antidiuretic hormone
HOMERIC TITLE	Telemachus

Olga

Sea is to sky as sigh is to sea. See is to sigh as sky is to sea. And what a sea, what a scene, as if seen from above, seen from above and not from inside these eyeholes. But the cider inside her inside these eyeholes we sadly now are stuck. Head hurts. Brightness hurts. Noise hurts. The wind is nice though. Carefully, now, weaving one's weary way around pavement crawlers, morning drunks and druggies, stepping over windwhipped dervishing plastic bags and scrunched-up chippy paper, splats of sick, upended boxes of unfinished doner kebab and chips. Seagulls squawk and circle above. Take me away, O monstrous inhuman weirdos, and drop me in the cold grey sea/sigh/sea?

Please?

One gull perching on the railing stares directly at us out of its immovable lichen-coloured dinosaur egg eye. Ei, aye, bataille, dabei. The Eye. Unblinking, unflinching. I know what you did last night, says the Eye. I saw it all because I'm prehistoric, see. It sees all. Seas all. All seaing all knowing.

Squawk.

Some early boyracers are beeping from the wheel of a souped-up red Renault, driving comedy-slow along the prom road. The bass from the subwoofer drills its way directly into the centre of our shrivelled brain. *Drive boy, dive boy / Dirty numb angel boy*. Blissed-out echoes, pools of euphoria, smacked-out messianic Trainspotting hands-aloft sweating. Inside the sound. *She was a lipstick boy / She was a beautiful boy*. Four lads, all strapped in with red racing harnesses, mega kinky in another possible world, hooting and laughing, making wanking motions.

–Give us a nosh, love. Blowjob for breakfast?

The driver is leaning out of the window as they pass. Flash of gingery shaved head and a pair of sticky-out ears. Red face and pink eyes. A comforting smell of weed and KFC wafts from the open window. All four lads in the car seem to be making identical blowjob gestures with hand and mouth. They're almost perfectly in sync. Like the boy band. Ha. Amusing how much they would hate that comparison. So bellow your lungs out at the receding Renault, words thrown right back at you by the wind. To be drenched in your own words. Like sea spray. Or pissing in the breeze.

–State of you lot. Go fuck yourselves! Go home and have a wank!

Fuckinell what cocktail of stuff was consumed last night? Hands feel like wonky starfish. Can't hold things properly. Nothing for it now but to flick the remainder of our last delicious Richmond Menthol in the direction of the receding sounds of the *fart-vroom* of the double exhaust and the *fart-hiss* of the dump valve, fiddle in our stupidly tiny pink PVC handbag for the work keys and gaze reluctantly at the frazzled figure reflected in the glass. How should I love thee? Let me count the ways. Plump and pockmarked, pale of face, wild and dark of hair, woven with one strand of itself into a knot on the top of the head, and crinkles of days-old mascara in the lines under the blackpools of the eyes, some of which two forefingers had rubbed away in a ten-second attempt to make oneself presentable after waking up in Lee Dunton's bed on Topping Street some thirty minutes since. A black shirt, waitressing standard, too small with its buttons almost bursting, encases one's upper half for the third day in a row, heavily infused with a triad of odours: chip shop grease, stale sweat and sweet perfume. Quiddity by Chipie.

Quiddity. Comes from a Latin word. *Quidditas*. And just as scents unfurl to open dusty chests of memories unbidden, so this ancient word is the creaking hinge of a door that opens up a portal to Last Night. Quidditas. Some kind of talisman. No idea what it means. But the word is a like a diamond. It shines in other languages.

She knew what it meant. She. Her. Look, she's standing at the portal to Last Night, beckoning. Gatekeeper to everything from Last Night, striped tigerish girl with lamplights for eyes, gleaming. But we cannot go there right now. Gleaming in the present, in the disappointment of the door's reflection, that insolent stripe of white stomach flesh. Gleaming between the waistband of the too-tight trousers and the bottom of the too-tight shirt. Visible whenever we stretch in any direction. Eyesore. Spray on more Chipie. A haze, surrounding us.

Armour, that is.

Once inside, the soothing repetition of the morning takes over: don stained black pinny, stuff hair into holey hairnet, roll up sleeves and start filling up the salts and vinegars. The music begins as soon as the lights are switched on. 'I'd Do Anything for Love (But I Won't Do That)'. Panpipe arrangements of Meat Loaf's greatest hits has been in the CD player for eleven months. Freshly sprayed and wiped down with sweet pink DIO fluid, nectar of the gods of hospitality, the place mats and coasters slide softly and greasily back onto the black wooden tables. Rising up, the same warm scent emanating from the damp cork of their undersides. The tang of vinegar battling with the soft beige odour of stale grease. Everything in order, clean-ish, ready.

The sound of footsteps. Andy, tramping in from the chipping shed. Today he is wearing Merrell sports sandals over white Fila socks pulled halfway up his calves. Stretched over his thighs, faded Mr Motivator cycling shorts with pineapples and palm trees on them. Stretched over his paunch, a tie-dye vest that says FAT WILLY'S SURF SHACK. The hairs on his legs stand out about an inch off the skin. They add fuzz to the edges of his shadow when he stands outside in the sun. Nestled in the fuzz of his chest, a medallion. Andy's glasses are the kind that react to the light outside, but the reacting element seems to be broken because they are always just a bit dark.

–Tie this pinny on for me, will you.

So leave the tray of salts and vinegars and gingerly, reluctantly tie the stained apron loosely round Andy's middle.

Andy and Scott would have been in for hours. Chipping potatoes and baking bread and pies. They hadn't laughed at the Chipie joke last night. Hadn't even got it. Or maybe they hadn't heard? It was witty but no one had laughed. Chipie and chippy. Of *course* they sound the same if you're from round here. *Homophonous*, you could say, if you were clever and went to sixth form and did your exams and moved away and went to university. *Chipie*. It's a fucking French brand. Sheepy. Shippy. Schippee. She-Pee. But of course everyone says it like it's 'tch', like 't'Chipie', the same way everyone round here says the 'ch' in fucking Michigan where our brother lives now. MITCHigan.

Let's all go t'fucking t'Chippy.

The Quiddity perfume, having just been reapplied and stowed in the coat cupboard, was the first item to have been purchased from the Duty Free shop in the Houndshill shopping centre that actually smelled the way it was supposed to smell, had really been purchased for seductive means, and was designed to be sprayed daily liberally and directly onto the brassiere in order for the scent to radiate continually outwards from the breasts. But the shirt and knackered self it encases always smell like chippy not Chipie no matter how many times we go through the wash.

Rachel

This is how it goes. Step carefully on every sleeper of the abandoned railway line, running through Poulton-le-Fylde station heading north towards Fleetwood. We are heading back towards danger. But what is we? A disembodied inventory of viscera maligned. Every part a Cheshire Cat frown. How then should we categorise thee. Let me count the ways.

A traumatised gut, the seat of emotional activity, mistrusted, misused and quarantined. A liver straining to process a high volume of intoxicants. Kidneys in need of hydration. Stabbing pains towards the lower back. A pair of staring eyes with swollen pupils and a forehead scored with lines like a musical stave. A tired, dried-out washing machine brain. Lines of poetry and songs flitting constantly across a sickening internal microfiche screen. Thin wrists and forearms patterned with a network of scratches and cuts from assorted stationery implements: compass, broken pen lid, snapped ruler. Long straight dark blonde hair. Eyeliner, smudged. Green hoodie, dubious skater brand with a bright orange cartoon impish devil on the front, purchased from the ground floor of Afflecks Palace in Manchester. Flared cords, £3 from Steals on Abingdon Street, too long. At some point last night it had rained;

trouser legs are stiff and dusty. Tide marks of dried muddy water. *I am large, I contain multitudes.* Of course it was a white American man poet who said that. Of course it was. A sizeable ball of world-weary cynicism, lodged inside us like a ball of undigested chewing gum. An actual ball of undigested chewing gum, amassed from schooldays, lodged inside us like a sizeable ball of undigested chewing gum. The metaphor and the real: both equally useless paperweights lining the cavern where the bleeding pumpbag should be. Yawning ribcaves, and (of course) the bloodhungry sawdustheart.

Keep a tight hold of the plastic Safeway bag and its contents. Check inside. One summer dress. Some small coinage, just shrapnel, weighing more than its worth. A Nokia 3200 phone with a plastic cover, pink with yellow flowers, battery low. Birds chirrup insolently in the sweetness of morning. What bucolic bastardry is this. Grasp at nameless white flowers and tall blades of grass with vague fingers, nearing the bramble-flanked entrance to the park between The Avenue and Poulton Road. What was someone saying last night about acid being laced with strychnine? Digital semi-paralysis is undeniably present – fingers half-frozen into gnarled claws, the shapes of which carry significance unknown but perceived. Still the legs drift on. Simpler beings to operate, legs. Scrambling up the bank to the bridge that goes over the railway line and leads on to The Avenue, then through quiet detached houses towards the main road leading up to Carleton. Birds continue their obscene and absurd concordances. Like butter wouldn't melt.

Focus attention downwards and the activity of stepping. Best foot forward. Spit spot! Play the childhood game of only stepping on the dark spots of chuddy on the pavement. Half scuffing, half hopping along Tithebarn Street, past the corner of Arundel Drive and the hairdresser's, past the bike shop and the newsagent's and the chippy heading for the bus stop, waiting for the number 14 bus that will take us back towards people and shops and space and sea, because there is nothing better to do, because we are meant to be taking it easy, taking care, not thinking about the mess of a first year at MMU, the last-minute train ticket, the possessions still in the room of the student halls, the confused roommate, the posters on the wall, the glow-in-the-dark stars and moons still on the ceiling, the CDs still on the windowsill. But that seed of a thought, the world left behind, crush it now. Look, here we are. After one year of living in the big city everything here seems tiny. Or I am now a gigantine bodypopping robot like the one in the Beastie Boys' 'Intergalactic' video. Foreboding orchestral music fades to gentle hip-hop, and one stride takes me directly from Poulton to Carleton. Every step a different colour, a different galaxy. Interstellar striding. To the left on the horizon lies the Tower. Three miles away as the crow flies. A few wisps of cloud hang higher. *I could eclipse and cloud them with a wink / But that I would not lose her sight so long*. Ha. Little do they know the Tower is actually a huge fucking aerial, both receiving and transmitting signals in languages not yet conceived. No, that's not quite right. It's actually a huge fucking magnet drawing us therewards. Wherewards? Herwards. Whowards? Herwards. My lodestone love. What the? Oh fuck. There's a her.

But hang on. The legs seem to be slowing of their own accord. The 14 is right there, waiting at the Castle Gardens traffic lights. But the legs don't want to go. The bodily inventory screams itself out again: brain, heart, liver, kidneys, every cell in fact, hurting now, needing rest. As if conjured from particles of dust, a woman's gentle voice – mother earth? Gaia? guardian angel? – mouths softly into the morning breeze two words:

Go home.

And you know she's right. As the lights go green and the 14 moves ahead to the stop, one woman bent over a wheelie trolley takes about an hour to get on, fiddle for money, pick up change, get her ticket then shuffle along to a seat, we are stuck, rooted to the spot, standing gormlessly at the corner, staring, unmoving. That sinking feeling when you decide *not* to do something. Either the heart is sinking or the entire world is sinking and the heart is standing still. But the world appears entirely oblivious. Look, there's the sun. *Busy old fool, why dost thou thus.* There's a dog walker, a runner, the odd car, someone whistling somewhere, a lad scuffing his way down Fleetwood Road with his bright orange newspaper bag. The whirring sound of the milk van can also be heard, though it's unclear from which direction exactly. Fuck. And here it is, emerging from Maycroft Avenue. Has he seen us. Fuck. Fuck. He has. From the milk van an overalled arm is raised and a head nods, somewhat formally. You could transplant Mr Mallinson into any previous decade of this century and he would be more suited than the current one. Exactly the same clothes all year round. Navy overalls over a knitted jumper over a collared shirt. Whatever the weather. Whatever the weather we'll weather the weather, whatever the weather it is.

–I thought you students were meant to stay in bed until the afternoon!

Can't seem to speak, so it will have to be enough to

smile ruefully, woefully, spread arms and shrug. But what is a rue and how does one become full of it? Does it have something to do with chimneys? Rue, flue. The tightrope between the metaphor and the real. Now there's an essay title. Did we just think of chimneys because Mr Mallinson is from the same era as chimneys? And what era is that? An era we are about to leave, here at the arse end of the millennium. But such grandiose theorisation is more than the brain can take right now, so just stay frozen in the smile and the shrug until the van is way past, turning right down Poulton Road, and then concentrate in order to relax the face and shoulders into something resembling normal and not this demented mime artist. Turn that frown upside down! Enough. Time to hide. Back to the bedroom we go.

Treesa

Don't go chasing waterfalls
Please stick to the rivers and the lakes that you're used to

A skip, a little bounce on the heels, waiting on the stretch of grass on the corner of Draycot Avenue and Rodwell Walk, humming the best TLC song, pushing Lulu's buggy back and forth slowly. Wednesday morning treat. Swimming and slides at the Sandcastle with a McDonald's breakfast on the way. Then Lulu goes to Mum's until teatime. Bliss. Lulu is wriggling in the buggy, excited. Knows where we are going. Holds her pink singing horse in one hand and a blue plastic spoon in the other. She likes to have something in each hand at all times.

Smooth hair against the wind and pull the ponytail tighter. Poor hair, flattened to within an inch of its life and pulled up high. Every day the same for the past few years, maybe apart from the odd night out. Against gravity though. And all the kinks ironed out. Not literally ironed out anymore, thank God. No more aching neck from sessions crouched over at the ironing board when Mum used to iron it straight for us under greaseproof paper, half-strangled head forced horizontal. No more, since Lulu and since getting our own flat, and finally we saved enough to get the amazing GHD ceramic straighteners from Argos. Make sure you put Frizz Ease on first or your hair might catch fire. But they really do get it all done in five minutes flat. Flat hair in five minutes flat. In our own flat. Flat, flat, flat yellow hair in a high ponytail pulled and smoothed and hairsprayed so tightly it feels like our eyes are pulled slightly upwards and sideways apart from the two carefully arranged front fringe pieces framing the face. The wind jangles the hoops in our ears. It's fresh, fresh enough to send goosebumps up the spine but not from coldness exactly. More from the pure freshness of the morning in the sun, chilly even in the warmth but also exciting, all mixed up together.

–Look, Lulubelle! Nana's here!

There's the knackered Polo. *Beep-be-be-beep-beep – BEEP BEEP!* At the wheel, Mum has my old sunnies on – the Miss Selfridge faded pink-to-blue aviator-style ones with the tiny diamante star in the corner. Trying to look cool in a *Top Gun* woman style. Funny that underneath I will always know that her blue eyes are our eyes and Lulu's eyes in turn. Mum's hair is freshly cut, the tips freshly frosted. Always the same do: no-nonsense highlighted short back 'n' sides, just like Scottish mums all over the world, probably. She is more tanned than ever today, partly from summer, partly from the sunbed in the back room. Every few days she lies down for exactly the length of the Hanson album *Middle of Nowhere* and tops up the colour. A long, tanned arm extends out from the open driver's window in an elaborate and regal wave. Clearly in one of those embarrassing moods where she thinks she's like a cool funny person.

–Milady, your carriage awaits.

–Muuuuuum!

–What?

–Stop being weird!

–What, don't you like the royal treatment? You can sod off, then. Me and Lulu can go to Maccy D's without you, can't we?

Lulu squeals at her name, and double-squeals at Maccy D's. Mum swings up out of the car to unbuckle Lulu. Swings out like it's a dance move. Every time, though, such graceful movements. This grace lives inside her. Muscle memory. Remember it from GCSE PE. Inside that movement is history, or herstory, or mumstory, whatever. Tells the story that Mum used to do gymnastics too, up in Glasgow. Can't believe the stories she tells about Glasgow back then. And we think it's rough here. Those stories about men who went to the dancing to murder women. Don't go doon that alley or Bible John will get ye. Even now, another shiver in the sun. What was the name of the place where she competed up there? Kelvin Hall, that's it. Place for gymnastics *and* athletics. Remember, we had the chance to go there too, before Lulu. With a Scottish mum you can enter the Scottish championships even if you live in Blackpool and were born in Blackpool Vic. Imagine that. No idea what the Kelvin Hall looks like but in our imaginings it has the same shining letters outside as that famous place that seems to be a market and a music venue all together, Glasgow Barrowland, all glitz and glam and neon lights, just like our Lights, you can see why they like it down here, all the Scots who come pouring in every September weekend. Glazvegas to Blazvegas, get pished and eat chippy chips, home from home.

Kelvin Hall. Sounds so impressive. But. Best not think about gymnastics and athletics right now. Got to keep watch for the sadness. Shut it away quick. Look, Lulu's glasses are wonky and smudged. Straighten and wipe glasses, and nose too. Even doing that, and imagining the state of her face later after an ice cream, it's enough to make you cry. Or laugh. Or both.

–How's she doing?

–Bit sniffly still, but she's alright. She's dead excited about today.

Buggy in boot, Lulu strapped in bumper seat, radio on. The only station it plays is Atlantic 252.

Lookin' back over my shoulder
With an aching deep in my heart

Lookin' back over my shoulder at Lulu strapped in, happily banging spoon and horse together. Lookin' over my other shoulder at Mum, whose mouth has curled up a fragment as she drives along St Walburgas Road. I know what she's thinking. Dad's song. Dad's song, because he's also called Mike and he's a mechanic, but also Dad's song because he whistles it all the time and sometimes plays it on the guitar. Even sings it sometimes, especially when pissed.

Lookin' back over my shoulder
At Lulubelle and Mum and me
We're going swimming at the Sandcastle
But first we're gonna get a Happy Meal

–Such a voice! Where's *Stars in Their Eyes*? Get Matthew Kelly on the line! Our Trees can stop traffic with her dulcet tones –

Ignore Mum because the whistling bit is coming up and that's the most fun bit, but annoyingly I can't whistle like Dad does it at all. His whistling is professional whistling – it kind of wobbles like he's playing an instrument professionally. And he can whistle through his teeth. You can only get that level of whistling after decades of practice, I reckon. Must be. It's like getting thousands of hours in at the gym – but no, again, no gym thoughts this morning. Look at the sunshine. Could even get our feet in the sea later.

I never dreamed it could be over. A happy-and-sad song. Both at the same time. Over there at the sports centre in Stanley Park someone is probably flipping right now. Tumbling. The feeling of being a rocket hurtling through the air. Defying gravity. But look – there's Lulubelle's little face in the rearview mirror. A weight in the heart. Nothing except love but it's heavy. Gravity's got me now alright. But look now – as if she could read my mind, Mum is shoving her second pair of sunglasses in my face, the stupid ones that came free with the *Sugar* magazine bumper holiday issue which Kayleigh had left round ours the other day. Thick black plastic rectangular frames and yellow lenses. Fuckin hippy shades.

–As if I would ever wear them!

–Alright, alright, calm down, I think only dogs heard

you. Here you go, and I think Lulu's Mickey Mouse ones are in the glove compartment. Don't want you to be left out, do we Lulu?

Lulu squeals and squirms at Mickey Mouse.

Sunglasses are thrice donned, I am *Top Gun* woman, Mum is a hippy, Lulu is Mickey Mouse, the windows are down, the roads are quiet, the sun is baking, the tune is cheerful but also sad. Sad in the happy. Wonder is there a word for that. But listen, here's the whistling bit. Give it your best shot. Can't do it like Dad does but most of it sounds okay until we get to the high bit. *I never wanted to say goodbye.*

–Pack it in, Trees. You're doing my head in.

Chapter 2

VOICE	Olga
SCENE	The Chippy
HOUR	11 a.m., 16 June 1999
PLEASURE BEACH RIDE	Flying Machines
SUBSTANCE	Vimto, Cinzano, Tobacco
ORGAN	Brain (primary visual cortex)
SYMBOL	Curlicue
COLOUR	Blue (sea)
FORMULA	C_2H_5OH
ART / TECHNIC	Multiplication
HORMONE	Cholecystokinin
HOMERIC TITLE	Calypso

We are all allowed to drink Vimto on shift but nothing else. No postmix fizzy stuff, no booze, just as much Vimto as we want so long as we don't stop working. But Vimto is pretty bloody good to be fair. Especially when you tip in a bit of vodka to top up the system on the quiet morning shift. Which we have obviously never done and definitely have not done on this morning shift right now. That would be obscene.

Carlotta comes in at 10:36. Carlotta has dark hair a bit like ours but definitely dyed. Reach up for the Cinzano bottle pre-emptively. A creature of habit, our Carlotta. What the fuck is Cinzano anyway. Today she is wearing a short black furry jacket – a bomber? a puffa? Who knows what's under the fur, which looks like half a child's gorilla suit. On her legs, shiny black PVC trousers, and clear, glittery platformed jelly shoes on her feet. The bomber jacket makes her upper half a perfectly round shape, and her skinny legs stick out underneath her, making her look like a lethal black poppy tottering on double stems. Her eyes are always rimmed with electric blue eyeliner, her eyelashes with blue mascara. Carlotta could be anything between forty-five and eighty. She's sitting at her usual table near the window. The Cinzano and lemonade, resplendent with orange cocktail umbrella, is placed delicately in front of her.

–Thanks, love. How are you today?

–Oh, y'know. Can't complain. I'd rather be on a beach in Ibiza but wouldn't we all?

–No thank you. I've had enough of that part of the world to last a lifetime. What d'you need Ibiza for when you've got all this?

She gestures outside, a skinny string with painted claws. The sun is shining right enough. For a second we try to superimpose San Antonio Bay on top of what we can see through the window: a chunk of the prom with a few cars crawling past; the sea, which is doing a fairly good job of blueing its blueness; and the knowledge of the Tower to the left, doing its towering.

–You're right. Who needs the Med?

Superimposition. Who needs the Med? Carlotta is paused while we indulge internally in some alternative thoughtpatternings. Where are we? Not Blackpool, that's for sure. Ibiza of course. Never been to Ibiza, but as a defiant psychonoaut I can go wherever the fuck I want and there's nothing you can do about it.

In San Antonio a few faint strains of Binary Finary's '1998' can be heard across the bay. It gives me some serious goosebumps, deliberately thinking about the frenzy of that tune at the same time as the panpipes' soft rendition of 'Heaven Can Wait' here in the restaurant. The way the tune comes from outer space and emerges through the middle of the synthetic sound, spiritual, evanescent, frenzied, while here in the restaurant the panpipes labour their way through Jim Steinman's melody. *And a band of angels wrapped up in my heart.* The band of angels is here too, in this imaginary song sandwich, imagining euphoric arms raised and feel goosebumps raised, because there is also, in that cheesy-as-fuck trance tune, a song, a vocal without vocals, just as right here Meat Loaf's voice inheres behind the panpipes, singing-not-singing. A band of angels. Boys in clubs, T-shirts drenched, arms aloft.

–You look a million miles away, love. Where are ye?

Good question.

Splattered and spliced across soundwaves and time-waves to a sweaty podium, Heaven & Hell two nights ago, a gaggle of gurning, grinning lads. And me still in my work uniform. Sweaty T-shirts. Sweaty hugs. Blackpool Balearic. But at the same time in the San Antonio in my head I can see a group of girls in tiny denim shorts and bikini tops straggling across the sand, barefoot, flowers painted on their faces. A hen party on holiday from Liverpool. Across this bay that same hen party could well be straggling across these same sands. Is it really that different? Common levels of toxicity. Strings of leaked and shared bodily fluids. What else? Letting go. A collective letting-go. The vomit and the stumble. Thinking of Lee Dunton. Fit. Sweet, too. Works on the rides at the Pleasure Beach. Thick muscles in his arms and legs. Shaved head and stubbly face. Quiet ways; quiet face; the gentle type. Doesn't say a lot, but get him on the podium in Heaven & Hell and something entirely different escapes him in wisps. Wisps of blue Aladdin's Genie escaping him. His face opens up. An easy grin. His big hands make curlicues in the smoky air. Graceful fingers and smooth moves. He doesn't know where they come from. These tunes are full-blown cheesy trance. Trance isn't utopian. It's nihilistic. Or maybe it's both. It's the sound of rave being commodified, oversweetened, extracted of meaning. Rich dudes with vans. These tunes are rave's entrails. We're not in a field and the party isn't free. The more commercial the better. But the lasers, man. The lasers.

Carlotta is one Cinzano down. She proffers her empty glass delicately.

–Top us up, will you love.

Andy is singing along to Meat Loaf in the kitchen, adding an extra layer to the cake of sounds: a mulchy falsetto interspersed with the 'booyakasha' and 'ere me now'. Potato peelings clump around the sound. He's on his first WKD of the day. Orange flavour is his favourite. For the Scots, of course, the rust of the Irn-Bru with the ice-clear vodka liquor.

Never been to Ibiza, but with a couple of grand to spare it would be ace to go and have a proper high-end type holiday there. Stay in a posh white villa castle high on a hill with a turret bedroom and maybe a host of tanned Ibizan men serving grapes and tapas and tinto de verano and sangria and beer and pills and lines of pure snow-white cocaine all laid out on silver platters. But then the portal slightly creaks open again and Rachel pokes her head out, all wide, sorrowful eyes like a bunny, and the Ibizan men fizzle out. Fuck's sake. Pull self together.

Carlotta lights a fag, takes out her book of crosswords, her pencil and her purple-framed glasses. She is humming along to the slow part of 'Bat Out of Hell' on the panpipes. The creak of her voice fires off some strange hungover neurons in the brain. *Then I'm down in the bottom of a pit in the blazing sun.* The crossword book is one of those free ones from *Hello!* or *OK!* magazine, and she is halfway through it. *Torn and twisted at the foot of a burning bike.* So in this song, the guy dies, right, or he's about to die, and his heart breaks out of his body and flies away before his very eyes. And wham, smack, thump, just like that we are back to Rachel and last night. Hearts and bodies and things about dying or at least wanting to die. Fuckssake. This is harsher than the average doom-regret-comedown-hangover combo. Did she. Did we. Ugh. The brain cannot. Not right now. And yet it starts playing, in short bursts – Olga and Rachel, us two, together, as if it's a *thing*, crawling round the flat pretending to be cats – Rachel blurts out a sudden monologue about depression and suicide then looks really embarrassed and folds up so small on the living room carpet that she almost succeeds in making herself invisible, except her striped fire-tiger eyes, orange, green, black, eyeliner smudged and dark, are still shooting their beams at us. *Did* we? But *what* did we? What did I.

How can it be that I want to punch her in the face. Extinguish those two tiger lamps, searchlights, stripelights, punch those lights out. And then cradle her afterwards until they are burning again. The kind of desire that feels so shameful you can't ever tell anyone about it except if you disguise it as a joke. I disgust myself at the best of times but right now feels like an entirely new level of self-loathing, hitherto undiscovered.

Enough. Snap back to the present, standing behind the counter. Gulp down the whole pint glass of Vimto. Heart racing. Head throbbing. *Did I punch her in the face?* We look down at our right hand. The knuckles are bruised and grazed from something. Who knows what, though. Nothing new there. The sight of the bruising sets off another reaction. An electrical imprint on the upper arm. You don't feel it, it feels you. Touching it gently – ouch – already know without needing to check that there is another bruise there, burning through our work shirt, and that it has been decorated in felt-tip pens by the hand of the tiger-striped lampgirl into a fantastical symbol of meteorology. Four seasons in one day. The cloud-bruise will change its weather signalling day by day, she said, commanding the storm, powerful, godlike, leonine, stoppit now Olga, ferfucksake. Today the storms shall be purple and red. Tomorrow, blue and green. Next week, yellow. Until the storm is over, you see.

Right. Yep. Clear as day.

Eric jangles the bell at the door. Lamplights vanish. Can feel our cheeks are slightly flushed. But a hangover will do that. It's not because of last night's memories crowding in suddenly, millions and millions of hot ghosts pressing at us, inside and out, bodies and brains and fires and desires, a sudden focusing of intensity. Aflame. No. Not that. Just a boozy flush. We see his moustache before we see anything else. Large, chevron-style, fagstained, off-white. With a moustache like that you don't need a personality, but Eric does in fact have one, and sometimes it feels quite at odds with the melancholy walrus-droop of his nosebeard.

–Morning, sunshine! What time did you roll into bed then?

Eric is winking as he shuffles over to Carlotta's table. Time to roll the eyes dramatically and then flutter the eyelashes. An expert transition from sarcasm to coquettishness in one fell swoop, while bringing Eric a pint of Boddingtons. The cream of Manchester.

–I was tucked up by ten. Lights out by eleven! I don't know what you're talking about.

–Oh yeah. Tucked up with who, that's what I want to know.

The daily battle between the cream of Manchester and Eric's moustache is probably the most entertaining thing to take place in a regular morning shift. The fact that the froth and the tache are now actually very similar in colour allows Eric to get away with a lot more than in his earlier days, so he does not worry too much, relishing the first glug, the sweating glass, the ale hitting his throat, gurgling in his belly. Fragments of their conversation reach us. Jigsaw pieces.

–You know you can call the police on them. There's a

special noise unit. They'll send the heavies round.

–Like pure melted butter it was. Never felt anything like it –

–And you just got him told, did you?

–The state of it, Eric – honestly, rats would be ashamed –

–You're not wrong –

–He said he'd posted the cheque two months ago –

–Raw sewage, I'm telling you!

–Cats better treated than humans, believe me –

–No one talks about it. The thinning of it –

–D'you want me to have a word?

–Sick, it is. No other word for it.

–Still, there's always a parking space, isn't there?

Carlotta seems to be, as always, entirely unbothered by the froth-fringed tache that is talking back at her and laughing as she gesticulates with her spiky claws and her bangles jangle.

A new bullet train of pain shoots through the head, the gut, the soul. Owch. So are we going to let ourselves think about it, then?

Of all the Olgas that have the potential to leap out and take the reins at any possible moment, Most Sensible Olga (who is called Daphne and is fifty-five years old and attends a Baptist church every Sunday and wears cardigan-and-skirt sets) makes a brief but vivid appearance. Her arms are folded.

Daphne: *You know you have to let yourself think about it at some point.*

Youngest-kid Olga (five-year-old Gary) sticks out his bottom lip in a sulk: *But whyyyyyyyyyyyy?*

Daphne: *Because maybe it's a new thing that you have learned about yourself.*

Gary: *Don't want to.*

Daphne: *If you repress emotions you'll only get headaches and nightmares.*

Gary: *Don't care.*

Intellectual left-wing man Olga (a flamboyantly dressed man called Charles, aged fifty) turns his silver-streaked head towards Daphne: *I'm surprised at YOU, condoning homosexuality. It's a sin in the Bible, for God's sake!*

Daphne, blushing the same colour as her plum twin-piece set: *Perhaps we need to be a little bit honest with ourselves and get this phase nicely out of our system before we find a man and settle down properly.*

Charles laughs: *Phase! Settle down! Hahaha.* He pauses, frowns, purses his lips and holds his chin with one hand in a quizzical fashion and squints his eyebrows, Bond-style. *Does this mean that you're a lesbian, though?*

The word, in our head, looks comical, obscene. Just imagine each letter as a balloon on a string. Capital letters. No longer HAPPY BIRTHDAY or CONGRATULATIONS. Silvery lesbian letters congratulating one on one's homosexuality. Charles hands the balloons to Gary, who doesn't care what they say – he's not great at reading and doesn't know what the word means anyway – but they are helium balloons, which are fun to bash around and sometimes let fly up to the sky and other times big boys make you breathe in the air which is scary air that makes your voice squeaky but then it goes back to normal.

Daphne looks fondly and maternally across at Gary: *That's right! It's an L for Lucy, an E for Elizabeth, S for Susan, B for Becky, I for Imogen, A for Angela, N for Natalie ... What does it spell?*

L.E.S.B.I.A.N.

Flashback to a moment last night. It was way hotter than we had imagined. In a temperature sense. Not that we had imagined it. Obviously. But if we had. It was hotter. She was hotter. A fast-beating heart and blood under the surface. There's a memory and a temperature and a scent but it's static. It's a photograph but we are inside it and there's no space between us AT ALL because we have dovetailed ourselves together somehow. We are the opposite of Tetris. Clothes and all. Edges gone. Melded. Smelded. Soldered. Smelt?

THWACK. Andy's wet dishcloth slaps across the back of our thighs. The smell of soldering disappears. A hiss and a fizz.

–State of you! Miles away. Where are you? Can I come too?

Whip round to see him standing there, smirking behind his half-darkened glasses.

–I don't think the boss is meant to hit the staff.

–I don't think the staff are meant to be on Planet Janet while on shift. Sort your head out, you. I don't care what you were up to last night. Just keep your mind on the job while you're in here, okay?

Automatic and surreptitious reach into front pocket of pinny containing our squashed packet of fags. Needed.

–Okay. Sorry. Yep. So ... is it okay if I just go and quickly supervise the van for five minutes then? It'll help me work more efficiently.

A nice sunbeam of a smile now for Andy. He rolls his eyes but nods briefly and jerks his head in the direction of the back door.

–Five minutes. No more. Then you're back and smiling sweetly and licking the boots of every sod who walks through that door. Oh, and you can lick my boots too while you're at it.

–Thank you! Yep, I promise!

Crouching down next to the bins outside. Lesbians. Dykes. Grown-up and scary women with short hair and leather jackets who go to protests and wear vests and plaid shirts and build sheds from scratch. I don't look like that. Neither did she.

Did we, though?

Did we?

What did we, though?

Let's just sit with it for a while. Breathe. Go with the inhale and the exhale. Sit with the roiling nausea and think about the nicotine rushing through the bloodstream and try to feel with the feeling that comes back in spurts – jolts – fits – starts. The feeling that something inconsequential can be something monumental. Both of those things. Where are we now? Not crouching at the back door of the kitchen, hungover to fuck, trying not to/pretending not to remember. Not that. Internally you're sitting on a coach journey, a really long one, one of those Greyhound buses you see in films, taking you from one American state to another overnight. You have all your possessions in a tattered holdall and you're American, wearing 1980s-style jeans and Converse, leaving one life and going to another. You did the whole 'will I, won't I get on this bus' and then you got on it. The bus takes you from your existence as a waitress in your home town to a new existence, probably still as a waitress but in a new town, a bigger town, a city in fact, where things are permissible and the quota of weird people is higher, where two girls can walk down the street holding hands and no one bats an eyelid, and they don't even look like the kinds of girls who like girls, they just happen to be in love so they're holding hands. Just like that. On the bus you're having the flashbacks because on the bus it's allowed. It's not allowed while you're sitting here at the back door, hungover to fuck, trying to mentally block out the sound of 'Two Out of Three Ain't Bad' being panpiped throughout the kitchen and Andy's occasional whoops and hollers.

No one on this earth can plumb the secret areas that I have in my head. No one.

Okay. So. Sitting on the bus, gazing out at flat landscapes rushing by. On some kind of highway. Listening to some kind of 1980s power ballad type of music that isn't so cheesy that it doesn't still cause the goosebumps to rise and perhaps one single tear to well in one eye and then make its way down your cheek, mirroring the water droplets that occasionally streak the windows. It's not raining outside. But the droplets come from somewhere. Just like us. Not crying. But the tear has come from somewhere. In the imaginary headphones are the fucking Pretenders. How apt a band to be playing in the imaginary headphones in the imaginary bus in the imaginary country in the imaginary film that an imaginary Olga is starring in right now.

Don't get me wrong
If I'm looking kind of dazzled
I see neon lights
Whenever you walk by

Neon lights. And fireworks in a smile. A neon lionsmile. That's about right. Fuck, a tidal wave of weird druggy emotion. It's all one. Love and heartbreak. Instantaneous.

Being extremely happy and being extremely sad are the same thing. I don't care what anyone says. This feeling, sitting on this bus, is extreme happiness and extreme sadness all at once. And it's filtering its way across continents back to the real – real? – the 'real' me, sitting here smoking my fag and letting the nicotine carry me away on the wisps and tendrils that filter down into my lungs and out of my mouth and into the atmosphere. Do I contribute to global warming every time I smoke a fag? Almost definitely.

So. What does the combination of landscape and music and life-journey-adventure create in my head?

OLGA. Stoppit. Just stop. And breathe. And remember.

So there was a girl last night. There was kissing. That part is remembered. There was more, too. But who knows what. There was definitely some bad behaviour. From this side. From me. Enough to create a black hole of regret or shame or doom or whatever word you want to attach to the feeling you get when you know you did something bad but you don't know what you did.

There's something fatalistic about it, though. There is no other way I could behave. Our desires are bigger than us. That's for sure. The moment that keeps flashing up and being batted down and swallowed like in that Hungry Hippos game, the moment is –

OLGA. Come on.

The moment is a jewel. A red jewel. A seed inside a pomegranate. No other way to describe it. That's what kissing is about. Never really knew before that moment.

There's all the acid to consider, though. The end of a bender. Didn't know what we were doing. Or did we.

But. That moment. It's like a leap out of time. But it's

like that for a reason. Sometimes things are too big to be thought about, okay? Too big. Too difficult. Some things need to be kept away, kept tidy, otherwise none of us would ever do anything ever. It would be like taking acid all the time. But are we talking about taking acid or are we talking about the kiss. Isn't there a famous painting called *The Kiss*? Passion distilled into tiny rectangles of different colours. Bodies composed of geometric shapes. Feels about right, actually. When I close. My eyes. I can go. Back there –

> And spontaneously we clutch each
> other as all around the particles of the
> world are falling away one by one
> around us—
>
> *You*
>
> *Are*
>
> *Stunnin*

Whose words were those. My words?

–MADAM!

Shit. Big Andy's voice clangs into the scene and all the particles are shattered into fragments too small to see. Back to ground level. Owchbrain. Particles? Wherefore art thou? I am losing it.

–That van has been supervised for long enough – you've got customers!

Chapter 3

VOICE	Rachel
SCENE	The Bedroom
HOUR	11 a.m., 16 June 1999
PLEASURE BEACH RIDE	Flying Machines
SUBSTANCE	Blood
ORGAN	Brain (frontal lobe)
SYMBOL	Crack
COLOUR	Red
FORMULA	vWF, GP1b alpha
ART / TECHNIC	Self-Love, Self-Hate, Strafing, Stabbing
HORMONE	Luteinizing Hormone
HOMERIC TITLE	Proteus

> Intellectual pleasure occurs as a result of the application of a code or a small number of logically connected codes to the message (this itself the source of the pleasure – a mass of variegated material is reduced to one system). In considering the speed with which the human brain works, we should note that the time span of intellectual pleasure or understanding ... is infinitesimally small. It is instantaneous.[1]

Ineluctible modality of cerebral fuckallery. *Fizzpop*. In the brain. The many in the one. Variegated into unilinear. Strings in a string. Wires in a wire. Veins in a vein. Cells in a cell. Always we come back to this weird quotation, sitting right in the middle of the purple inkbook, copied from a library book now forgotten. Intellectual pleasure. Meaning: brainfucks. Yes please. Now we're talking.

What are we doing right now? Afternoon bedroom sitting. Atlantic 252 on the radio. *Baby when you're gone*. Buckfast drinking. Dried blood all over the sheets. Note with little surprise that we appear to have opened up the main wound again. Smashed a beer bottle in the toilets. Again. A familiar reassuring throb through the right arm.

So. Let's talk speculative neurobiology. The 'let us' presupposing a party of more than one. When in fact we are but one. *One body, many voice*s. Address the cupboards with their squiggles and scrawl, the half-empty bookcase, the CD stand, the boxes, the years-old posters of Manics' Richey and Nicky Wire in leopard print, Shirley Manson, Radiohead. The brain cell *fizz-popping* is an audible process at this point in time. The blood alcohol level is such. That. We. Can. Make. Up. Science. And that is fine.

These sharp, splintering flashes of insight. They come

1 Jurij Lotman, *The Structure of the Artistic Text* (1971), p. 58; Rachel's underlining.

at a cost. They arrive when the brain's defences are lowered. When it is dried out, shrivelled and detaching itself from the skull like gum from the sole of a shoe. As a brain cell shrinks into nothing, it pops out its last dying breath – its magnum opus – and you are rewarded with a final moment of Pure Comprehension. The *fizz-pop*. Owch. Drinking the dregs of the Bucky from a plastic cup that appeared from who knows where. Sitting on the floor because lower centre of gravity is more sensible at such times. A strange drubbing feeling overcomes the nervous system every now and then. Smaller motor-neural twitches follow. Unusual cocktail in the system today.

Observe the self clinically. What will happen to us next. Holding the purple inkbook limply in one hand. Hard to gather together the atoms of the physical self convincingly enough to grasp things properly. At such times. The purple inkbook is lineless. The page we open is blank.

Draw then. Release yourself from the yoke of language. Connect pen to paper. Just let yourself draw what comes. Drawing therapy. What's in a line? Open up a line. Lines are what I make on myself. The addition of dimensions. Topological woman.

A line says: This, right here, this is enough.

Draw a human head with the top sliced cleanly off, hanging down by the skin. A sizeable saw must have performed such an operation. Draw the saw next to the head. Out of the head are flying pills of every size and shape.

Defiant. This is what I want to draw, here in this private afternoon of nesting in my own monstrous and bloody alcoholic afterbirth. The head stares back at us. On the paper it looks more anatomically accurate than we would have imagined ourselves capable. Maybe they aren't pills.

Maybe they're all the newly coined ideas a person will have in their lifetime, escaping into the ether like the dreams that the BFG catches in his glass bottles. Stopper them up now, quick. Precious gems. Currency.

So what must we call these cerebral fizz-pops? Epiffanny. Whatever. Aha. Whatever: the nightmare from which we are trying to awake. Blame *Clueless*. The soul of the commonest object. A clock tower. A vulva. An insect. A cipher. Olga. What if one person makes the entire world panepiphanal? Perhaps this is the definition of love. Or monomania. *Rachel, a character in her own self-writing novel of the divided self, a narc in all senses of the word, is watching her own literary and emotiononsensical development from the outside, and it is sickening her*. It's breathtakingly simple.

Better not to think of errant girls as transistors for the self; better not to think of girls as conduits; girls fine-tuning the blade you use to stab yourself; better not to think of girls, a girl, the girl, the new significance, the new hollowed-out cavern inside us.

Better to exercise the fizzing popping dying gasping brain cells a bit. Better to reminisce, better to think back longingly to those first few lectures at MMU and the titles which had sounded so dry. Phonetics. Semantics. And yet knowing now that they are the building blocks of everything that makes us human. Meanings of words and bits of words. Making and remaking the world through an infinity of frameworks.

Better perhaps to write a poem. Resist the urge to channel this new girl, this new frequency, through every module enrolled, tried, adored, failed, then exited. Or perhaps better just give ourselves the credit that inspiration is its own thing. Focus now. When the black mouth of the world splits open it is not this new Olga person but the world. Olga is not the world. Remember this.

Swiftly pen four lines in the inkbook.

To play the game of catching strains of phantom scents
To learn the tricks of clutching straws and tasting crumbs
To charm the snake that bites its tail to spite itself
To chase the double random path of tangled kites

These are the most plaintive, pathetic lines ever to grace a piece of paper. Tear them out immediately. Turn to page one of the inkbook. Think about structure instead.

On the first page in the purple inkbook, the letters STRUTCURE proudly head the paper, all capitals, the misspelling even more boldly displayed because of the size and design of the lettering, all angles and lines, no curves, standing proudly next to the date of the lecture, 15 January 1999, and some doodled structures that look like scaffolding that holds up a building. Cos structure's like scaffolding, innit. But not a very stable scaffolding with that spelling, eh? Although, there's a strut and a cure inside too. And a suture. Well that's a relief, eh? The pen strokes are bold and signify excitement but the misspelling signifies that we had definitely been still buzzing from the night before and were not of completely sound mind. And the signification of lettershape was boldly defiant against the point of the lecture topic, though we hadn't known it until fifty-five minutes later.

The point had been, we guess, that the word STRUCTURE written on our page like that kind of fits the concept STRUCTURE. Which we then learned was kind of the opposite to the point of the lecture. Oh well. The point had seemed to be that the squiggles on the page that we use to write bear no relation to the thing they're signifying. And that really did blow our tiny little mind. It blew it because it somehow cemented the idea of secular worship. Worshipping the arbitrary sign. It happens everywhere, all the time, from birth to death. Nonsense to capitalism. Eh? Bear with me, tired brain. Being a toddler obsessed with the Shell sign at petrol stations. Dad said we used to say it excitedly, over and over. Shell sign. Shell sign. And there you have it. The coining of a religion in miniature. A sign by any other name.

Thinking about the word *arbitrary* fits this moment perfectly. The light comes down through the window. The inkbook and its squiggles are the most reassuring thing right now. Edwyn Collins is stating on the radio that he has never met a girl like you before. And his hands are bleeding and his knees are raw. Look down. The stripes of our old dressing gown are somehow resonating and pulsating along with the beat of the song and simultaneously with a throbbing that we feel through our body and especially in the wound on the arm. The bloodpulse.

But does arbitrariness actually mean that nothing really means anything? Or is that just the kind of thought that comes from the end of a bender? Are Bit Rare Ee Ness. The game of splitting up words into smaller words that we used to do at school. I'm App I'm Anne. Where the fuck did that come from. Is it only in the North West that we insult people by calling them 'pieman' for no fathomable reason? Who ate all the. Are Bee Tree. Here groweth an Arbi Tree. But most people would just say random. And random itself can mean anything, which kind of proves its own point. To be random, to be a random, a random as random as a noun. A random, you know, a weird person you meet at the bus stop. But a random can't just *be*, intransitively. You're only random to someone else. Random as object rather than subject. Sounds discriminatory, doesn't it?

The right to be random! Rights for randoms!

Ugh. Where do these voices come from. Inside, yes, but where, who, wherefore, wheretofore? Remember the glamorous guest lecturer who had told us all that Virginia Woolf used to hear the birds singing in Greek. Wish my own voices were as erudite as that, sitting here on the floor, helplessly letting them all chug their way round and round the internal caverns of whoknowswhere while gazing into middle distance, noting and hearing the words *middle distance*, wondering exactly what constitutes *middle distance*. Berating the mundanity of the constant self-theorisation. Am I a random to myself right now? Absolutely. When the hand that clutches the drink bears no relation to the brain that controls it. See, I power these terms, these concepts. I make them my own. Multiplicitous demonic goddess I am, bending concepts one moment, shrinking and fawning the next. And that, my friends, is random.

Fizzzzzpop.

But back to the science bit. Bouncingly coiffured Jennifer Aniston in the shampoo advert. *Here comes the science bit – concentrate!* Imagining the entire human communication network as a spider with an infinite number of legs, pinned and petrified, mummified, stretched across a vast set of axes. Structures hang there, right there in front of us in the afternoon light, invisible yet palpable, like infra-red alarm systems. Don't touch any or you'll set off an alarm! We are Catherine Zeta-Jones in *Entrapment*, nimbly lifting herself up, over and around them, glutes and quads taut in yoga gear. Minus a pervy Sean Connery looking on.

Mirror mirror, capture me now. We look vaguely towards the mirror, stick out one leg from our seated position on the floor, diagonally up, toes pointed, pouting face.

Daft apeth.

The old excitement comes back, even now, looking at those letters. From STRUTCURE to structural-ISM, and when you add the -ism to the mix it's like pure baking soda. It's catalytic. Structural-ISM felt almost fetishistically appealing. Why? Because it was the first time that we pondered the process of something that sounded kind of interesting becoming an ism, and why it did so, and what happened to it. Because to make something an ism seems to cement the thinking of that thing as a structure itself. As a prefix. It prefixes the world with itself. Do I prefix the world with myself? Of course. But no one else follows Rachelism. Why do some things deserve to become universal isms? What does it mean? Baking soda. Something gains traction is all.

Shifting in the afternoon light. The next page in the purple inkbook has quotations from Roland Barthes, Ferdinand de Saussure, Claude Lévi-Strauss. Curly handwriting signifying the seriousness that came from this poetic, philosophical, theoretical writing that they seemed to do. The sheer Frenchness of the names of these dead white men had felt exciting in a serious way. So serious. It felt serious copying down their words, and serious reading them back again. As if nothing they wrote could ever be wrong, as if scaffolding your own writing with these quotations meant that nothing *you* write could ever be wrong. Even these words, these sentences, feel completely different since last night, since Olga. But remember: the Author is dead anyway, yeh? Or so the French philosophers tried to tell us. And yet, while they were alive, the careers of these dead white men depended on us maintaining the illusion of the exact opposite. It's all nonsense: it's all Wonderland logic. We, signifying humans, are all just scrambling around together on a huge ice rink, bumping into one another. Or those of us lucky enough to be at university are able to pay entrance to the ice rink, skate hire, and off we all wobble. Let go of the railings, they won't help you. Dictionaries differ wildly. Everything is up for grabs. Defining seems to be the key to things. Make up your own definitions; make up your own terms. If you are working on the definition of something you are positing yourself as someone with something to say.

And we have things to say. Rachel Gillian Charlotte Watkins, a big fucking stalking peacock with a large piebald shrivelled audible grotesquely patternfeathered fuckoff brain. Let's do some more stuff to it now. M People drift in and out. *Search for the hero inside yourself.*

Let's think more about the traction of an ism. The acceleration of it. Politically all isms are a bit dubious, are they not? When you study theory you study all the isms. But. Impossible to lump them all together. Each one is different. Easier to define what theory is not. The nots are the shared qualities. Theory is not dogma. And perhaps the reason this -ism suffix is so seductive is that it represents the translation of abstract noun to dogma. Perhaps we could say ideology instead of dogma. And perhaps ideology and dogma are the same things to different people. Here we come unstuck again. The variegated string. The rope made of twine. It's all one. One of Olga's sayings. Borne out during a strung-out night. Everything comes back to everything. It's all one. Meaning. Who knows what to Olga.

Meaning. A number of things and equally one thing to us right here right now. Meaning. The theory of univocity which can be found in the philosophy of the poststructuralist philosopher Gilles Deleuze, which can be found in the thought of seventeenth-century philosopher Baruch Spinoza, which can be found in the thought of scholastic philosopher John Duns Scotus. The multiple in the one. This is everything and nothing. Something and nothing. And now the surface really tips into Wonderland. But also makes perfect sense if you think of your own self as nothing but a surface being slowly perforated, and this is what happens in the danger zone of a sudden bloom of obsessive love.

> *A strafing of the surface in order to transmute the stabbing of bodies, O psychedelia.*[2]

What a swoon of a sentence. Nothing has ever before or will again articulate what appears to be our life's project at all levels so perfectly. It sounds like it was written by mad theatrical genius Antonin Artaud but in fact it was written by another French dead white man, Gilles Deleuze, in a strangely wistful and romantic mood, perhaps after tripping, it was 1969 after all. Perhaps in a similar state to us right now. Did Deleuze ever consider strafing his own surface? Strafe my surface. A very specific command. A kind of specialised erosion, boring holes, letting things in and letting things out. Love and inspiration are not really different. It's a multidirectional process. It appears to us now that we will dedicate our life to this until in maybe around one decade's time we will go the way of Virginia Woolf because we cannot see any other conclusion if we are to live the life

2 Gilles Deleuze, *The Logic of Sense* (1969), p. 182.

we are carving/is carved/we are carving/is carved out for us/carved out of us.

As we turn the page to the word PSYCHOANALYSIS we see that it is appropriately encased in a rectangular sign hanging on an open door. In the background, a hastily sketched room with a sofa and a desk at which sits a bearded, bespectacled Sigmund Freud. At the same time, in our peripheral vision, we notice the words that we had scratched into the paint on the radiator, aged fifteen.

There is a crack in everything
That's how the light gets in

It's from a song by Leonard Cohen but the idea is more ancient than that. We know Rumi has it first. *The wound is the place where the Light enters you.* Many men have said this kind of thing. Only men, seemingly. Have any women done their version of this kind of proverb?

Look down at the self-made opening in the arm. No light getting in there, just dust, seemingly. Dust in the sense of consciousness in the sense of sin? Maybe. Dust, dirt, infection. *Fizz-pop.* Sudden insight into why we need to rend our skin and soul. The flow is perhaps outward, not inward. And like a true narcissist we seem to be more interested in the things inside us that need to get out. Or. Perhaps there is a contra-flow. A bi-directional flow. Blood and feeling. Orifices and objects. The crack and the light. It made a lot of sense.

Maybe we could try and rewrite it now. Find a blank page in the inkbook.

The light and the dark (all one) both inside and out (all one) needs to get both inside and out (all one).

Yes, that's more like it. Our inside is our outside, or it should be. Meaning: how it feels to be raw. To be inside out. To wear not just the heart on the sleeve but the entire viscera. There are multiple reasons why the objects in the natural world that we feel most akin to are all the washed-up bits of sea life found on coastlines cleaner than this one. Jellyfish and crabs. Because their insides are their outsides. And this is why we keep coming back to flaying and cutting and tearing and scratching and tearing. Because it is the literal rendition of how we feel. Insides and outsides are the same. All opposites are the same.

Olga made this statement too, about opposites being the same. Last night she said it, off the cuff, contextless. Olga who didn't finish her A-Levels. Olga took some tabs of acid and we took the beginning of a literary theory module and we ended up at the same place because that same place is that everywhere is the same place. It's somehow more about the intensive work done than anything about time or place or location or situation. Like running on a treadmill still expends energy even though you don't get anywhere. *Work done.* Remembering Mrs Hartman talking about it in Physics. Mrs Hartman. Getting anywhere near Mrs Hartman, even in shadow memory format, produces instant all-over body blush.

Do we really believe this? What do we really think about universality? Relativity? Difference? How do these words relate to one another?

Give it some thought. Off the cuff, right now. Make your brain do it.

Yes now, in this limbo afternoon.

Universality is bad because it discredits the particularities of context, and context is everything if you are a political being. It is harder to be seen as a political being if you are a girl. If you are a boy you are immediately understood as a political being. If you are a girl you are understood as a decorative being. Last night, standing there in her red lipstick and her stained chip shop uniform, Olga taught us feminism.

Thinking back to the clever English Lit boy-students in the MMU Literary Theory seminar. They would probably have an aneurism if you said they were not political beings. We can see the outrage now. *What do you mean apolitical. I bought the giant Che Guevara poster at the freshers' fair along with all the other boy freshers.* But. Even once we all started studying literary theory, Marx was the only political figure who registered with them. With their cherished copies of Kerouac and Bukowski. Skinny legs in Pop Boutique flared cords from Afflecks Palace. Richard Ashcroft, Paul Weller, Ocean Colour Scene, retro mod lookalikes, 1960s longish haircuts. Clarks Wallabees and the perfect Gallagher swagger. And a lip-curl of distaste at the mention of identity politics. These cocky boys made us nervous and hate ourselves further. These are not my boys. Not boys for me. Look up at the noticeboard. The envelope all ready to send to *Select* magazine is still pinned up there from two summers ago, sealed and stamped, encasing the ad:

> *Fed up of Oasis-loving homophobes; looking for eyeliner-wearing gender-bending Manics-loving punk boys to share makeup and dresses and stomp around in DMs.*

Whoever could have foreseen running away from uni, coming back home and instead falling for a girl. A *girl*. Desire for the same. Or another one of my kind. It feels taboo. Strange how your brain tricks you into not going into certain places when maybe you have been in those places all along. It is very clear to us now that together Olga and I could take over the world. Together we are a – what is it? Oh yes. A matriarchy.

Turning to the next page of the purple inkbook we can see *Aestheticism* penned in elaborate faux-brushstroke calligraphic writing and decorated with curlicues and foliage coming out from all sides. We had drawn it during the first week of term because it had seemed like a perfect expression of how we had been feeling that day. Now it already seems like the work of another person entirely. Cringe at the sight of it. Privileged and diseased torpor. *The Portrait of Rachel Smith*. Mirror mirror, capture me now, reclining on my carpet, swathed in a stripy kids' dressing gown, shadowed staring eyes, old makeup smudges, dusty vague slow fingers, throbbing wounded arm, shrivelled besmirched and overweirded brain. Staring at these grand words we learned and captured and entrapped ourselves with.

Aestheticise!

Who said that?

Aestheticise everything!

Did Olga teach me this without saying the word itself?

Did she teach me it from a steaming bath full of rose petals and an entire glass jar of expensive Neal's Yard stolen lavender bath salts?

I think she did.

Did she also teach me politics from the same place, chunnering away in the rose-petalled bath while I poured her another glass of wine about how she was a member of the youth wing of the Communist Party because she had lost faith in Labour after Blair had come along?

I think she did.

She made the edges join up.

Fuck her.

And so. Here we are in a bloody mess, hiding in our outgrown teenage bedroom in our parents' house and no Olga to join up the edges of the spectra. Forced to do nothing but turn these recent pages onto which we bled, inked, drooled our excitement at the vertiginous opening of new multiple worlds. So. To aestheticise politics or to politicise aesthetics? Is it another one of those getting-to-the-same-place things? Do we get to a dangerous place with both? Fascism. Ah yes, it comes back. Walter Benjamin's essay 'The Work of Art in the Age of Mechanical Reproduction'. Reading the yellow-stickered DO NOT REMOVE library copy that had been so multifariously underlined, footnoted, endnoted, sidenoted, decorated with unhelpful marginalia including spurting penises and comedy breasts that you feel you are reading Something Significant before you have even started, which sets you off on a different kind of journey. And then getting to the last sentence and it being *fizz-pop* central. *Communism responds by politicizing art.* Fuckin ace! And yet. Opposites coming back to the same place again. Remembering that Mr Yardley told us in Year 8 History that communism and fascism, if taken to their furthest extremes, would end up at the same place. But the last two sentences in the Benjamin essay give that idea some direction, some motive, some force.

Fizzzzzzzpop. We are entering the arena of the obsessive. Vine leaves and thorned roses crawl about the purpled words that came next:

Renaissance Love Poetry. The discovery, conquering and colonisation of the woman's body masquerading as the discovery of new worlds, new planets, new harmonies. A little sketch of a serenading bard standing underneath the lady's window, strumming the lyre. Learning about the traditions of medieval love poetry and instantly we knew we were just like this figure Petrarch. Petrarch from the womb. Petrarch of the fourth dimension. That is all it all boils down to. Love as the entire world condensed into one silken scarf pulled through a golden ring. It doesn't take a brain fetishist weirdo like this one to understand that when you direct a certain level of libidinal energy into or onto a person it barely matters where they are in the world. It barely matters who they are. They have no idea. It is actually nothing to do with them.

But if Olga wasn't permeating our entire world right now, would we still be channelling this energy, this force? Does it come from her or does it come from us? How many people are we? How many is one? We think we know the answer to this, swallowing a lilac Xanax, which sets off the deep purple of the inkbook and the darkening red of the blood.

N.A.R.C.

Our glistening bleeding arm needs some attention. It had healed to a thick purplish welt since the last time. As it healed it made us think of the word *wort*. Because of its raisedness. Like it was full of something. Congealed blood. Purple bladderwort. Now burst open again. A cut in the surface. Does it do something or say something through its articulation? Art. Ick. You. Lay. Shone.

Are we expressing? Is the wound a poem? What is the opposite of performative language? A linguistic performance?

It's all one. They are actually the same thing.

Think about the simplest, most childlike theory we had learned during those months. Speech Act Theory. It had come as a surprise. A whole lecture seemingly about the sheer power of language and the way it can *do* things just by *saying* things. *I hereby pronounce you*. The book of lectures from the 1960s that sounds like a kids' book. *How to Do Things with Words* by J. L. Austin. *Peter and Jane Do Things with Words*. Examples not included in that book include: Take me. Have me. Fuck me. Mock me. Hurt me. Fuck me up. Do it. Surrendering words. A whole new category. It's easy: just preface anything with 'hereby'. I hereby give you permission to do what you will with me.

Weird how it strays into kink territory immediately. The difficulty of separating the sexual contract from the emotional. And perhaps therein lies the problem.

Interesting how the use of *hereby* legitimates the use of *therein*. Interesting how the use of *therein* legitimates the use of *hither*. Perhaps even *thither*. Wonder what will pop out of me next. Popping *out*, sniggery euphemisms notwithstanding, merely meaning of course, in this case, the lateral popping out from one cell in the mindspace to another cell in the mindspace. It's more like popping *sideways*. In the vein of David Hoyle doing our absolute favourite thing he has ever done on his *Divine David* show: The Divine David Makeup Masterclass. How he pulls his words about. Plays with a transatlantic drawl. Puts a dripping faux-French ending on words. Never seen or heard anything so wonderful. *The Absolute Symbol of Beauty in an Urban EnviroMON.* And guess who also loves David Hoyle. Olga. Of course Olga likes the absurd tipping into the macabre. And of course we do too. Or we do now.

You are Sin.

Yeeowch. A sudden full-body whack of a memory flashback. Me, saying those words to Olga, last night.

Look, your hair is made of snakes. You are Sin.

Did I really call her Sin? Did I make her into an allegorical figure? What kind of pretentious knobhead says something like that at a party? This kind, obviously. Her hair had been made of snakes, though, at the time. Fair enough. But the implications of it, now in our bedroom reflection phase, make the entire sorry self thrill with mortification. And not in a good way. How predictable, how *unimaginative*, to make her into the *Ur*-femme-fatale figure. Damn the desirous intoxicated brain, stuffed full of John Milton's *Paradise Lost* with its soap-opera-level melodrama, creatures like Sin, Death, God, Satan. Harpies, fiends, grotesque and monstrous fallen angels. How is anyone meant to navigate the world of normality, never mind the world of the absurd, and not end up rewriting humans as symbolic figures? Not even the Fiend himself would do such a thing.

The fact is, the words, when spoken, were true. When the world tips upside down, the words you speak are the only thing you have. We are all sociopaths in that moment. What moment do I mean? Oh, you know, the moment when you've taken a tab of acid and your head is full of Judaeo-Christian creation myths written as epic poetry and the impressive phrases of French philosophers and you meet the girl of your dreams who is actually the personification of Sin complete with snake-hair and evil intent. Those moments. In those moments you are only as true as the words that speak you.

In the inkbook on the page dated 13 February 1999, the word 'Deconstruction' is enclosed in a kind of diamond Tardis-like structure. This weird phenomenon Deconstruction had made us think of magic more than anything else we learned at uni in those months. It spawned iterations of itself in us instantly. The constant, frustrating, beautiful attempt to define a theory that defines itself as *not* being a theory. Paradox, again. Eternally trying to define the thing that resists the definition. Of course there has to be some frustration in there somewhere. See how it's all sexual? Fucking all of it. Language's progression mirrors the structure of desire. The. Inability. To. Ever. Get. To. The. Thing. Itself. But. The. Eternal. Desire. To. Try. Libidinal chains. The ouroboros. The snake that bites its tail to spite itself. And so it seems we have a cyclical thesaurus that speaks us. A whole wealth of terms that mean slightly different things but are all interconnected. Seminal. Seminary. Seminar. Spawn. Satan. We cannot not think of Olga in amongst these terms. It is driving us mad.

Focus. We had learned how the idea of language *doing stuff* rather than just *saying stuff* went from *Peter and Jane Do Things with Words* to *Jeter and Pane Contort Words into Unimaginable Shapes and Nothing Is Ever the Same Again.* You see how there is no difference between the theory of deconstruction and taking acid. To deconstruct something means to take it apart bit by bit, you imagine, and always we think of Lego pieces being disassembled methodically. But there is something about the process of the taking apart of the Lego pieces that means they are fundamentally changed. And so it is with the brain. There is no hope of putting the pieces back together again in the same way, or even retaining the desire to put them back together. Because you realise that opposites are the same, that centrality is an illusion, that originality does not exist, that marginal, weird meanings of words are on a plane with the generally understood ones, that words work of their own accord against your will, that you are just a tool being spoken by a force that goes beyond, before, above, below, through and underneath you. Never had we learned anything closer to a dark art in school or uni before learning about deconstruction. You learn about what happens in this seemingly pedantic etymological trickery and it spawns nothing but further pedantic etymological trickery. And last night, the acid trip and the dark underside of the world, everything splitting apart and showing its underside. Simultaneous brainfucks, multiple thought-trains with no tracks because they are flying. Particles deconstructed.

It's. All. One.

Fizzpop. Having the stuff of your psyche forced through the mincer of these frameworks, it is painful at a visceral level. At a visceral level, and we mean of course the viscera that inhere within as well as the heart on the sleeve and the guts stretched across the skin and the soul that flies out, out, out of the cuts in the arm. It hurts. But it is impossible to learn these things and not live your life through them. Secular worship alright. We worship the scaffolding. Amen.

Do others do this.

Do others feel this.

I am asking you.

Yes, you.

Here's a joke for you. What do you get if you cross a psychoanalyst with a Renaissance poet? The answer, no doubt, would have been found within the lecture that we had missed due to a mega-bender. Chastising ourselves the morning after, we spent exactly fifty minutes sitting in the library with two books in front of us, reading a random line of Jacques Lacan's *Seminars* alternated with a random line of John Donne's *Selected Poems*.

Cheeky fuckers, both of them. And yet. The gravitas piles up over the years. Decades for Jacques. Centuries for John. Gender fucking bias. Preordained. Pre-decided. It's easier to become a Famous and Important Writer if you're a man. Olga taught us that.

Well, it had seemed that knots were important somehow. A line from Lacan: *The knot is the only support conceivable for a relation between something and something else.* And what do we need right now? A knot, any knot, to allow us to relate something to something else. Because right now the loudest voice we can hear is another dead white man, the poet T. S. Eliot, standing on a beach somewhere on the south coast. On Margate Sands, connecting nothing with nothing. And somehow it makes sense. When we connect nothing with nothing, the only thing we have is the connection, the knot.

The inability to grasp both objects and thoughts in this current hungover-to-fuck state is annoying. What to do when such a thing happens. Make this variegated system into one. Condense the scattered atoms of the self into one knot. A medicinal orgasm purely to focus the elements inside you into one area and produce enough tired endorphins to maybe allow oneself to take a shower or make a cup of tea or both.

So. Detach body from brain.
Or. Perhaps keep brain involved this time.
Allow self to think about girls. In this context.
Fuck.
Touch girl self with a girl's hand.
Girl squared.

Girl^2

Give self orgasm.
Come.
Quickly.

All that I desir'd and got.

'Twas but.
A dream.
Of thee.

Feeling as yet incomplete. *Not enough for I have more.* Religious metaphysical poets are the horniest of bastards. 'Tis a pity they were all such fucking misogynists. We could have done Donne better. *Nor free, except you ravish me.* Carry on touching grimly away at yourself regardless until you come a second and then a third time. Now all your muscles are tensed hard and bristling and you feel sore at the core of your coreless core. Rubbed dry.

Well, I think that thanks to Joyce we are reaching something I had not imagined. I had not immediately imagined it, but it came to me with time – to consider Joyce's text, the way it is made. It is made exactly like a Borromean knot.

Consider the entire body as a flayed erogenous surface. The grater that grates itself. Inside the same as outside. What would that look like. A Möbius strip. More. A Klein bottle. More. A cylindrical, hollow, self-consuming orifice-phallus. More. A nonsensical object. I wish. The ideality of. What was Jacques Derrida's unfinished PhD thesis going to be about again? The ideality of. Something. Butterflying questions. Less numb now though. It has worked. The self has gathered somewhat. Feeling is throbbing through us. Tears well but not from a regular type of crying. A wank and a cry. A cry and a wank. A crank and a why. A useful morning ritual to remember you can still feel. Some nausea is filtering through now. Some guilt. Dried blood still everywhere. Sweating inside our dressing gown. A head full of new desires. There could be more than Olga. More girls that could do this. Could fuel this. Fuck.

Take your aching self into the bathroom, disrobe and step into the shower. Do not look at body. Nineteen years is just a quiver of a self. A cerebral fizz-pop is just a mini thoughtgasm.

Rachel Gillian Charlotte Watkins permits a few tears in the shower. Total conceptual and watery blending. A drop of wine pervades the whole ocean. Even the Stoics cried sometimes. A conceptual fucking fuck. New project: becoming-harpy. Agony and ecstasy and triple screaming heads.

Fuck her.

Chapter 4

VOICE	Olga
SCENE	The Empress Ballroom
HOUR	12 noon, 16 June 1999
PLEASURE BEACH RIDE	Pasaje del Terror
SUBSTANCE	Ectoplasm
ORGAN	Brain (amygdala)
SYMBOL	Black hole
COLOUR	Green against black
FORMULA	$C_{37}H_{34}N_2Na_2O_9S_3$
ART / TECHNIC	Running (pursued)
HORMONE	Adrenaline
HOMERIC TITLE	Hades

Terry/Tiresia can be seen through the window of Cash Converters. Looks fit today in her blokey work shirt and trousers, even when clearly hungover and knackered. Interesting how everyone has a crush on Terry. Lads, lasses, and everyone in between. With blue eyes and long lashes, Tiresia is perfect for her real job, which happens after the sun goes down: donning huge and fantastical wigs and outlandish dresses, showing off her amazing pins in stilettos, accentuating those cheekbones with stripes of shadow, then singing songs, telling stories, making weird art onstage and mixing blackest of black humour with strange, life-affirming surges of determination that the world isn't as messed up as we have been led to believe. There is some hope. Prefers the female pronoun but can't get away with it at work. It may be nearly Y2K but Cash Converters are just not that progressive yet.

Terry has glitter at the sides of her forehead and in the stubble around her jawbone. Through the mass of telly screens, food mixers, CD players and vacuum cleaners displayed in the window, Terry is standing chatting to a colleague and the glitter is winking under the lights. Look at that. Always under her own mobile spotlight. Glitz and glam even now, in the day job, with bags under the eyes.

Lean in, press our nose to the glass and flick a quick V in her direction. Terry notices while pretending not to notice, smoothly continuing the conversation, so we screw up our face with tongue pressed into the space above the chin in 'stupid' expression and Terry is now trying not to laugh while listening to Linda or Brenda or Wanda or whoeverthefuck it is. We then mime smoking a fag and after a minute or so Terry manages to say something to Linda/Brenda/Wanda that allows her to grab a jacket and 'take five'. With a surreptitious finger she points to the left. Round the corner we go.

–My favourite person!

Terry bursts out of the back door and clasps us to her. Fag smell and faint sweat and booze vapour trails and spiced warmth of CK1 cologne. That smell combination. Makes you want to cry, somehow. Probably the hangover talking. In the daylight, Terry has eyebags that you could climb into. And fall asleep, probably.

–How do you do it.

–What?

–Stay up all hours and then do a day shift in here! And not fall asleep standing up!

–Says you!

We eyeroll, then nod.

–Yeah, fair enough. At least I can go and sleep now!

–Lucky basta... – ohhhh no, listen, come with me – quickly.

Terry grabs us by the arm and pulls us away, setting off at a pace across Alfred Street, trotting together round the corner to Leopold Grove and towards the back of the Winter Gardens.

–Don't look back!

–Where are we going? Slow down, Tez, I'm gonna spew!

–Just come on, I'll tell you in a minute. In here.

Ducking into the back entrance of the Winter Gardens. We are both breathing hard. Sweat on foreheads. Smokers' lungs. A small cacoughony of catching-breath. Everything around is a bit blurry.

–What the fuck? Who did you see?

–It was Darren.

–Fuuuuuuuckinell.

Terry's blue eyes, eyebagged eyes, now hunted. Prey eyes. Fair enough. Darren Ricci. Bad for both. Bad squared. The secret about Darren. Secrets, multiple. Not just money owed. More than that. Terry knows that Darren knows that Terry knows. The secret. And no one else can ever know. No one can know, either, about last year. Darren, Mark and Wayne Ricci. The Ricci brothers. All under one roof. A force to be reckoned with. And reckon with all of them I have. Wayne, the oldest, evillest and best in bed. Nasty fucker. Fit though. Fuck him. I did, of course. For a while. But Mark. Another kettle of stinking rotten fish altogether. Don't want to think of – too late. Last year. Face down looking at the carpets of the bedroom next to the bedroom I had fucked his brother in. Brother to brother. Went from joke to deadly serious in a split second. A no. Was not. Enough. Deserves all he got. Yes I told. This time I told. I wasn't the only one. No regrets. He's inside now. Where he belongs. But of course Darren still stalks the streets. Loose cannon Darren. Just enough of a sense of justice to feel that he must stand up for his brother.

–He won't find us in here.

–Oh my god Tezza, do you realise where we are?

At the same time we look up at the curved and intricately stuccoed ceiling of the Empress Ballroom. Grandeur! And why not.

–Milady.

–Why, I thought you'd never ask!

We take the lead, this time. Take Terry gently by the arm. Gracefully, solemnly, together we waltz. One-two-three, one-two-three. A rush of adrenaline and fear and relief and we are laughing, bubbles, cackles, waves upon waves of hysteria until Terry joins in and off we go, carousing, gliding around the ballroom amongst the odd frowning shopper nipping through the building towards the Houndshill. Two sets of two eyes creased up and streaked with tears of laugh-cry-laughter while all around the world is whirling.

–Okay stopstopstop. I really will spew this time.

The world takes a bit longer to stop. We cling to one another, anchoring ourselves together in a sea of unsteady air.

–Eurgh, I feel seasick. Why the hell did we do that.

–More exercise than I've done for months!

Tottering over to a couple of blue, slightly threadbare velveteen-upholstered chairs, together we flop. Wait for fastbeating hearts to recede.

–So what colour would you call this? we ask Terry, thumping the velvet chair. Terry sighs.

–You never get tired of this, do you.

–Nope!

–Ok, so it looks like a kind of ... grey. Maybe a kind of pale green?

–Nope! It's blue! Bright blue.

Terry shrugs and we laugh.

–I just can't get my head around it.

–It's not rocket science, chuck. It is brain science though, actually. Haha. A One-Woman Wonder of Modern Medicine, me.

–What's it called again? Tridentia? Trickantia?

–Tritanopia. Blue–yellow colour blindness. You know what the worst thing about it is?

–What?

–Who is normally affected by it. Alkies and old people. It comes with cataracts. Only one in ten thousand people has it from birth.

–Well, you know, Tezza, you are one in a million ...

–Whatever. Fuck off with your weirdo massive technicolour vision. I happen to be in extremely learned company with my condition.

Terry preens an imaginary speck of dust from the shoulder of her work shirt.

–Why? Who else d'you know who's got it?

–Only the Father of Western Literature as we know it.

–Eh? Who's that then? Shakespeare?

–Nope. Older.

–Erm ... whassisname ... Geoffrey Chaucer?

–Guess again! Older.

We squint, frown, think, shrug.

–I dunno. My brain can't think any older than that. Was there even literature before that?

–Course there was. Think ancient Greece.

–Dunno. Can't think. Who?

–Homer! You know Homer, right?

–Uh ... guess so. But don't know anything about him except, you know, Homer Simpson.

–Well settle in, love, because I have a theory for you.

I could probably make millions if I wrote this down. But I'm gonna premiere it here, just for you. Ready?

We are nodding, already smiling. Tezza and her stories. Love it.

–Okay! So. I have a theory. Okay, okay, it's not completely my theory, I tell a lie. It was one of my teachers at primary school who got me thinking about it. Mr Bannister. I was about eight. The lads were taking the piss. They always took the piss anyway, y'know, because of, whatever. Being a girly boy. Playing with the girls. Anyway, when they found out about the colour blindness it just added another level. Every day was hell. But one day Mr Bannister took me to one side and told me something. They had just been laughing at me because I was colouring in the sea – we all had to draw posters advertising Blackpool for summat-or-other – and I had picked a green pencil to colour in the sea. *Snot green sea*, they were saying. Some cleverclogs had realised that if you said 's'not', as in 'it's not', it sounded like snot. So they were kind of chanting. *Snot-green-sea. Snot-green-sea.* And pushing me around and making nosepicking signs and calling me Snot Green Terry. Ugh.

Terry shudders and shakes her head.

–Anyway, Mr Bannister gave them all a bollocking and then he said to me very quietly, he said, Do you know what, Terry. One of the most famous stories ever told was by a man in ancient Greece. That man was called Homer and the story is the *Odyssey*. Odyssey means journey. It's a fantastic story and it's still known about all over the world. And you know what? He gets the colour of the sea wrong.

–How did he get it wrong? we butt in.

–I'm getting to it! Apparently, in the *Odyssey*, Homer never mentions the colour blue. Not once. But the sea is everywhere. The whole journey is across the sea. He describes it all the time. But he never mentions the colour blue. He says it's like the colour of dark wine or something, which I think doesn't really make sense to your regular punter, am I right?

We nod.

–So I think Mr Bannister was telling me this to cheer me up, but basically, being someone who knows about colour blindness, I reckon Homer had tritanopia. He couldn't see blue, but he wrote this amazing story and he began the whole of literature.

We consider this carefully. Affect a lofty gaze.

–So you're basically saying that your special needs really *are* special.

–Fuck OFF! Terry shoves us, gently.

–Hey, d'you reckon it's safe now? I need to get back.

–Yeah. Let's just go carefully.

Linking arms, we tentatively retrace our steps to the back of the shop. Okay. The old heart, now racing for another reason. Okay. Talk to Terry. You know it will help. Screw up courage. Get the words out. We're nearly at the back door again. Grab Terry's arm.

–Listen, can I tell you summat?

–Course you can, what's up? You haven't been threatened by Dean or Max or any of that lot again, have you?

–No no, it's nothing like that. It's –

–Are you *blushing*, missus? What the fuck? Wonders never cease!

–Don't take the piss, Tez, or I'm not saying anything!

–Okay, okay. Terry smooths her face down with one hand, wiping the smile away, and looks expectantly at us, immaculate eyebrows slightly raised in concern.

Deep breath. First and maybe only ever time to say this out loud.

–I met a girl last night.

–So what?

–*No*. The emphasis of the *no* is serious. It was like –

And we are shaking our head, unable to carry on the sentence. What can I say, anyway. I don't have words for that. What was it, even?

–It was like a *love* thing.

Face is properly red now. Can feel it. Terry does not laugh, although somewhere, probably, there is the urge to.

–Well, that's alright, isn't it? Who is she?

Terry's reaction. So casual. You met someone. A girl. Who is she. It's a thing. Panic stations. Can't do this. Abort. Abort, now.

–Aaaaah, I actually don't know if I can even talk about it. I don't know where she lives but I think maybe Poulton or Thornton way. But the thing is, *I can't really remember what happened* ...

Terry does laugh at that, although gently.

–Story of my life, darling. Don't worry. No harm done though, right? Are you going to see her again?

–I dunno.

We look at the floor. Face still red. Ashamed.

–I can't remember how it ended but I think I might've told her to fuck off or something.

Deep breaths. We haven't even talked about the fact that she is a she. Terry doesn't care. Of course Terry doesn't care. This is why we ended up here, of all places, without even realising. Tezza. So wise, and doesn't judge, ever.

–So what can you remember? Did you kiss her?

–Yeah. A lot. But it was different to any other time that I've kissed a girl. You know, when you're messing around or showing off or whatever. This was the real deal. It's making me feel sick thinking about it.

Terry is laughing properly now.

–That's not the normal reaction I'd expect with a love thing, is it? Instant vomit-recall?

–TEZZA! You said you wouldn't take the piss! It's fucking terrifying!

–Okay, okay. I'm sorry.

Terry takes a long drag on her cigarette, examines her nails, exhales extravagantly.

–So you've met someone. You were off your face. Nothing new there. I'm guessing she was too. You don't know what happened. You're completely knackered and hanging like a bastard and coming down and whatever else is going on in there.

Terry places one finger on our forehead and taps it gently three times.

–So *forget* about it. For now, anyway. Go home and get some kip. Have some for me, too.

We nod, slowly, blush receding. 'Tis true. She's right, I am dog-tired. To the bones. So tired that sober sleep is scary. Drinking is easier than sleeping.

–Look, I've gotta get back in. Linda will be telling everyone I'm out t'back necking my girlfriend –

We shove her, roughly, mock angry, but grinning anyway.

–Fuck OFF!

Truth is I would be proud to be Terry's girlfriend. So why the fuck am I so shy about Rachel the shining luminous brighteyed wildcat girl. Arrrrrgh.

–Take care of yourself, flower. Get some kip.

–Says you!

Terry grins now, too.

–Come here.

Terry hugs us and we hug her back. Warmth and energy. My battery pack. Replenishment.

–Hope it's quiet today. Maybe a quiet pint when you finish? Send me a message!

Terry's eyes are rolling.

–A quiet pint, she says. How many times have I heard that from you? Six hours later, seventeen tequilas down!

–SAYS YOU!!!

Our pouting kiss – the Perv-Smoulder, Tezza calls it – blown, across the wind from outside to in, to Terry's receding figure, is momentarily framed and slowly obliterated by the hydraulically squealing self-closing firedoor.

Chapter 5

VOICE	Olga
SCENE	The Industrial Estate
HOUR	1 p.m., 16 June 1999
PLEASURE BEACH RIDE	Big Dipper
SUBSTANCE	Sausage barm
ORGAN	Gut
SYMBOL	Winged envelope
COLOUR	White
FORMULA	$C_{18}H_{19}N$
ART / TECHNIC	Telecommunication
HORMONE	Serotonin
HOMERIC TITLE	Aeolus

BUCHANAN STREET: ABOVE THE CROWDS, AIMING FOR THE CLOUDS

The empty top deck of the 14 with all the windows open is not a bad place to be after a dead morning shift. Nausea is barely present, surprisingly. Just relief. Okay, and some nerves, about going back into college. The scene of The Dropping Out. But this time, it's important. So, we say sternly to ourselves, use the time to get your head together and think about what to say to him. Going back into those stale-smelling common rooms. The Rossall and Arnold kids, even the Baines and Hodgson kids, mingling with the Collegiate kids and the kids from over Wyre. All those becoming-adults. Almost-students. Some of them driving actual cars and parking them in an actual student car park. In their navy-blue polo shirts and their baggy jeans. Eager and nerdy and well-meaning, some of them. Sure some of them started carrying briefcases. Hanging round the sweaty table tennis room at lunchtimes. Others trying desperately to be quirky or dressing like full-on moshers in Slipknot hoodies. And then some of them posh, undeniably, effortlessly, an extra sheen to their skin and their hair and their teeth, playing tennis at private clubs, going abroad on ski trips in winter.

Is that why we left? Because of them? A small monster of shame clutches at the internal organs momentarily. Fuck off. Get thee gone. Not helpful. Focus on the matter at hand. It's okay because I've written a whole bloody play off me own back, haven't I? The notepad, slightly battered and stained, is in our bag. Don't need A-Levels for that.

What will he say though? Just imagine. Aim high for a second. No point in not.

DEVONSHIRE ROAD: YOUR NAME IN LIGHTS

Imagine that he, Mr Avocat, knows of some kind of national competition that you can enter. Young Dramatist of the Year. There's always a Young Whatever of the Year, isn't there? Young Musician of the Year. Young Chef of the Year. Young Wanker of the Year. Ha. Can think of many contenders for that. But really. Imagine. I know I'm good. I fucking know it. Some of me is in that play. And I reckon it deals with stuff he could only dream of. And maybe he does dream of it. But, ugh. No need to go there. No idea about the private life of teachers, thankfully. But there is something in him that's soft. It's not the way some men look at me. Thank fuck. I wouldn't go to him if it was. No, it's something else. So, he might help. Just imagine. Mr Avocat hands the leaflet over. It's a national competition. *It's worth a shot. You're a talented writer. Just type it up and post it to that address.*

It's a London address. Mr Avocat lets me use the computers in the computer room even though I dropped out of college months ago. I type it up and post it off. A few months later I get a letter at home. CONGRATULATIONS, it says. YOUR PLAY HAS BEEN DEEMED THE MOST PROMISING ACROSS OUR NATIONWIDE COMPETITION, AND WE INVITE YOU TO LONDON, WHERE WE WILL PUT ON YOUR PLAY AT THE NATIONAL THEATRE.

And then no need to move back here. Stay in London, get the one play under the belt, start writing the second, befriend some rich arty types, move into a pad by the river Thames and live out the bohemian dream.

LAYTON INSTITUTE: DIRECTOR'S CHAIR

Five-star reviews in the *Guardian* and the *Times* and a front-page story in the *Gazette* with an interview. LOCAL GIRL FINDS STARDOM IN LONDON. OUR YOUNG THESPIAN HITS THE BIG TIME and the subheading OLGA SHAKESPEARE?

So which playwright do you most identify with, Ms Adessi? Well, my first love was always Mr Shakespeare. I learned all his sonnets off by heart, sitting on the school bus. It was soothing. *O me! what eyes hath Love put in my head.* But there's a point where I feel I take things further than our Will, you know what I mean?

RODWELL WALK: REALITY BITES

Strips of grass and scraggly trees on the right-hand side of the road. The way into Grange Park. Harold Pinter, more like. Never would have known who he was if it wasn't for the Manics. Spitting out Plath and Pinter. White, box-like detached houses on the left. Nastiness and depression. Red tiled roofs. *Which have no correspondence with true sight.* Fevered madness, of course. That way madness lies. And that way I lie. And I do that so well. I'm no fucking Shakespeare. I couldn't write a sonnet. But I know I can write an existentialist play or a surrealist poem. I like surrealism because it feels realer than realism. Realer than real.

POULTON ROAD PETROL STATION: FRENEMY

Fuck, Nikki Rawlings works in there doesn't she. Duck, hide, don't let her see you. Hang on. You're on the top deck of the bus. She's in the shop. Don't be a fuckin idiot. But still. Causes a chill in the bones, and for why? It's not like we ever did anything to her. She just hates me because I've got a voice as good as hers but I've also got a brain. But she thinks I'm weird. I am fuckin weird! But so is she!

> *O me! what eyes hath fuckers put in her head,*
> *Which have no correspondence with true sight;*
> *Or, if they have, where is her judgement fled,*
> *That censures falsely what they see aright?*

Inside the headphones, Jeff Buckley. *Lilac wine. Sweet and heady, like my love.* But no: not thoughts for now. Don't think, just go, just do. All doing, no thinking. Spectacle first, theory after. This is bigger than last night. No wild girls, no perfect kisses, no hot, cold, hot memories. Not for now. Focus. This is your future. These dusty men, these teachers. Nothing but gatekeepers, remember. Gatekeepers with weak wills. Gatekeepers led by their cocks like every single man on this planet. And coming back to this place means nothing other than the attempt to get through a bloody gate. No one else is going to hand us a key so we've got to work for it. Got to exercise some persuasion. And the art of persuasion is something we can do very well.

So. Check face in compact mirror after alighting from the bus. Makeup definitely verging on doll-like. But a teenage doll who got a bit older and went out a lot. Dolls with bags under their eyes and gritty remnants of dirty, off-white powder in the bottom corners of their handbags. Blue eyeshadow, rouged cheeks, red pout. But this look will be useful, just you wait. More Chipie, of course. Half comforting, half just another reminder of work. It's the Chipie that comes before, during and after the chippy. Oh, but what will he think, seeing us like this, clearly in work clothes, clearly on a road to nowhere. Goodfornothing, that Olga. Wasting her life wrapping chips in paper. Should be ashamed. But to bow down in shame, to assume it at least, will help the cause, surely. Channel the real feeling into a stronger version of itself. That is the real key of acting. If only. They. Could see. The fire inside of me. The weirdness, the bullying, a payoff, surely.

The Kabin on the corner of Mowbray Drive has fucking amazing egg mayo barms. But will egg mayo be friendly towards the growling torpid octopus in the gut? Initially yes. Then absolutely no. But ultimately yes. The trick is to go small and gradual. Don't stuff your face or it will just come back up. Too much mayo is not a good idea. How about a BLT. Yep. Healthier. Salty and crispy and lettuce and tomato and stuff.

Ah no. Sausage and bacon and brown sauce. That's the one.

The clock inside the Kabin says 1:13 p.m. The prescribed meeting time is not until 2 p.m. The sun is hot. Belly growls. When was the last time we ate? Was there an attempt at the eating of a yoghurt at some point last night? A Müller Crunch Corner. O yes. Much hilarity. Each chocolate-covered O a tiny doughnut galaxy. Rings around the world. Or worlds around the ring. Zing: another flashback. Rachel saying something weird but it sticks in the head like nothing else. *Imagine the entire world as a scarf pulled through a golden ring.* But what had been the point? And a word. *Entireosphere.* A good one. Keeping that. Oh yeah. And. My own failed joke about torus and Taurus. They sound the same, see. Homophonous. In every accent? Think so. But. No one knows what a torus is. Rachel did though. She's fucking smart, her. Scary smart. One feels inadequate on all levels. Such luminous skin: she's trying to fuck herself up, I can see, but she's so fresh, there's all these layers of health underneath the scars, I don't understand why she does it but I do know that I want no part in her fuckuppery.

So. Time to stroll while munching from its white paper bag the glorious soft white barmcake that gently embraces the crispy salty goodness of bacon *and* sausage *and* brown sauce. The belly does not complain too much – in fact we feel a surge of joy when the salty tang hits all the tasting corners of the mouth and the bite is soft, soft, then crispy warm comforting hotfat grease. This was a good idea.

From the Kabin's ticking wallclock to Scanlite's proud digital display. Analogue to digital, right there. The Information Age is just another age like the Stone Age and the Iron Age, right? Except instead of stone or iron as our raw materials we have information. Computers as power tools. Back when we were wielding rocks to bash other rocks and make fire, never could we have conceived of this. Some red bits on a black screen announcing the time as 13:18 and the temperature as 20 degrees Celsius. Scanlite Visual Information. Whoever would have thought. But why do the black bits have that particular shape? Look closely and they are like elongated diamonds. Not quite diamonds, though. Something scratches at the corner of the brain from Physics at school. LED is a Light Emitting Diode. Is that LED?

What is it? Radio Wave 96.5 is down here too. Murdering your ears with the classics since 198something. Radio waves, now there's a thought. Not waves like the sea. Not waves like light. Waves like sound? What is sound? What is the worst sound of all sounds? Why is the sound also the space between two adjacent islands? Nails on blackboards. Sawing through metal. Sawing not soaring. Only in the dulcet tones of the fair North West do 'sawing' and 'soaring' sound the same. Saying sawing sounds stupid. Adventures in pun. Pun porn. If pun porn existed I would have it covered. But did I even say it out loud? No one will ever know. When the insides and the outsides get mulched around it's impossible to tell the difference between the internal and the external voices. WARNING. KLAXON. Is a klaxon ever used in a non-comedy sense, I wonder.

Klaxon. Metaphor extended.

Ugh.

A double beep in the handbag. The 3210 has so many more sounds than the 3200. It's so much smaller and sexier, too. Metallic buttons, not rubber ones. But the gut lurches as another flashback clangs its way into our memory. The scrawling of numbers with a biro onto a skinny arm decorated with white and red scars. Did I give her my number. This will be her. This will be her. The certainty of it thwacks us even harder than the flashback. Pull out the phone.

1 message
received

Lee D.
WHERE DID U GO
SEXY

Ah, fuck. Be still my. Not her. Not her. Sighing, we chuck the phone back into the handbag and take another bite of the butty as the labouring heart gradually slows back down to a canter. But the food feels weird. I have a cement mixer instead of a mouth and they forgot to add the water. This bite isn't going anywhere. Swallowing feels wrong but we do it anyway. The phone beeps again. Fucking Lee. He knows I'm working today. I remember telling him before we passed out.

1 message
received

Ra chelion%$&*
Hi is this Olga?

Not Lee. Not Lee. A girl. *The* girl. Even the word *girl* sounds different. Fuuuuuuuuuuucking hell. The remainder of the bacon and sausage falls out of the barmcake onto the pavement and we do not fucking care because last night apparently we typed a number in our phone and the number goes to the shiny liontigerlamplightgirl from last night and it is *impossible* to tell whether this feeling is unbelievable ecstatic bliss OR the exact feeling you have when you die OR when you overdose on speed or another nervous system stimulant. Or perhaps just a minor pulmonary event.

It is that, alright. Fuuuuuuuuck.

Type as quickly as we can, hammering through the letters on each number with a forefinger. Quick, before I change my mind. Look round to see if anyone else is looking and then laugh aloud at self. Furtiveness! Fuckssake. What the. Argh.

Hi liontigergirl, how are you feeling?
I am rough. Just finished work. Had
loads of fun with you last night. X

And off it goes. The little envelope. Carried on Heaven's breath itself. Nothing to stop it flying through the digital ether on its little wings and reaching its destination. Whothefuckknowswhere. How far from here? How long does it take? The butty, now pavement trash, has lost every single inch of its appeal. Is text messaging instantaneous? Don't think so – not quite. Standing a few metres away from the Doc Martens shop, staring hard down into the empty cavern of the phone screen looking for the words '1 message received' to appear, but they don't. Not for two, three, four, five minutes.

Electrical storms could be happening up there in the skies. Who knows. Space revolutions. Satellite rebellions. People climbing up the masts and chopping the wires in protest at the way our lives are changing due to these little beeping handbag fuckers. Oh well. It's just some dark pixels on a grey screen with a girl at the other end, somewhere not too far from here.

Fucking digital tumbleweeds. Phones need a screen-saver of that. Fuckssake. Heart can't take it.

Phone chucked back into handbag. On to the photo shop. There are some incriminating photos to be picked up. Nakedness, massive spliffs, lines of whoknowswhat, unkempt pubic hair. Fun in Lee's shed. Fun in Lee's bed. Just at the moment that we hand over a fiver to the man in the shop, the little handbag fucker beeps again.

Ahhhhhhhhhh shit.

1 message
received

Ra chelion%$&*

Me too. Dying today. Or
want to die. Can't decide.

Is that it? A huge fucking great stone inside us, suddenly. And perhaps ... relief? Maybe we'll never see each other again and I won't have to worry about that lesbian word balloon any more. The man hands over the photos and our change and only then do we remember to feel embarrassed about the contents of the photos. But the photos have changed into badges of normality and we almost want to get them out right there and show them to the man. Look, look, see. Just some healthy heterosexual hedonism going on here. Nothing weird.

L. E. S. B . . .

Double handbag fucker beep.

1 message
received

Ra chelion%$&*

It was amazing to meet you.
Hope we can meet up soon.

This girl is weird. No one sends two messages in a row that could have fit into one. And no kiss. Why does that matter though.

And how to reply is the question. Not how, actually, but whether. There's the rub. Can't do this right now. Imagine before we did it this way, before we sent text messages. Before phone calls even. Writing letters that took weeks to arrive. My darling Rachel. Dearest. Yours, Olga. Fuck *off*, brain. But really, though. Imagine in those times. Lesbians in dresses or perhaps in men's clothes, shunned by society, or maybe accepted as an eccentric, depending on your social class maybe. Or studied by medical men as an ANOMALY. Me and this girl, in 1920s Paris. We have loads of money. We take rooms on a fashionable avenue. We have a statue of Sappho in our entrance hall. Artists and writers come and visit us. It is cool to be us. She wears a suit and monocle like that character Cissy in *You Rang, M'Lord?* I wear bohemian scarves and flapper dresses with sequins and bright red lipstick. Sometimes we swap our clothes and roles around because no one is there to tell us otherwise. Glamour! But here we are, on Mowbray Drive. Palmer Quinn's Electrical Wholesalers. Chadwicks Kitchen Showroom. Signage. Plumbing. Flooring. Roofing. Bathrooms. Screwfix. Travis Perkins. Joinery. Paint. Ashworths Beds. Central Tiles. The Blackpool Power Tool Co. Self Storage. Woodburning Stove Centre. Timber. Computers. Cars. Vans. Employees on lunch hours. Empty fields and hedgerows all around apart from the two-carriage Northern Rail train trundling across from Poulton to Layton. At the end, the three low, wide, grey concrete blocks of the Blackpool Sixth Form College, Highfurlong and Collegiate. An appointment to keep. As if to mock, the giant digital display outside the Digital Solutions shop declares that it is now 13:51 and 23 degrees. *When I do count the clock that tells the time*. Inside our head, the bright lights of Showbusiness. Still shining.

Chapter 6

VOICE	Olga
SCENE	The Sixth Form College
HOUR	2 p.m., 16 June 1999
PLEASURE BEACH RIDE	Revolution
SUBSTANCE	Cake
ORGAN	Ear (synaesthetic)
SYMBOL	Sphere
COLOUR	Purple
FORMULA	3:2
ART / TECHNIC	The Classroom Drama of Sacred Geometry through Quadrophonic Speakers
HORMONE	Glucagon-like peptide 1
HOMERIC TITLE	Scylla and Charybdis

So. For the first time we enter the Sixth Form College building through the visitors' entrance rather than the student entrance. All pale lilacs and greens. Has it been done up or is it just posher at this end of the college? The receptionist looks about our age. Bored out of her skull sitting there all day, surely. There are doodles on the notepad in front of her and some writing scrawled on her hand. Hi, I've come to see Mr Avocat. He's expecting me. Olga Adessi. Look, to see my name scrawled there in the visitors' book feels surreal. As does being handed a visitors' badge. As does taking a seat. All strangely muted, but that could be the state of mind, remember. Strangely stretched and elongated, everything still is. Muffled too. But the soft gravel of his voice is like instant coffee. A judder into the present.

–Ms Adessi. *Enchanté*. We meet again.

Mr Avocat's grey dusty sweep of a fringe is exactly the same. Red bowtie unchanged. Slightly stooped stance identical. Strange large black shoes as always. Like brickies' boots. One noticeably curled more upwards than the other. Smile gentle. His inclination an almost-bow.

–Follow me.

Solemnly, now, processing through the soursmelling chairscraping echoing common room. Youths in skater jeans and baggy T-shirts draped and lolling across chairs. The little tribes seem so childish now, even a year on. Mosher types with baby mohawks and DDR jackets. Townie types in trackies and clean white trainers. Nerdy types in almost-school uniform. Britpop lads with mod hair. A scant few goth types with whitened faces and blackened eyes and Marilyn Manson hoodies. Nothing has changed in a year. A battalion of vending machines, some working, some not.

Hoots, calls, chatter, plastic cups of coffee, paper bags of chips, the hot dog maker, the plastic cheese toasties, Mary's Bar making up Pot Noodles marked-up threefold. Stale pre-lunchtime cooking grease scent pervades. And together, as though heading up a regal wedding retinue, we enter the empty classroom. One of the carpeted ones, quieter, comfier, lending itself more to sleepiness. The classroom smell here also unchanged. Memory flood. Here I was the best fucking Titania this room has ever seen. Fucking morons stuttering over blank verse. Said Shakespeare was shit. Why the hell did they choose to study it then. But focus, now, on the task in hand. And lo, and so, just as we try to escape our pasts, just as we must assume our parts. Remember how impressed he was when I recited all those sonnets. This is nothing different. Act it, then. Do what you do best.

MR AVOCAT: So, Olga, what can I do for you?
OLGA *(beaming)*: Are you still doing *A Midsummer Night's Dream*?
MR AVOCAT: Indeed we are. Your Titania will take some forgetting.
OLGA: I still fancy Kenneth Branagh.
MR AVOCAT: I don't blame you. But that is not why you're here, is it?

Olga bows her head.
The feint. Assume modesty. Assume diffidence.

OLGA *(guiltily, as if t'were a crime)*: I've written a play. I wanted to tell you about it. I want to get it on the stage.

MR AVOCAT: Wonderful! What's it about?

OLGA: Identity. Power. Sex. Death.

MR AVOCAT: Fantastic! So what happens in the plot?

OLGA: Well, there's this young woman. She's a businesswoman. She works in London. She's at the top of her game and she's only in her twenties. She's amazingly successful, and amazingly beautiful, and also amazingly evil. She wins the best deals. She wears the highest heels. She wears tailored pencil-skirt suits. She also works as a dominatrix. Men in higher positions than her who live in the poshest suburbs pay her hundreds of pounds to visit them in her pencil-skirt suit and walk over their backs in her stilettos. She doesn't need the money but she likes the thrill. Because power isn't ever enough for her. She needs to feel power in work and sexual power. But she can't form relationships. She doesn't know how. She doesn't know how to do them without the power thing, without playing one person off against another or twisting people's words or actions to use them against them. Because. She's got it the wrong way round. And. She's unstable. Existentially. She doesn't feel like she can carry on existing. It ends with her suicide. She throws herself off the roof of the office building where she works. The twenty-fifth floor. She lands in the middle of the street. In Canary Wharf. That's one of the financial districts of London. Her body's all smooshed up.

Mr Avocat shifts ever so slightly.

MR AVOCAT: It sounds compelling, Olga.

Olga's heart races ever more, though this is entirely imperceptible as she leans forward smoothly. Her eyes do not leave Mr Avocat's for one second. Her eyes are doing something else. Dancing, or suggesting, or laughing. Almost independent of the will. The engaging eye. Engaging of its own accord.

Olga leans forward further. Mr Avocat leans a fraction of a centimetre further away.

In for the kill.

OLGA: Can I tell you my theory about this?

Not a request. A statement of intent.

I think this is basically what everything in the human race comes down to. Everything. Power and desire. They're all linked up, all these little constellations of power and desire. One person desires another, but they desire the next person, who desires someone else, and the one who has the desire doesn't have the power, or they don't think they do, but actually what no one realises is that the whole thing is the wrong way round. The person being desired is not actually the one with the power. They can't get what they want either, but power isn't actually about getting what you want. The person carrying the desire is the one with the power. Because power equals desire. It's like petrol. It's a fuel. That's one of the lines in the play. That's what she says. She kills herself because she can have whatever she wants – she can have any man she wants and secure any business deal she wants, and she realises that the only thing that keeps us alive is the wanting. And that's the one thing she can't have. The happiest people she can see are the men who pay her to walk over them in heels, or tie them up and humiliate them, or invent contracts where they're not allowed to do the things they want to do the most. They're the happiest. They've got all the power because they've completely surrendered themselves. She's got everything, which means she wants for nothing, and she's got no petrol to keep her alive.

Mr Avocat looks ponderous.

MR AVOCAT: Did you come to my extra classes on approaches to literature, Olga? Do you remember learning about how people use psychoanalysis to read literature? It might be worth revisiting some of that ... you might find some of it interesting.

OLGA *(impatiently)*: I don't need to read psychoanalysis to know that desire fuels us. Do you think the play works?

Mr Avocat's reply is intercepted by the entrance of Mr Thornton, whose dark eyes narrow at the sight of Olga. A small smirk disturbs his lips.

MR THORNTON: Well, well. The wanderer returns. Nice to remember what you look like, Olga.

Olga blushes, rarely.

Mr Thornton, Head of Music, is tall and broad. In his forties. His eyes are dark and his arms tanned. Paternal. Kind. Passionate about harmony. Looks like a Roman centurion. Olga sighs internally. Manipulation of Mr Avocat may have to be aborted.

MR THORNTON: Yes: I believe that once our classes moved to 3 p.m. on a Friday I did not see you past Christmas. How *are* you? How *is* the pub on a Friday at that time? Quite peaceful, eh? Just before everyone else finishes *working* and goes there after 5?

Olga is silent, rarely, temporarily.

OLGA *(beaming at Mr Thornton)*: I've been writing a play. I want to get it on the stage. I have to work Friday afternoons. I wasn't in the pub. I loved your classes. I came to every one I could.

MR THORNTON *(ignoring Olga, to Mr Avocat)*: I was wondering if I could pilfer your copy of *The Threepenny Opera* this afternoon, and also was wondering when would be a good time to catch up about the Other Thing.

MR AVOCAT: Ah, the Other Thing. *(Sighs)* Perhaps tomorrow, first thing?

MR THORNTON: Fine.

MR AVOCAT: Olga has written a play about power and desire, Mr Thornton.

MR THORNTON: Has she indeed. *(To Olga)* What are you calling it?

OLGA: I'm not sure yet. I've got some ideas. *High Rise.*

High Heels. Killer Heels. Fuck-Me Heels. Something along those lines. What do you think?

MR THORNTON: I think steer clear of the expletives if you're aiming for a mainstream audience. Don't you agree, Mr Avocat?

MR AVOCAT: I do, Mr Thornton.

Why do they do that. Call each other Mr This and Mr That in front of students. Such a pretence. Sounds so stupid. And I'm not even a student here anymore. Talk about performance.

OLGA *(brightly)*: Can I not call you by your first names now I've finished? Are we not equals now?

Roman eyebrows are raised.

MR THORNTON *(sternly)*: What do you think, Mr Avocat? My initial response is that promising students who finish the class earn the right to first-name terms. Promising students who drop out, I'm not so sure.

MR AVOCAT: By that ruling, Olga, as you did manage to finish my class, you may call me by my first name.

OLGA: What is it?

MR AVOCAT: Eric.

Olga shifts in her seat. Says nothing.

'Eric' shimmers in the air, clunky, unfitting.

MR THORNTON *(booming)*: I have it. Ms Allegri, instead of giving you my first name I shall bestow upon you the formality of address with which you have addressed me for the time you attended here, and in the spirit of goodwill I will give you another further parting gift. Mr Avocat, do you have a spare further five minutes or so?

'Eric' nods, the momentary shadow of his own link in the chain in the form of his own unspoken power/desire for Mr Thornton flitting across his greyish face, similarly enthralled at Mr Thornton's commanding baritone.

Mr Thornton strides to the CD player in the room. Switches on the speakers. Reaches inside his blazer pocket. Puts in the CD and a piece of jazz music begins. Scuttling saxophone, frenetic, deft. Webbings of sound. They reach the corners of the room. A kind of sticky buzz. Fractal. Opiate.

Olga's brain reels.

MR THORNTON *(commanding the room)*: Do either of you know what this is? This piece of music happens to be John Coltrane's 'Giant Steps'. The album of the same name was released in 1960. This piece is now a standard for students of jazz harmonic progressions. It moves in major thirds in a downwards progression, from a B to a G to an E flat, and has further third relationships. I won't bore you further with the intricacies of these. But it also happens to be something else. Coltrane was on to something when he wrote this. Something else entirely.

Olga closes her eyes, utterly ignorant of jazz harmonic

progressions, unable to read music yet multifariously entranced. My crosswire senses. Going crazy with this. Difficult to focus when so stimulated. Purple. Not music so much as alien dust, a kind of flour, shaken rhythmically/arhythmically over a patterned thing, a doily, only more complex, forming who knows what. Icing on a swirling galactical cake.

MR THORNTON'S BARITONE: Now. It's a well-known fact that Coltrane drew a diagram, a tone circle, which came to be known as the Coltrane Circle. All harmonic relations can be rendered geometrically. But rather than the conventional circle of fourths and fifths, Coltrane draws his own version. The relationship between music and geometry has been around since Pythagoras discovered that the pitch of a musical note is in inverse proportion to the length of the string that plays it, and this led him to think about the music of the spheres.

OLGA *(excitedly)*: I know all about the music of the spheres. Pythagoras, right, he said that the planets must produce a sound because they are objects moving through space, and the space between each planet is a musical interval. And the sound of these intervals together produces a harmony. But we can't hear it, because it's all the time, and to us it just sounds like silence. And if silence was a sound that was all the time, of course it would sound like silence. And what we think of as sound is actually just varying degrees of the absence of the music of the spheres. Right? We think of silence as a thing that never changes. And sound as the thing that varies. But couldn't it be the other way round?

Mr Avocat and Mr Thornton do not reply. They are not listening to Olga. They are listening to Coltrane.

COLTRANE, INSIDE OLGA: The sinew, the spin, the muscle, the lean, the purple, the black, the climb, the sweet, the change, the grin, the appeal, the return, the speed, the hilt, the swing, the tip, the hip, the step, the tap, the trip, the swell, the grin, the top, the hat, the tilt, the stop, the shuffle, the scream, the breath, the trill, the short, the long, the centre, the sides, the ebb, the flow, the catch, the drop.

THE SOUNDS INSIDE COLTRANE, INSIDE OLGA: The car. The cough. The fern. The knee. The car cough. The car cough fern. The cough fern knee. The fern knee. The Car. Cough. Fern. Knee.

Carcoughfernknee.

Chapter 7

VOICE	Treesa
SCENE	Sandcastle Waterpark
HOUR	10 a.m., 16 June 1999
PLEASURE BEACH RIDE	River Caves
SUBSTANCE	Chlorine
ORGAN	Intestines
SYMBOL	Water
COLOUR	Blue (swimming pool)
FORMULA	HClO
ART / TECHNIC	Deception
HORMONE	Relaxin
HOMERIC TITLE	Nestor

Look at us three. Scooshing through the water, three generations, mum, mum/kid, kid. Stepping through the pretend mini-waves lapping at the shore of the pretend desert island. Steering clear of the monsters that lurk at the deep end – the grillmouthed underwater beasts that make the big waves only suitable for the big kids. Lulu in her happiest place, in the middle with one hand holding mine, the other hand holding her nana's. The Sandcastle is a tropical fake paradise. Fake palm trees all round the café, which serves chips and coffees. Weirdly comforting in here because it's the same steamy temperature all year round, whatever is going on outside. So today it's a bit warmer than the summer breeze outside, but a lot damper, and steamier, and dripping. All around are beige-coloured fake rocks, fake mini-waterfalls, fake mini-waves. The thing Lulu calls the water jump. Stand and watch the water jump from one place to another. Little water worms shooting through the air. Caterpillars. Fireworks of water.

My swimming cozzie is a very dark grey, almost black, the colour of shadows. Lulu's cozzie is the opposite: neon pink and neon blue. It has fish all over it. When she's squirming in the water she is a fish. Or a little seal. No fear. Faster in water than on land. A proper water baby. Mum's is striped orange and yellow in weird old material – not Lycra or Spandex, something more baggy. Really old-fashioned and embarrassing. Mum doesn't care though. She holds up the back of her hand and wiggles her fingers. Natalie from next door has been at her nails again. Natalie is desperate to get into beauty school but these wonky pearl-pink plastic triangles edged with trails of glue are not a good sign.

–What d'you think of me nails.

–Dead glam.

–Not me, then.

Mum snorts.

Wonder will Lulu want stuff like that. When older. Better to let her decide for herself later. Lulu is squirming. Knows what is coming. The falling water and the underneath water and the worlds of water. The mini-slides. The jumping water. The little things to stand on and watch the flying water. The water mushrooms. The spaces in between the jumping water to stand in and the bigger spaces where you can make your own water shapes. The little pipes that make the water jump through the air. Flying water worms.

–Water jump.

–That's right! Water jump! And water slides. You ready? Let's go!

Mum swings Lulu up onto her hip.

–I think you could do with a new bikini, Mum. It looks like it's from the seventies.

–It is. What's wrong with it? Still does the job.

–You could get a nice black one. Bay Trading've got some on sale. I saw them in there yesterday.

Mum snorts again.

–Black sounds boring. You and your muted colours! What's wrong with a bit of bright. *She* understands.

Mum indicates Lulu on her hip with a jerk of the head. Lulu whoops.

–Whoop! Let's go, let's go! Water. Water jump.

–Water jump!

It's still pretty quiet at this time. Two boys in orange swimming trunks are running up to the Thunderfalls. Lulu never wants to go on the big slides. She prefers making things with the water. Watching the water jumps. Making her own water jumps. Making big splashes. Kicking the water up. Holding water in her fists. She does the water in different shapes.

She has made me think about water differently. This feels like it is an important thought and yet it will be immediately forgotten as soon as Lulu acts up and needs attention. But it stays for a little while. Just let yourself think it. Yes. Making shapes out of water. Interesting. Lulu acts like water is solid. Not a liquid or a gas. Something that stuck from chemistry. Kind of fun thinking that everything is one of these three things. Or changes from one to the other. Particles whizzing and banging. Fun. Fun also when Lulu acts like water is a living thing. A character. With feelings of its own. Angry water, she says, next to a big splash. Sad water, she says next to the weeping willow-like fountain.

These thoughts don't come along very often in a sea of feeding and buggies and toddling and lifting and catching and chasing and wiping and cleaning and shouting and sighing. Hard times. It is hard. No point saying it's not. But. No point being depressed. No time to be depressed. Mum's cousin Mick who lives in Brighton has depression. The picture of him up on the wall in Mum and Dad's living room, standing outside the grey block of flats with its stark sign. NESTOR COURT, next to Preston Rock Garden, next to Preston Park. But hundreds of miles away from Preston. Wonder why.

Depression, though. A real thing you get diagnosed with at the doctor's. Wonder could our Lulubelle ever get that. Look at her, slapping the water with her fists, kneading it, making water pies. Hard to even imagine her old enough to feel depressed. Lulu is all that she is, right now, in this moment. Mick tried to slit his wrists ten years ago. He drank a bottle of vodka and swallowed a pocketful of paracetamol and sat in a hot bath and razored his wrists. But someone found him in time. And now he goes to therapy and doesn't drink and doesn't really go out of his flat very much. He takes Prozac. Prozac sounds like some kind of glamorous American teenager drug. A cool drug. But really it just means that Mick is quieter, thinner, has stopped drinking, stopped crying, still smiles when you see him but has an extra look in his eyes. Something behind the smile, which is a bit wider than it was before. Or maybe we are just imagining it.

Hard to know what depression feels like. Sometimes there are hints of it in Dad, the softest-heartest bastard in the world, especially after he's had more than four beers and his eyes get that kind of infinity-sad light behind them, either drinking cans at home in front of the telly or sometimes when he used to come back from the pub and say, 'Alright, sunflower' and put his dry-rough hand gently on my face. 'My sunshine girl', he would say even more rarely, but only ever after an all-day session, while Mum rolled her eyes and picked up whatever large bundle of stuff she was sorting at that particular point in the house and strode off into another room.

But the bundle of stuff is important. Another important thought. Hold on to it, quick! Even though the tone of Lulu's shouting is leaning towards crying and upset, just hold on to that thought. Mum's carrying and sorting of bundles of stuff: washing, shopping, pots, pans, cooking, cleaning, gardening. That's how she loves us. Never heard Mum even say the word 'love'. Not in any sense. Pretty sure Mum's parents didn't say the word either. Una and Barry Paterson, didn't get past early fifties, born and died in the Gorbals, which is in Glasgow. Mum says the Gorbals are unrecognisable now. Said they'd torn down the slums decades ago and rebuilt. Said it had a theatre and students walking round it and clean-looking high-rises with sensible numbers of people living in each flat.

And now Lulu is practising her swimming in the shallow end. Yep, Mum shows her love by doing stuff and never making a song and dance about it. She just does stuff for you. Without you asking. Without you even knowing you need that stuff doing. You'll come back and find something done and you'll know Mum was the one who did it. She does it because that's how she shows her love and because she's a mum and that's what mums do, expecting nothing back, which is the hardest thing to learn. Every time you successfully do something – change a nappy, get the kid to sleep, carry the kid from one place to another without waking them, feed the kid something and manage to get more than 20 per cent of it into their gob and not on the rest of them or on the floor – when you do these things, nothing happens. No scores, no medals, no one standing over you saying congrats, good job, well done. Nothing. Nothing happens because you do all of this stuff just to stay level. It has to be done. Just to keep things okay. Such a change from school, where they reward you for every tiny little thing – for setting foot inside the building, if you're on the truancy blacklist, for good behaviour, for good marks, for good coursework – especially if you're lower down and not in the top sets. Pretty childish, especially if you're in Year 11. But to go from all these childish awards and rewards to *nothing* – no rewards for all the kid-feeding and kid-bathing or the carrying of bundles of stuff around from place to place – is fucking hard. What I woudn't give for a gold star when Lulu has slept the night through, or a good mark, let's say nine out of ten, for giving her a healthy meal that she likes and eats. Maybe Liam can give me one later. And a grade. Ha. Bad joke.

But.

The reward is right here: look, Lulu is smiling, splashing around, doggypaddling in a circle. Her face is the sun. She is my sunflower: she faces me and grows towards me. Wonder if that will catch on for me when feeling sentimental. Probably not. More of Mum than Dad in me. And Mum doesn't really call me anything. Lulu can flap about in the water and just about keep herself afloat now – and Mum is whooping, Well done Lulubelle! We're all gonna get ice lollies after because you've been such a good girl and you've done so well with your swimming.

And me, what about me? I've been a good girl all fucking year. But Mum knows that I want ice lollies too – always Twisters, never anything else – and she knows this when she says it. And to be fair, Mum loves Twisters too. We probably both love Twisters more than Lulu ever will – she can take them or leave them – but look, down at the other end of the pool. A purple swimsuit encasing a familiar figure. Purple and lilac berries decorating Sue Wilson's posh-looking cozzie. Sue Wilson is quite tanned from her own sunbed, though not as brown as us, and you couldn't get much more different body shapes between our Mum and Sue. Like a stick of celery standing next to a plum. A warm, spiced plum. And which would you rather hug?

So lucky that year to have Mrs Wilson as Year 11 Secretary. She knew our life story between 1991 and 1996 better than almost anyone else. Going into the office to hand in endless slips of paper, notes about absences, reporting things, being reported, being collected, waiting for taxis to the doctor's or hospital, or just needing to see a face who was not a kid or a teacher – always we would be looking for Mrs Wilson. Hazel-eyed, shimmery lilac-brown smoky-eye-shadowed Mrs Wilson, who now wants us to call her Sue since leaving school but we feel too shy to do so.

To see Mrs Wilson here in her purple and lilac cozzie is a bit embarrassing. She is here with her own grandkid, Lila-Jade, one year older than Lulu. Lila-Jade sees us and runs along the side of the pool.

–I'm nearly big enough to go on the big slides now, she grins, hopping and shivering in her faded *Toy Story* cozzie, which sags off her bum because it's lost its elastic. She doesn't stay still very long; grabs Lulu by the hand and off they go, darting in and out of the water worms, chasing the splashes, making their own splashes. Lulu is shorter and tubbier and slower than Lila-Jade by a long way. We watch them. Easier than looking at Mrs Wilson standing there, which ever since leaving school has made us feel like squirming, as if we are still just a kid no older than Lulu.

–How are things, Teresa?

'Sue' Wilson directs her gentle smile at us.

And we are water. Water inside and out. We are squirming right now, inside and out.

–Alright thanks.

This feeling of being too big and too small at the same time. Being near Mrs Wilson is like being near a radiator. It's like feeling the warmth and wanting to go near it. But up close like this you feel hot and trapped like you want to run away. Think what it would be like if she was your mum. Just imagine her giving you a hug right now. Warm and round and comforting but also squidgy because we're all wet and chloriney and dripping. You could disappear for a minute into her body. Being hugged by Mum is not like that. Not that we can remember that many hugs. We can remember being lifted up, swung up high, carried around, but not hugged so much. We definitely remember not wanting a hug anyway. Eurgh, I don't need a hug. I'm not soft. But of course hugs aren't just for softies. Easy to know this now, all grown up aged nineteen when Lulu comes for a hug and just says, 'Hug' and puts her arms out. And hug her we do. Lulu isn't soft. She's brave and stubborn and completely daft like Liam. She likes pretending to be vehicles. Planes – trains – cars – boats. Motorbikes. Lorries. Any moving vehicle. Her favourite game.

On GCSE results day Mrs Wilson gave us a massive hug. Knew the secret that barely anyone knew. Knew what was growing in our belly. But didn't say anything, just smiled, a more motherly smile than she had ever smiled before, a mother to a nearly-mother, softer and browner-eyed than ever before, and wrapped her arms around us and all we could feel were our own cheeks burning up. The weirdness of it, at a time when everything around us was weird and just getting weirder by the day. At school getting results and being hugged by Mrs Wilson, who had come out from behind the desk she always sat behind especially to give us a hug.

You'll be brill, she said quietly in our ear. You are brill. You can do it. Come and see me any time. You're going to be absolutely fine.

It wasn't as though we had been super keen on more studying anyway. Gym was the thing we were the saddest about by a million miles. Studying would have been Blackpool and Fylde College, NVQ or BTEC in something, hadn't decided yet, maybe sports science or sports development.

The A in PE was the thing we were proudest of inside that stupid little envelope with its piece of typed paper, or would have been if we didn't have this cringe-making, heavy-growing alien lump of a thing inside us, weighing us down, making us hot and fat and tired and embarrassed and upset at the slightest thing, feeling like everyone could see, even though no one could see yet, not even us. We looked the same, maybe our skin was a bit greasier, a bit spottier, we thought we could imagine our neck looking somehow a bit thicker, our cheeks a bit rounder, as if there was some motherly way about us that we had suddenly grown. But it was almost definitely in our imagination. Results day was hard though. Mrs Wilson and the blushing crushing hug made it slightly better.

And now, all together in our swimming costumes. Here we are. It is embarrassing to meet people unexpectedly while wearing a swimsuit. Mrs Wilson looks unembarrassed.

–How's work?

–Oh, you know. Same old, same old. Lovely and quiet at the moment but not for long! How's yours, Lou?

Mum shrugs.

–Same old. Can't complain.

–And you, Teresa? Are you getting some hours at the shop again?

–Yeah, twenty hours a week or so. Gets me out the house.

–And how's Liam?

–Yeah, he's fine. I don't see him much! Sometimes we meet him on his lunch break. Take him butties. Like today.

Mrs Wilson looks at Mum and narrows her eyes slightly. Lowers her voice slightly.

–Did you hear about Simon McLeod.

–No? What about him?

–He's gone. Fired. All hushed up. No one knows why.

–Really? But he was lovely! Wasn't he?

–No. No he wasn't, we say, a bit louder than we had planned, heart pounding even louder, it feels. He wasn't lovely. I'm glad he's gone.

Do not say why but it's still all there, inside, a rotten sack of stinking memories. October 1994, Year 9, the dark, musty corner room adjoining the sports hall, the huge hanging net bags full of basketballs and netballs, the tub of rounders bats, the bags of sour-smelling bibs, the piles of multicoloured cones, the stacked benches and chairs, the stinking lost property box, all encircling us like silent spectators while we stood in the middle in our favourite leotard holding a piece of chalk, rooted to the spot with burning cheeks while Mr McLeod's voice went on and on in the darkness, saying things he shouldn't be saying, but so hard to put your finger on it because it was all mixed up with stuff he should be saying, stuff about gym, stuff about the GCSE options, stuff about progress, about performance, but then other stuff too, stuff we didn't even really understand, stuff about our body, stuff he wanted to do. With us. To us. Weird stuff. Sick stuff. And then the touching. Definitely no touching should have happened there but touching definitely did happen, not just there and then but during gym lessons, but in the storeroom alone with him it meant much more, it was a bigger, louder, scarier gesture, the touching. We had just waited until he had finished saying all the stuff and doing all the touching, waited until his mouth stopped moving and making sounds, and then turned and fled.

–Always such a hit with the mums, Mrs Wilson is saying. Winning ways. Winning smile. Lovely teeth. Lovely legs. I shouldn't be saying this. But – she whispers – they're saying he couldn't keep his hands to himself.

Mum sucks in a breath and kind of whistles, only backwards.

–Bloody hell. Never would have thought it. And with that gorgeous wife too. Not that it makes a difference. Bloody hell. It's never the ones you think, is it.

–Did you ever see Mr McLeod do anything strange, Teresa?

Mrs Wilson's kindly gaze is serious, concerned, interested.

We are finding our mouth completely dry, empty of saliva, empty of words. We struggle, for a second. Cannot speak. Shake head rapidly. Keep shaking it, longer than we should, so that Mrs Wilson looks a bit more concernedly at us, and then Mum too, and there are four eyes staring at us while we're shaking our head faster and faster. Is that a tear we can feel at the corner of one eye? Fuckinell! No. Not the right thing to do. Stupid anyway. Over nothing. Over something that was nothing.

Swallow, finally, calmly. Draw something from somewhere, some kind of calm, some kind of extra thing we learned from labour. Deep wells of extra stuff inside us. Stuff to keep us going when we can't keep going. And this moment here, with these four eyes on us while we struggle to gulp air down a dry throat tunnel with no sound, this is nothing. Just a speck of nothing. Forgotten in a second.

–Don't think so, we finally manage to say, carefully, looking at each of them in turn. But I'm not surprised he's gone. I'm glad he's gone.

Chapter 8

VOICE	Rachel, Olga
SCENE	The Pier, The Superclub
HOUR	1 p.m., 1 a.m., 16 June 1999
PLEASURE BEACH RIDE	Playstation
SUBSTANCE	Doughnut
ORGAN	Oesophagus
SYMBOL	Vessel
COLOUR	Beige
FORMULA	$3\alpha,7\alpha,12\alpha$-trihydroxy-5β-cholan-24-oic acid
ART / TECHNIC	Ingestion, Ejection
HORMONE	Leptin
HOMERIC TITLE	Lestrygonians

I'm an upple litset by the talk you rot –
But I'm not so think as you drunk I am.

Rachel

FROM THE EJECTIVE PERSPECTIVE

I have studied the continualism of alcohonuum. I know the which in ways we bend and fall, the lyrico-anarco-cynico swoonstakes. Know that I understand, stand under, I who knows, who knows. The repetition only slightly different, repetition only a bit different, only subtly different, each time, every time, singly, singingly, stingingly. The bits in the middle and the difference. I know, I've bent down, bent double, peered, beer-goggled, goggle-eyed into the gloom, goggling the gloop and the gloom, glaring and gleering. I've done it everywhere. Things that become part of us and then leave us later. Parcels of us, ejected. Parcels of us, stained. Earlier on today. Sucking on the dregs of an orange Calippo. O that delicious fake orange chemical sugarwater. Will it stripe my insides orange I wonder. But what colour are your insides anyway. When they're inside. It must be completely dark in there. No light should be getting in. So do colours even exist?

Dozens of thousands, millions perhaps, have thought this. What am I and the what that comes out and am I fundamentally changed. When I come out of one end and smell the same as when I come out of the other end. When I come out of the wrong end. When I am slick, when I am black, when I am red, when I am cream, when I am orange. Chameleovomit. When I am green. When I am lumpen. Bread sauce, when cooling, a bit of skin on the top. A roux.

A stew. The roux and the rue. Stewed rhubarb's glossy pallor. Takeaway chunks in red red wine. Curry at both ends. When I am a chip, a whole chip and nothing but a chip. Ingested whole into the hole no chewing. A whole Wotsit divested of its orange spacedust. A whole Twiglet divested of its rust. The mind boggles. The gut contracts. And then the later, liquid phases. Somewhere between oil and bile. The amphetamine emptiness. Nothing inside. A special kind of high. The heave and the ho. When we all imagine that the toilet bowl is a large type of cruising vessel. A wave upon the what?

I go to five shops in Poulton. I buy a Mars bar and a Caramel from the newsagent's on Breck Road, two roast pork barms from the cooked meat shop, an iced bun and a jam doughnut from Burton's in the Teanlowe Centre, then a 30p mix, a packet of Rainbow Drops, a disgusting cheap brick of fake-chocolate-covered flapjack and a packet of white chocolate buttons from Bargain Booze. I eat them on different benches, ending up in the park.

At home, I can only do it when I'm alone in the house and listening to 'Reasons To Be Cheerful' by Ian Dury & the Blockheads. The juice of the carrot. The smile of the parrot. A little drop of claret. Ha. More than a drop is needed here.

Lumpen. No other word comes close to describing all of this, in its multiple stages and its multiple substances and sensations. Flesh and food. Food and flesh. All lumpen. The lumpen bulimitariat. Joining the ranks. Becoming lumpen, consuming shiny purple-and-silver-foil-wrapped confectionery items which then become gloopily and abjectly lumpen. Injesting, digesting and then ejecting. Making something part of yourself and then violently ejecting and rejecting. What crude symbolism could we attach to this. Fleshsyrup. Bloodgloop. I want to eject myself out of myself. Of course. What else could it possibly mean. Oh yeah. I like the taste of food in my mouth but I have a fatal fear of gaining weight. Oh yeah. Let's try not to attach gravitas to such lumpen processes. The way we read it before we read the philosophy and the way we read it after. But still the process is the same.

The trick is to think the hardest you possibly can about being thin while guzzling. There's a wildness to it. The extremest of juxtaspositions lends a temporary logic to the process. Consume in order to shrink. It makes sense. Topsy-turvy logic, the best kind. It feels like freefalling, freewheeling, skydiving, bungee jumping, anything that involves launching yourself off a precipice and the bit that happens before you hit the bottom. When you hit the bottom you have to eject everything as quickly as you can and erase all traces and even all memories so that you don't become one with the lumpenness. Careful to get rid, or you will be no better than the pool of whatever disgusting oil-slick congealed syrupy gloop sits inside the toilet bowl. Though I am a novice. It does not come easily. In certain moods it has to be accompanied by all other possible ejections too. I have to be crying, wanking, shitting, pissing, noserunning, leaking in every possible way, and then it all comes out. These sessions are tiring. It takes time. I disgust myself. Sometimes that helps.

OLGA VERSUS DOUGHNUTS

I buy five doughnuts from the pier for a pound. The girl at the doughnut kiosk looks about twelve, though taller and wider than me by quite a margin. She has braces and is wearing a Deftones T-shirt. She looks smart. I can hear Rage Against the Machine playing. *Fuck you I won't do what you tell me.* She'll be CEO of her own company by twenty-eight. Got that determined look.

You have to eat them immediately, while they're still warm. The grease soaks through the paper bag in seconds and makes its secondary trace of a greasy imprint on my canvas bag and a tertiary trace on my jeans where the bag rests at my side. Deeeeelish.

Grease, eh.

I fuckin love a sugar rush. It streams its way through the veins, or I like to imagine it doing that: little sugar-rockets firing themselves, hurtling themselves through sticky bloodtunnels. Clogged tunnels, my imaginary dad says. He's turning fifty this year and at the imaginary doctor's they told him that if he doesn't stop it with the imaginary gelato and the imaginary tiramisu and the whateverthefuckelse they eat for afters in Italy he's on his way to developing type 2 diabetes. He stands there on an imagined street corner, gesticulating Italianly, pronouncing Italian words, crisp white shirt stretched over Italian paunch, grey smartish trousers, smart Italian shoes. Shiny tanned Italian balding head. His face, indistinct, but very Italian. Ancona paints itself around him in uncertain colours: nothing but the Dolmio advert to help us here.

A sea port, yes, and lots of happy families eating on large tables that seem to be in the middle of cobbled streets. *Put the Dolmio smile on your face.* Smiling nuns sucking up strands of spaghetti and managing not to spill any of the delicious tomato sauce onto the whites of their wimples, sitting next to beautiful smiling melted-chocolate-eyed kids also sucking up strands of spaghetti, sitting next to glamorous women with curled fringes smiling while seductively sucking up their own strands of spaghetti while good-looking young men gaze adoringly at the glamorous women while manfully sucking up their own strands. The young man gazes too long at the beautiful woman with the flashing earrings and spills some tomato sauce on his shirt. Everyone laughs. And of course the whole scene is presided over by the creator of this wondrous dish: the stern but loving matriarch, with obligatory huge mama boobs encased in some kind of flower-patterned housecoat. Next to her is my dad, traditional Italian papa wearing a waistcoat now over his pristine white shirt, expensive-smelling aftershave, handsome even with his balding bonce and his beer belly. Dark eyes and hair, dark stubble and a wicked heartbreaking smile. He is Tony Soprano.

Do those families exist outside adverts? If they did an advert over there for a delicacy from round here, how would that go? And for what. Readymade frozen microwave chippy dinner, made by Young's, Birds Eye, Tesco. *Just like the real takeaway experience.* Steaming cardboard packets on plastic trays passed round the living room while *Neighbours* is on. *You can taste the paper wrappings.* And why not? It's the future. Synthesise, synthesise. No less real than real. We've all seen *The Matrix*. The notion of the real, moving forward.

Kids scrabble for a go on the Game Boy. Teenagers are straightening their hair. Toddlers are opening all the cupboard doors and pulling everything out. Dads are absent echoes. Mums are standing at the microwave heating everyone's chippy dinner box and after everyone else has been sorted the mums reach for tubs of pink powder because the next advert is Slimfast. *Give it a week. See the weight come off.* The magic pink powder causes hallucinations, which are demonstrated at the end of the advert: the tub of Slimfast powder has some kind of magic belt around it that tightens, causing the rigid cardboard tub to develop a waistline.

Mum certainly doesn't help us to build a picture of this absence. Stormclouds rumble even at a mention. The darkening shut-up-shop of the face, the thinning of the mouth. Shutup shutup shutup. She is always standing over something and never just standing. The fried eggs. The kettle. Buckets of dirty washing. And maybe a casual comment tossed at me like a balled-up sock: not overtly aggressive, but a gentle warning. Least said, soonest mended. What you want to know for. Good for nothing. Men they are all take take take. Italian men especially. Good for nothing. Lazy bastards. Just you be careful. You got plenty of condoms, yes? No risk-taking. O my frowning downturned Matka. If you knew the number of abortions I have had, would it make you cry? O my twinkle-eyed strong-armed handsome roguish life-loving life-giving imaginary Papà. If you could see me now, eyes shut legs open as Lee Darren Mark Stuart Mike Chris Rob James Kieran Dan Simon Ben Tom Jamie dive in, would it make you cry?

RACHEL IN HEAVEN

Watch the twitching of the bouncers' jawlines as they chew gum manically and flex muscles. Inside, the pervasive smell is one of feet. Heaven plays R&B while the kids grind against each other grimly. The carpets never quite dry out; my heels stick to them as I head for the ladies.

Always the same. Knees folded over, trouser legs soaking up the dampness on the floor, god knows what the dampness is, best not to think, especially when thinking hurts. It hurts and yet it is bringing me this joy. Always the same. The clarity of it all. *The poet is an airy thing, a winged and holy thing; and he cannot make poetry until he becomes inspired and goes out of his senses and no mind is left in him.* Socrates. Don't buy it. The poet is a gritty thing, an especially earthly and crawling insect-like thing, and she definitely cannot make poetry until she becomes so thoroughly saturated in her own selfish self-indulging self-absorbing self-feeling self-seeking SELF that she can no longer – oops! – navigate vertically but finds herself crumpled into a comma shape, folded, paralysed in this grey-white box, enamel, porcelain, lino, metal, plastic, this brutal overlit box, just enough room to clumsily arrange limbs. Elbows grazed, crunched, bruised, banged against the hard seat, neck extended right down into the bowl, my own personal porcelain harness. A bridle. Where to, madam? Who is at the reins? Don't look up. Hold on tight. What type of vehicle is this? We are at sea. I declare we are at sea. Hold on to yer hats, lads. We're going down. It's not got chunks, mind. It is an oil slick. A slick move there, madam, if you don't mind me commenting. The silver lining. The black oozing oilslick lining. Lining the bowl. No overspill. Beware the black oil. Remember that *X-Files* episode. Black oil seeps into the eyes. Mind you don't fall in now.

Strange visions in this pigswill. Seabirds. After that oil tanker got wrecked a few years back. They soaped them. Each and every one of them. Who? Who would? Who went? Flew to the aid of the seabirds, scrubbing wings, bloody Fairy Liquided them all, soapsud sink baths, no less, each one singly, then letting them go, all fresh and lemony, all degreased, no longer buoyant, lost their essence, lost their stink, would they even know themselves?

Always the same. The spin cycle of it all. Washing machines. The walzers simulate this motion. Sugar. Adrenaline. Spinning. Round and round, upside down. Swaying. Rollicking. I tell you, we are at sea. Just make sure you keep your eyes open or you'll pass out. Sore eyes. Streaming eyes. And nose. But open eyes. Just. The extremity of it all. Is this what I have to do? Is this one limit it's possible to reach? Do I feel strung out? Am I a guitar string, tight, tense, ready to twang, a ledge, a cliff edge, a summit, a point? Have I reached some kind of *significant point*?

Heave.

The liquid I imbibed, this nectar I desired to add to my makeup, viscous flammable sticky aniseed tincture, is being rejected, ejected, expelled. Never quite enough gone though. I am good at this. Harder when alone at home in the sober daytime after secret adventure binges across carefully selected corner shops across town, playing my very own private bulimia mix tape at full volume, crying-retching-gulping-scratching in the bathroom. No. This is dead easy in comparison. A glottal fricative bark followed by a silky-smooth splash into the bowl. Is this enough? I have more.

It was the Sambuca Swallows that did it. Flaming black sambucas again, party trick, ridiculous, dangerous, a dribble down the chin and you'll spend the rest of your years looking like a ventriloquist's dummy. A line of skin, eaten away.

First of all you knock it back. All of it. Don't swallow. Hold it there, swill it around, throat closed up, tongue pickled and floating in this oily suspension. Grab hold of the lighter sitting on the bar. Insert young and impressionable audience here. A few worried faces. *But is it safe?* Concerned bar girl. Course it is. You've seen them fire-eaters, right? Just like that. The throat creates a vacuum, blows it right out. You've got to be decisive. Take it like a man (ha). You have to light yer own. No sidekicks here. Do it quick. Flint, strike, flame, hold flame aloft, then whoosh! Down into the oral cavity. Right down. And the liquid is burning. Burning off itself. An inverted Christmas pudding, flaming blue, until you open up your gullet and let it down. The throat is soothed rather than irritated. The heat is sweet. The fumes are potent. It loosens the tie, loosens the resolve, loosens the tongue. Loosens a whole lorra things. Slackens theconsonants, lengthens the vowels. Relaxes the fundamental organ.

O no.

Little discarded shot glasses. Apple Sourz, sambuca, sugar and alcohol. Hairspray and deodorant. Impulse and Lynx. Tommy Girl and Chipie. Hundreds upon hundreds of spilled Smirnoff Ice bottles. Shards of glass glisten under the lights. In Hell the dance floor is dark, surrounded by raised podiums and cages with dancing poles. The lasers are green. Swathes and sheets of them knife the air as you hear the beginning strains of that tune with the sexy vocal. 'Silence' by Delerium – an extended version of Tiësto's In Search of Sunrise remix, which is 11 minutes, 35 seconds long. You know the one. It gets blasted across aqua aerobics classes and into runners' headphones everywhere because of the swell and the build and the beat and the liquefied synthesised emotion holding up that breathy voice. There isn't another trance tune quite like it. Fags are held high in euphoric bluster. And here it goes.

Commercial trance is in the blood. All the invention had left acid house music long before we reached puberty and all of us here sweating it out in Hell right now are its embarrassing legacy. *It goes like this, the fourth, the fifth, the minor fall and the major lift*, a thousand tracks laid down in a simulation, a synthesis, of some kind of harmonic nirvana. Repetitions of the bass note, four beats in a bar, simple. It's always a female vocal. Ethereal. A powerful voice lost in feminine ragged breath. The three-step bassline, used scores and scores and scores of times, fourth-fifth-sixth and then back down again. Bodies are swooning all around. A waterfall of bodies, muscles writhing and contorting, more tree than human, grins stretching all across their faces, arms stretching like branches to the source of energy and power – the DJ booth. Movements and sounds are tracking and replicating themselves slowly and softly across the aural cortex. How can this ever be repeated? Streams and ribbons, threads and layers of liquid gold surrounding me until I am wading, bathing, drowning in thick molasses of sound. Haunting. The minor key. Why can't I ever grab on to the minor key and possess it, no matter how hard I try? It evades me, darting through the dark tangled forest of itself. What *is* that synth sound they use? Does it have a name; is it openly marketed, bought and sold; is it possible that amongst producers this sound and all its permutations are common parlance? How could someone market such an unashamed sensory manipulator? Is this sound not the lowest common denominator of music? Is there an iota of 'art' within this fifteen-minute epic? Is it anything but a power ballad at 140 rpm? If it were slow, would I cry? *Cry*? Why am I in the middle of a weekend holiday crowd thinking of crying? Is anybody else around me thinking of crying? Is euphoria even possible? Is it possible to discern the harmonic threads of this particular synthesised sound? Have they scooped up an entire orchestra, liquidised them until they are blended smooth, a thousand polyphonic instruments and only one voice? The scope is monolithic. It is absolutely all-encompassing.

Heaven holds a sense of wonder
And I wanted to believe
That I'd get caught up
When the rage in me subsides

F-G-A minor and back again. Always. *Why*? How? Why do they want to string you out like this? Do they realise the power they have? Men in production studios with families and four-wheel drives and paunches, men who were probably full of gutbusting hope and desire at one point, men who danced and felt hope at sunrise in Ibiza in the late eighties when Ecstasy promised a genuine subcultural alternative, men who now have goatee beards and multiple houses and evening slots on Radio 1, how can it be that these middle-aged men have the power to control a room full of two thousand youths? Keening, grinding, gurning, aching, screwing up face, screwing up hope, screwing up everything into a ball, a knot, a clench of muscles. So beautiful it hurts.

In this white wave
I am sinking
In this silence
In this white wave
In this silence
I believe

Stare at your hands. Their constriction says everything. They cannot extend, they cannot unfurl, they are hopeless embryonic spasms seeking to clutch, clench, fold inwards unto themselves, go back to the womb, disappear. At this point, this fine pinprick of a moment that has been honed and sharpened by the swell of the crescendo, the bubbling of nasty white foam in the pit of the stomach, there is nowhere left to go. Nothing to remember and nothing to clutch on to. The moment crisps up and becomes a sliver, a shard, a shrivelled wisp of onion skin in the frying pan of the skull.

Chapter 9

VOICE	Olga and Rachel (combined, internal)
SCENE	The Lights
HOUR	12 a.m., 16 June 1999
PLEASURE BEACH RIDE	Alice's Wonderland
SUBSTANCE	LSD
ORGAN	Brain (serotonin 2A receptor)
SYMBOL	Web, Crystal, Entireosphere
COLOUR	Spectrum
FORMULA	$C_{20}H_{25}N_3O$
ART / TECHNIC	Scattering, Pixelation
HORMONE	Adrenocorticotropic hormone
HOMERIC TITLE	Lotus-Eaters

To enter Alice's Wonderland you have to be eaten. You and your entire world have to disappear through the Cheshire Cat's mouth. The only organ that can regenerate itself is the liver. Liver, a giver, a liver of life. From Blackpool to Liverpool: the city of the black pool to the city of the pool of light. A man with an arm round his toddler daughter (Jung and easily Freudened) is at this point sitting in the front train car and heading directly into the toothfringed black hole of the Cheshire Cat's mouth. Nonsense with teeth. Don't be scared of the Cheshire Cat, for he is nothing but a grin. Man and child, together on the Alice ride, thinking about the city of life and the city of death. The pool of life and the pool of death. It was all a dream, of course. The music that can be heard on the Alice ride is not anything connected to Alice in Wonderland but rather 'I've Got a Golden Ticket' from *Willie Wonka and the Chocolate Factory*. Confused? You'll get used to it in Time. Yes, in Time. Listen to the Caterpillar's advice. Late! Late! Watch out for the terrifying dog with the fiery eyes. The tubular tunnel is rotating around itself. The giant playing cards are peeling off the walls. Are we upside down or is it an optical illusion? And look – here is a giant Alice – the Proto-Alice – illuminating the dark.

Up the coast to Liverpool, the bust of Carl Gustav Jung rests there on Mathew Street. The party street, next to the Science Fiction Theatre. And you know, in the film *Tomorrow Calling* the character played by Toyah Willcox asks the haunted photographer to seek out Science Fiction Temples. It's all connected. A manhole on Mathew Street marks the spot where the ley lines meet. This man, sitting on the Alice ride here right now with his toddler daughter, daydreaming about the bust of Jung and thinking that there should be a bust of Sigmund Freud right here, in the city of the pool of death. Lifepool, Deathpool, Lightpool, Darkpool. And again, down south, town of brightness, Brighton, Bright Town, at this very moment some anarchists are spraypainting the viaduct with a slogan that reads LOVE ONE ANOTHER. Each letter is sprayed in a different colour. Walk under the viaduct on Chatham Place and you will see it. Deep underground, a triangle of interstellar ley lines really do link up these three points: the viaduct in Bright Town, the bust of Jung in the Pool of Life, and right here, the Alice ride in Black Pool. Don't you know the story? Synchronicity is just the tip of the iceberg. The KLF were on to something, man.

Science Fiction Theatre, Liverpool.

Science Fiction Temples, Blackpool.

Ley lines.

Pleasure Beach. It's all there in the name, man. At the end of the day, everything can be *boiled down* to the phase transitions between the three fundamental states of matter. The boiling down being, of course, one of these processes: the alchemical distillation, or the extraction of a jam from fruit, or the reduction of a spicy sauce.

But we digress. Particularly, and universally, of course, here, in this case, with the Pleasure and the Beach, what we are actually talking about is the meeting of solid and liquid. The impossibility of drawing the line between solid and liquid. The waves that lap on the sand. The grains which are tiny crystals which together form a liquid which burns to become glass which is transparent like a liquid and mimics the hardened liquid of ice. And so on and so forth, the phrase mimicking nothing but the pouring forth of an analogy, perhaps ad infinitum, we aren't sure yet. Let's see.

Back to the Pleasure Beach. The waves lap on the sand. A liquid on a solid. Wave and particle. The flow of Pleasure and the grain of Beach. And so we go through the gates with the letters in lights – PLEASURE BEACH – and the smiley face that could be a UFO.

–Where are we now?

–The Pleasure Beach, of course. Just think of it like a giant theme park.

–Tautology.

–Eh?

–A tautology is when you say the same thing in different ways.

See, the sign says

The Pleasure Beach: It's a Holiday Out of This World!

But it is *in* this world and *out* of this world because it is the *whole world*. The Pleasure Beach is not just the Pleasure Beach. The Pleasure Beach is the entire town is the entire world. Its dimensions escape their dimensions and extend to fit the space around it.

The entire world, then, is these old rollercoaster trains and their rickety whiteness. The newer, spangly red-and-blue metal legs with rattling rainbow train cars hurtling past. Sky high. Redbrick terraces around. Shrieks. Ice creams. Stag parties in drag, thick hairy thighs in mini-skirts. Hen parties in Playboy rabbit ears or high-gussetted red *Baywatch* swimsuits. Kids in neon Lycra cycling shorts and shellsuit tops. Dads in T-shirts saying *I'm Not Drunk… But I'm Working On It!* Mums with hard white thin spaghetti straplines against lobster chests. Whole families in Umbro football shorts and Nike Air Max trainers. Sitting stationary in the Haunted Swing and the entireosphere orbits around *you*. Autoheliocentricity. What headfuckery is this. Nausea squared. Soaked bums after the Log Flume and then the queue for the Big One on your first time. Don't believe the hype. It's just the feeling of dying for three minutes and then the disappointment of standing up straight on solid ground again. What even is G-force? It's like being in the engine of a rocket, man. It's like the whole world being squeezed through the orifices of your skull. It's like your whole being squeezed through a tube of toothpaste. Oh, and they never tell you until the very end that you've got to take off yer glasses or they might imprint themselves forever into your eye sockets or your actual face. So you won't be able to see anything anyway and maybe that's for the best. The red of the track and the blue of its skeleton legs. Blue of sky and blue of sea. Twisting the spine of the track and the hard weight of the air at the bottom. We don't live in a town, we live on the sea. Air and water and thousands and millions of metallexoskeleta. If you don't know what I mean, just look up. Tower and coaster. These structures will outlive us.

So we are walking under THE LIGHTS, man. So said Carl Jung to Sigmund Freud as he witnessed the construction of Valhalla right there on the seafront as Sigmund stumbled off to the ghost train. Stars. Stars in stars. Stars, in stars, in faces, in lights. Your face, inside a star. All the stars, strung up on lines, lighting up the road along the prom. You know, the important ones. Like Princess Di, Ken Barlow and Vera Duckworth. The tram with the rocket lights shooting its load at five miles an hour. Snails. Shells.

Seahorses. Tendrils and fronds. Flashing webs. Butterflies. Caterpillars. A grasshopper. Flashing wires tripping me to fuck, man. CASINO. Fronds upon fronds; green fountains or green crowns. Frankenstein's Monster. Skellington heads. Ghosts. Googly eyes googling round ghoulish heads. Egyptian mummies popping out of sarcophagi. Big M for McDonald's we drive under. Multiple Ms; M&Ms; M-upon-fuckin-Ms. Glittering critters in the dark.

And spaceships! Shooting beams at one another across the road. The beams fly across and up into the black. We are *in* space, man. Spacemen in spaceman. Light beams made visible. Glittering rings in the dark. Jewels and unseen precipices. Down that black hole is the sea. Strings of green jewels now strung along each side of the road. We see

FUNLAND

And: the Tower! There it is!

The Tower, brought to you today by

F
A
N
T
A

Huge orange capital letters climbing up its trunk.

Eggs. The eggs leading us along the road and their obscenely swollen shining faces. The lady one with the lipsticked pout and the circles of rouge on the round eggcheeks. The clownish one with the sinister eggsmile. The blue one with the glasses. A tram rattles and roars past, its brakes screeching. The egg with a wobbling duck's beak. Another clownegg with downturned mouth. Unhappy clownegg. Was Humpty Dumpty always an egg? Plants. Planes. Planets. Fireworks. Pandora pouring out the contents of her jar. The tram with the steam train lights and the Fisherman's Friend sign. A trombone. Wobbling pins across the road. Stars and zigzag lines. A pirate ship scene. Pouring teapots. Hotels strung around with lights. Dancing musical notes. Lion man faces with swollen cheeks. Flowerpot faces. Sunflower smiles. A flashing static steam train. Harry Ramsden and his squirting dolphin duo. The Fab circle. The Wagon Wheel big wheel! It means the world. The world goes round, dunnit? Traffic lights mean love. Red for love. Green for love. Amber for love. The cat who throws the darts. Mr B's Golden Mile Centre. Random circles of light. UFOs everywhere. Prize Bingo. The Bispham Kitchen tram. The Sealife Centre. Oasis and its two flashing palm trees. Happy hours every hour. Central Pier. Chicken Express. Silcock's Fun Palace. Burgerland. Gaiety's Karaoke Bar. Tall proper Blackpool Transport trams. Cream with green piping. Normal trams. Ha. Normal is splitapart. The Wall's Ice Cream tram. Leering monster faces next to mermaids. An assortment of genies escaping a miscellany of bottles. Colourflash extravaganza. Star. Twinkle. South Pier. Lucky Star. And now we have all the stars of *Corrie* lined up in their hall of fame. Deirdre. Ken. Alec. Bet. Raquel. Vera. Curly. Faces in stars. A pair of red demon's eyes leads the tram through the darkness. Playing the race game. TIME EXTENDED. Playing the dancing mat game. Vengaboys. Up. And down. And up. And down. *The Vengabus is coming. And everybody's jumping. New York to San Francisco. An intercity disco.* Blazvegas. The Donut Factory and the Clifton Hotel. The Savoy Hotel. Creative Advertising. And somehow we're back to the White Tower Casino helter-skelter and the Millennium 2000 blow-up red slide. A teenage lad in a Fila jumper walks nonchalantly down the slide with a bottle of Mad Dog in his hand. Defying gravity. Kids battle to save themselves in a rowing simulation game. Defying reality. And then we reach the gates. Your name in lights! Dressing room lights. Lights is nothing but bulbs is nothing but beams is nothing but bodies of light. Hard bodies. Light as knife as penetrating fucker. Light is to knife as to knight is to ... life? We are naught but knights. Knaughts. Oh Lord, help me. Angels of light.

And wait – it's not Carl Jung and Sigmund Freud. It's two teenagers on acid, tripping their way through the Pleasure Beach. Look – their eyes are wide black plates. They look at one another with recognition and relief so strong it's true love immediately because everything else has got really, really, *really* weird. Lines and smoke are coming out of everything. It's all pixelated like N64 games – it's like we're in *Super Mario* or *Sonic* or fuckin *Zelda*. You can see the bits of everything. Things that don't normally breathe have started breathing. There are new things in the sky. Fuckin angels, man! And new life everywhere, and dimensions we don't know about, and there's nothing really to stand on because – wait! The ground and the sky are the same thing, and then there's the sea over there, which is ridiculous. What even is water, anyway?? The only thing in their field of vision that they recognise is one another. They are each other's anchor. They're walking through the Pleasure Beach just looking at everything in awe, sometimes guffawing so hard they almost vomit, stepping more and more slowly and carefully until they reach the queue for the Big One. Whose idea was this again? The world's already the Big One. A fuckin great rollercoasterer, underer, overer, upsidedownerer. Hook, line and sinkerer. Did Forrest Gump say that? No, wait, he said something else.

Ah yeah. That's it. Life is like a box of chocolates.

And in saying the word, somewhere, *somewhere*, a box of chocolates is opened, each one a different flavour, texture, colour, sensation: each one its own planet, its own galaxy, its own solar system. The stuff that's inside of stuff. Stars inside stars inside stars. Starry-eyed starcrossed starry-wheeled catherinewheeling unstoppable forces of synthesised *stuff*. It's all connected. Golden spires. Silver webs. Garden gnomes. They know. Stuff inside stuff inside stuff. Russian fuckin dolls. Or is that Russians fucking dolls? No wait, that's the future. We are no longer teenagers but are suddenly centuries old; we are Futurians; whiteclad and silverclad alien beings consuming nothing but pills for food and pills for sleep and pills for moods like crying and happy and excited and love and sex and then pills for dying and more pills to stay dead.

–See? It doesn't matter if you're on drugs or not. A theme park can be the entire world just as the entire world can be a theme park.

–Panepiphany. Panepiphemera. Panepiphenomenon.

–Panewhatnow? Just stop trying to be clever and listen. I'm trying to explain that the world is a playground; the playground is the world; nothing exists beyond the trashy flashes of the lights and the zooming *sugar rushes* that will become metaphors for the coming-to-fruition of the mainstreamising of lesbian culture, a story set in our richer southern sister and televised for the nation in 2004, but wait, we are getting ahead of ourselves – we don't even know who 'we' are – but what we are saying is that *this is it*. When insufferable bigoted middle-aged Jack Nicholson asks long-suffering eyebagged singlemumwaitress Helen Hunt whether this is as good as it gets we don't just say yes – we say in fact it doesn't get as good as *that* here.

–*Fruition*? You mean, like fruit?

–*(Sighing)* No. And yes.

Here we go again.

Fruition: a working definition by Olga Adessi and Rachel Watkins (the Lotus-Eaters), plus a Miscellany of Stimuli a Stimuscellany of Mimuli a Screamooscellany of Muesli &c.

–So there's this image, I reckon it's quite famous, I've seen it in magazines and stuff – it's of a woman unzipping her jeans and a whole load of *stuff* is spilling out. It's like a cornucopia. Berries, leaves, vines, fruit. It's really beautiful. D'you know what I'm talking about?

–I *think* so ...

–That's what I'm feeling like right now every time I say a word. Or every time you say a word. All this *stuff* pours out. Not words, or maybe also words, but at the same time, *stuff*.

–Oh my god! That sounds brill. What stuff is coming out of my mouth right now?!

–Mmm, it's like a kind of tangleweed – I dunno if that's even a real thing but it looks like that, almost like cartoon vines all tangled together with cartoon thorns and roses.

Stop and look at her for a minute. There. From her mouth: small round petals escaping in a cluster: pale pink, pale blue and then darker colours of lilac and fuchsia, all mixed together, pearly petals in a dense mass, moving slowly like a wave of honey. Beauty. Am transfixed.

–WOW I can see it too!

Those petals are familiar – they look like – hang on, brain – we can get there – r h o d o d e n d r o n petals. The hilarity of this word hits me – THWACK – in the face.

–What are you laughing at?!

–It's – your words – they're like petals – they're like – *rhododendrons* ...

She is also now laughing uncontrollably.

–What is it now?!

–It's just – *dendrons*! What a word! What are *dendrons*?!

And each time she says *dendrons*, actual dendrons shoot from her mouth – these are straight, tree-trunk-like branches but horizontal, with multicoloured leaves, again in a cartoon style. And when she speaks more slowly, the viscous, wavelike outpouring of petals. And when she looks at me, silent for a second, lips slightly pursed, a lotus flower grows.

If I kiss her I will eat this lotus flower. Sacred lotus, *Nelumbo nucifera*, one single flower, pale yellow centre fading outwards to delicate white, slender, gently pink-tipped petals. Bloom. Around her lips, flat green lily pads. Your face as the smooth centre of a pond or lake. Never have I ever. What magic is this. To bestir such depths. To put one hand in cool green. Water. Touch the surface of waterlipskin just once, twice, thrice, in slightly different and overlapping places. Diffracting circles. Ripples upon ripples upon.

But no. It snaps away and disappears before I can move a muscle. And then, of course, muscles, the fibres, the hairs that twitch, the flanks of racehorses, straps of flesh under skin. Expand and contract. The heave and the ho. Squeeze another language out, right there.

–We need a name for this.

–For what?

–This language.

Her eyes get it. Waterfalls of – beams of –

But NO. The eyes could do, are doing a whole other thing, but that is not for now. Eyespeak and mouthspeak is too much. Eyespeak is another dimension.

–Well, there's an ancient Greek philosopher, Diogenes Laertes, hang on, not him, he wrote about it – hang on – Chrysippus – he said that if you say something it passes through your lips. Literally. It's about things being literal. Not metaphorical. Everything that you can think of that's a metaphor is actually real.

–Crispus???

And sure enough, a concatenation of crisps bursts forth from her mouth, with the word, as the word, dancing in the manner of the crockery items in Disney's *Beauty and the Beast* when they sing 'Be Our Guest'!

Hysteria. Utter. The hysteria catches a whiff of itself and manifests as steam, as from a kettle, slowly whistling from the top of her head. Uh-oh. Head. Where is this headed. Triple-headed. It's all a dance of the literal and the –

–CRISSSPUSSS!!!

And as we laugh the crisps dance their way gaily into a formation of a giant cat's face, Cheshire's cousin Lancashire, Crisp-Puss, a giant catface shimmering in the air. Its eyes are two red Pringles tubes, spinning like Catherine wheels. Its teeth are the jagged ends of Nik Naks and broken Monster Munch. Striped tigerish fur made up of spiralling Skips in lines, like a football field, against lines of shimmying Wotsits. Marmalade Crispuss. Magisterial. The Cat. We worship.

As Crispuss fades, back to the important business of naming. What it is. That we are doing.

–Literal. Everything is literal. That's it!

Litter-all. Argh. And sure enough, dancing rubbish threatens – you smell it before you see it – but a snap of the fingers and a new word must be pronounced to ward away the literal procession.

–*Fruition*. That's it. That's the name of our language!

–And we are speaking what?

–Fruition! We speak. And it comes to fruition.

Fruition is perfect. When it comes. To fruition. When I come to fruition. From her lips are cherries, bananas, grapes, pineapples. We have found it. The opening up of an orifice and the pouring forth of bounteous fruit.

Wait – are we actually just talking an orgasm. Don't think it because it will happen. Don't think it. When you think something it passes through your –

–Are you thinking what I'm thinking?

What did I tell you about eyespeak and mouthspeak. Pressure cookers we are, bubbling, boiling, steaming. Dangerous. Something about this *will not happen*. Or will it. Well, will it then. Will it. Whirl it.

But whose thoughts are these? Who is speaking now? Which one am I? Which one is she? Which one are you?

And who is the third that walks alongside you?

Eyespeak. A connection, but silent and still.

–We're on exactly the same page here, aren't we?

–I know. I can't explain it, but –

–Stop trying to explain it! You don't need to explain it.

–It's amazing.

–I think we need to be alone soon.

–Yeah.

–Soon? Or now?

–Now?

–Okay.

–Okay.

Rushing rushing rushing rushing rushing. Grab hands and rush out of the door. We. Don't. Get. Far. Only semi-conscious. Hot. Tangled. Bodies. Barely. Conscious. Falling. Hall. Carpet. Blackout.

(Flashes in the pitch-black tunnel. Photos, £6 per shot: souvenirs to take home. Petrified contortions, grimaces, gurns. Those with foresight flash bras, boobs, flick fingers, flick out tongues.)

–Submersion ... a kind of tunnel ... is this what a submarine feels like?

–Wait ... is this some kind of internal conversation? Can you hear me? Where is this coming from?

–Um ... not exactly sure but ... yeah I can hear you. Are we in the womb? Or is it the sea?

–I can feel a dull ache, dredging the depths of ... Can you feel it?

–Yep, I can feel it. Are we underwater?

–It's more like a pang. A pang of desire. Like a wave. Or a knife. Sharpened by sand.

–I'm the sand and you're the waves. Friction equals momentum. Our entire existence is being played out along this line of friction.

–Are you here?

–Yes I'm here but I feel desperate. I feel serene. Liquid.

–Sand.

–Liquid.

–Sand.

–Heat. Heat turns sand to liquid glass. Look into me, as in a mirror, a mirror that you can climb into.

–Come on. Flooding and yet building. We are like two underwater cars, slowly filling up with water. Come on. Say it.

–Say what? What do you want me to say? Come back. You're whirling. You're dispersing.

–Come on. Say it. Say it. Not enough. Say it.

–*(Together)* Say it.

–Not enough. Forever and always. Atoms and aeons.

–Spear it then.

–Spear what?

–Spear the small white –

–Spear the small white glinting –

–Spear the small white hardsharp glinting nib of me.

–O thy nib. Thy noble nib. Rock thy nib.

–Cunt. Say what you mean. A cunt, glinting.

–Did you say cunt?

–Thy noble cunt. Rock thy cunt.

–Phew. Fizzing: twitching. Like radar. Circles that radiate outwards.

–Or gas fire filaments. Heatwaves. Infra-sensory. Red glow. Is this dangerous? Are we dangerous?

–Don't be so bloody narcissistic. Of course we're not dangerous. This doesn't even exist.

SNAP. Blinded by this unexpected flash of cruelty. We are in love. One of us has hacked a hole in the other's chest and climbed in, bloodred talons digging into soft tissue. It doesn't matter which way round you look at it. The talons clutch and release, clutch and release, keeping us breathing, tearing away at the old pumpbag inside us.

On the surface, climbing from an invisible momentum up to a new and frightening height, erveyinhtg is sartgne. Yroue' nto srue waht jsut hpepaend. oYu on lgneor konw waht is noamrl. Terhe is oen tinhg ouy nede to konw:

Did ...

Volatioin ... (nope)
Vlatioion ... (nope)
Vatioioln ... (nope)
Vtioiolan ... (nope)
Vioiolatn ... (nope)
Voiolatin ... (nope)
Violation ... (finally)

Occur?

Wlel, ddi ti?

And ... woh
ohw
hwo
owh
who was the violet tear
and who was the viola ted?

Rde nda yleolw nda pnik nda geren ...
Ograne nda pprule nda beul ...
I cna snig a rnaiobw,

Snig a rnaiobw,
Snig a rnaiobw oto ...

A few strands of seaweed dislodge themselves from the corner of the brain. Four eyes open stickily. What has happened here? Gravity has increased to the power of itself. Whatever that means. It means that we can't move a muscle. The we being you, me, us. Not Deus but meus. Perhaps we have fused and turned from magma into stone. The waves and the sand, the pleasure and the beach, now twisted awkwardly round one another like quotation marks, lying together on the blue carpet of the narrow hallway. Four hands wedged between four thighs. But not clear whose hands are whose. A lustcloud, hanging over us. Both faces out of sight, squashed into the carpet under a web of hair. Try to move and every sensation is an extreme of both pleasure and pain. Friction of the carpet. Paralysis of the limbs. The weight of two bodies, not added together but squared. Girl^2. When you have been upside down on a loop-the-loop for a while, the redblooded headthrobbing becomes too much to take. Violent deepfried candyfloss narcotic vinegartang: more reasons to vomit here per square mile than anywhere else on this godforsaken island. Four eyes close stickily.

Chapter 10

VOICE	Multiple, past and present
SCENE	Blackpool and surroundings
HOUR	Multiple, past and present
PLEASURE BEACH RIDE	Pepsi Max Big One
SUBSTANCE	Blackpool rock
ORGAN	Musculoskeletal system
SYMBOL	Fossilised footprint
COLOUR	Grey
FORMULA	C_3S (Ca_3SiO_5)
ART / TECHNIC	Spinning (stories)
HORMONE	Parathyroid hormone
HOMERIC TITLE	Wandering Rocks

Blackpool and the Fylde Coast

A History, Geographical and Social

Interspersed with Modern Tableaux from Our Beautiful Town

STONE AND ELK (PREHISTORY)

Sea. Ice. Limestone. Shale. Triassic rocks. Desert. Islands of sand. Mosses and meres. Mudstones. Siltstones. Sandstones. Till. Peat. Forest. Bog and swamp, oak and yew. Fylde is to field as to level green plain. 'Tween Ribble and Wyre. Estuary. Dunes. The Poulton Elk. Spearheads of flint. Forests now submerged. Charcoal. Salt lines. Metals and pottery. Sheep, chickens, cattle. The Thornton Wolf. Bronze axes. Druids' eggs. Blue woad-painted bodies. Houses of reed and log. Grain crops.

Straight Roman road to the Fylde. Four Lane Ends. Roman port under the ICI plant. Roman grave under St Michael's Church. Roman baths under Kirkham. Spanish rabbit warrens in the Fleetwood dunes. Britannia Inferior. Exodus Romanus. Gwrast the Ragged, King of Rheged. Cumbric *pen* and Old English *hyll* become Pendle Hill. *Rhos* becomes *rossall* becomes *moor*. Eccles. *Norse breck* becomes Norbreck. Anchorsholme as dry land in marsh as anchor for boat. Vikings and Saxons and Angles and Danes. St Chad's. Cleared woodland plus *leah* becomes Cleveleys. Promontory sheltered by oaks plus *ness* becomes Hacmunderness becomes Agmundrenessa becomes Agmondernes becomes Amounderness. Vikings in Knott End. Knots of stones on the beach. Famine. St Cuthbert in Lytham. Wattle and shingle.

TREESA AND THE CANDYFLOSS
Seafront, 12 noon, 16 June 1999

Call on me
Spin spin sugar
Crawl on me
Spin spin sugar
Stinks on me
Spin spin sugar
Twists for me
Spin spin sugar

One calm hour, just to wander and faff on the beach. Bliss. Or it *would* be, if it wasn't for a wide grin, hanging loosely between a pair of ears stuck onto a shaved skull, that arrives out of the sky and plants itself squarely in front of us.

–Oi! You ignoring me?

Liam is grinning for Britain. Grinning for the world. Clutching his hand is Lulu, whose flushed cheeks are smudged with stickiness and fluff. A faint odour of spun sugar and caramel wafting from the pair of them. They've been on the pier. Some of Liam's teeth have fallen out due to drugs and sugar, but the front two have dug their heels in and remained. They're like pirates, the way they're reeling around. High on sugar. High on life, Liam would say. Baby pirate and daddy pirate. Lulu clutches a giant fluffy unicorn in her other hand. Its horn is multicoloured and made of plastic.

–Hiya, Lulubelle! What've you won?

She says nothing, only thrusts the unicorn towards us. Grasp it and examine its cheap stitching, its synthetic fibres, its inhuman face. It is streaked with sticky pink.

Lulu snatches it back.

–He sing a song – listen!

She squeezes the life out of the unicorn, bending over and hugging its belly close to hers. The unicorn's head jerks upwards as if it has been electrified and from its throat comes a startlingly loud, tinny voice:

The Vengabus is coming
And everybody's jumping
New York to San Francisco
An intercity disco

A few seconds of this and the three of us are in harmony, bending over, screwing up our eyes and laughing. Lulu is beside herself, shrieking and stamping in her Barbie wellies. So sweep her up into our arms, making a noise like a plane. *Wheeeeeee.*

–Can you lend us a tenner? Just until payday? We went a bit mad on the slots ...

A gentle shake of the head. And so, with another smile flash, Liam the gap-toothed Cheshire Cat hoists Lulu up onto his shoulders and we walk on. Another half an hour before he has to be back. The imprint of the smile is left hanging in the air. Inside Liam's smile is the entire universe: stars, planets, solar systems, smudges of sticky, sweet life smeared across the darkness.

ROMANS AND WITCHES (400 BCE–1500 CE)

Kilgrimol forest becomes Fieldlands becomes Fylde. Spectral monks drowned in floods. Ceorlatun becomes Karl Tun becomes Carleton. Village of free peasants. A battle of Saxons and Danes at Weeton. Boggart Pit on Mains Lane. The demon of the Fylde. Water dragon of Marton Mere.

Pool Town becomes Pewton becomes Poulton. Normandy stamps 'le Fylde' on the end. Skip Pul becomes Skippool. Markets and tithe barns. Wharves and Wyre train. Kirk Ham becomes Kirkham. Ducking stools and scold's bridles. Cruck cottages of the Fylde. Lethum becomes Lytham. Manchester Square – the Black Pool. Benedictine priors. Frecla Tun becomes Freckleton. Laa Ton becomes Layton. Biscop Ham becomes Bispham.

The Roman fort on the river Lune becomes Luneceaster becomes Loncastra becomes Lancaster. The County of Lancastershire. The Red Rose of the House of Lancaster. All Hallow's becomes All Saint's Church, Bispham. Ancient sundial and Zodiac signs. Schingel Tun becomes Singleton. Cockfighting in Mains Lane.

The Stanleys and the Derbys. The uncrowned Kings of Lancashire. The Stocks in Poulton. Black Kirkham rides a black horse and wears a black cloak. Layrbroke Manor becomes Larbreck Hall. Lancashire Witch Trials. Dorothye Shawe accused of WITCHERY AND DEMDYKERY.

RACHEL AND THE PURPLE INKBOOK
Talbot Road, 6 p.m., 16 June 1999

Hop off the 14 in the bus station. Walk round to Blacks. The army of women who work there are stalking the narrow aisles with their colossal tubes and cardboard blocks of wound-round material. Make a beeline for the bit at the back with the biggest, weirdest, fluffiest, most gorilla-like material. Gorilla suit material. This part of the shop is our favourite. It is like another world. Things feel outsized and alien. All we want to do is climb into a space somewhere amongst those tubes and hide and be somehow comfortably squashed by those heavy, wound-round giant sausages of material. Instead walk round to the other most exciting part of the shop: the stands and carousels on the other side, with their craft materials. Assorted shapes and sizes of googly craft eyes. Assorted sizes and colours of pipe cleaners. Assorted shapes, sizes and colours of felt shapes. Buttons upon buttons upon buttons. Scissors of various sizes and specialities. Polystyrene balls of assorted sizes; what the hell are they actually for? Felt-tip pens. Pencils. Needles. Stickers. Kids' stuff that glitters. Glitter itself. Tools of various kinds. Glues. Tiny knives. Tiny hooks. Tiny clasps. Everything tiny and bound for construction in a tiny world but sold there as parts, components, elements, Legolike, ready to assemble themselves at the behest of a thrifty crafter. Reassuring. But one of the women has started to stare. We have been here too long. Time to leave. Walk down Deansgate to Abingdon Street, then find Steals. Upstairs in Steals is another good way to hide. There are rows and rows of cut-price flared jeans and cords up there. All around £3. Green, grey, blue, demin, black, white, off-white. But again, the women working in there are staring.

In the purple inkbook, in the first few pages. From prose to poetry in several moves. *Prose it must be, because there is nothing burning inside me with a ferocious enough intensity for a poetic medium.* And so prose it is. And yet now there is this Olga. Or this Olga thing, because it is the thing and not the person. Olga brings forth sonnets. I puff them out like they are feathers and I am something overstuffed. *Dark joy or shining pain may be its end.* No intensity for the poetic medium. What does that even mean. Shitting out poetry. *I want to tell you just how much it kills.* No direct address. Keep going. *The one that stabs me, tells me how she loves.* The pain and the love. Misdirected. Directed to whom? *She stabs me, though the one who stabs is me.* I use the one I love to stab myself? *Through you I stab the hole inside my heart.* To stab a hole? Not quite right. *She holds the sword but does not stab the wound.* I need my own role in this. *I stab the soul through she who holds the sword.* Or. *Through she who holds the sword I stab myself.* Girls as conduits. I possess them. The ultimate act of arrogance. Possess another body, not just against their will but without them even knowing. Make a doll of them and get inside it. And when you think she is inside you, it is actually the other way round. You are inside her, or this other voodoo version of her that you have created, navigating her from the centre like she is a spaceship.

Not cool.

Sorry.

Try again. *We hold the sword with fingers interlocked.* Too much togetherness and our real fingers have never been interlocked as such – yet – or have they?

She holds the sword I use to stab myself.

Yes. Makes sense.

MYTH AND LEGEND (1500–1700)

No one has ever got to the bottom of Marton Mere. Banks by Chain Lane. The lake and the gynn. Spen Dyke. Peat-blackened water. The Black of the Pool. The Houndehill in Laton becomes the Hound Hill becomes the Houndshill. Cardinal William Allen of Rossall Grange. Salt cotes at Preesall. Burn Naze Salt. Gezzerts becomes Gazette Farm. The Cottams of Cottam Hall. Protestant parents of Catholic saint. Smugglers at Wardleys Creek. Hambleton Hookings as large mussels with pearls. Tallow and flax from Russia. Rauðr Klif becomes Rawcliffe. Newton-with-Scales. Edeleswic becomes Elleswyk becomes Elswick. Ale and rum at Skippool. Recusants and pursuivants. Priest holes. Lancashire Witch Trials. Ducking stool + pond = duck pond. Bank of the Black Pool. The headless boggart of Whitegate Lane. Fosse Hol becomes The Foxhall. Slave ships from African countries bound for Preston. 'Ambleton 'ookers down Skippool Creek. Otters in Marton Mere. Spen Dyke Mermaid. The Fylde Hag.

PASAJE DEL TERROR
Pleasure Beach, 5 p.m., 16 June 1999

Ey ey ba day ba wadladie day
Ay um ba day
Ba day ba wadladie day
Ey ey ba day ba wadladie day
Ay um ba da- ay um ba da-da-da-da-wadladie day!

From Bilbao to Malaga to Orlando to Cancún and now Blackpool! Pasaje del Terror. Beyond the Limits of Fear. Once you go through that door you must keep walking and never look back. Do not touch anything or anyone, and maybe, just maybe, nothing and no one will touch you.

Find the door marked 666 and knock three times. Someone or something will answer. Beyond these gates you will reach your final destination. Travel closely. Travel quickly. Rattling chains, above, below, all around. *Whisper*Sound and *Whisper*Sense. My spidersense is. Flashflash-strobe. The sense of something. *Whisperuponwhisperss* Subliminal? *Whisper*Something beyond. Just a scare maze. *Whisper*. But what is behind. *Sssssssssssssssssss*.

Smalljumpscare

Smalljumpscare

H U G E

J U M P

S C A R E

Crawling carrying mumbling stumbling trembling. Something soft slushing. *Sssssssssssssss*. Wet whispers.

Dark dark dank. Crawling crawling over under skin. Wetskin. Slugskin. Velvet but damp. Damp corpselike softness. EEEEEEEEEEEEE. Rotting mulchlike scenes projected onto walls. Only flashes though. AAAAAAAAAAAAAAAAAAAAAH. Something catches. *Whisperuponwhisper* Something squeals. Are they real or machines. Hold hands. Keep together. *Whisperuponwhis-persspersssperssssssss* SCREAM – CURDLE – SCREAM – BLOOD BLOOD COBWEBS BLOOD – running through a door of teeth – falling into a cage of ribs – did I fall against grabbing arms? SQUEALS. Are they real or are they machines. A clown leaping amongst curtains. It is It. Cannot look. Huge painted smile and snarling gnarled mouth. S-S-S-S-S-S-S-S-S-S-S-S-S-S-S-S-S-S-S-S-S-S-S-S-S-S-S-S-S-S-S-S-S-S-S-S-S-S-S-S-strobe/strobe/strobe/strobe/strobestrobestrobestrobeeeee-e-e-e-e-e-e-e-e-e-e-e-e-e-e-e-e-e-e-e-e-e-e-e-e-e-e-e-e-e-e-e-e-e-e-e-e-e-e-eeeeeeeeeeeeeeeeeeeeeeeeeeeeeeeeee I think it's time to get out of here. The gentle nursery rhyme tinkle. Faint against the screams. Do not fear the Masked Man. The hooded Reaper carries his scythe and holds a leash to which a white-faced vampiric character is attached. A strange kinky duo in a room of rattling chains. Gurgling and creeping but who is doing the creeping. Now we are running all of us. The desperation takes hold. The pulse goes everfaster. The exit door materialises and we spill out into a pub, the running must stop, there are onlookers, amused, bemused, sipping pints to bestill their beating hearts.

Nichola from the Wirral stops and looks straight at us with tear-streaked cheeks.

–Do not go in there. I'm telling you now – do *not* go in

there. It's not right. I know it's just actors but I've never been so scared in my life.

Nichola stops and looks down at her whiteknuckled hand, which is clutching her pink sateen scarf that says BIRTHDAY GAL.

–It's my birthday today.

–How old are you?

–Fifty-five.

A HISTORY OF BLACKPOOL'S SEA BATHING (1700–1960)

Bathing machines. Dippers for Ladies and Bathers for Gentlemen. ***At Black Pool near the sea there are accommodations for people who come to bathe.*** Description of the Sea Coast from Blacke Combe in Cumberland to the Point of Linas in Wales. Raikes Hall. Lane Ends Hotel. The Circus. Billy Buttons the Clown. Bailey's Hotel becomes the Metropole Hotel. Forshaw's becomes the Clifton Arms. Public Houses No. 1. No. 2. No. 3. Mr Forshaw's Bathing Place and the First Promenading. Elston's Hotel becomes Yorkshire House. Post offices. Stagecoach from Manchester. Booze from the Isle of Man. 1784, Mrs Bailey's Bathhouse. The Packing Ground. Bowling Green. Mr Bailey's Tavern. Mr Forshaw's Tavern. Mr Crooke's Post Office. Mrs Hodson's Tavern. Mr Hull's Tavern. Mr Bonney's Wine-House. Mr Elson. Pul House. Weaving factory at Bispham. Norbreck House. The black and the pool are married.

Twenty-seven windmills! Concerts from the Musical Society of the Gentlemen of Preston. ***Description of Blackpool in Lancashire, frequented for Sea Bathing.*** The Blackpool Parade Act for Promenade Development. Henry Banks. Bank holidays. Wakes weeks. ***Sea Bathing for the Working Classes.***

THE BLACKPOOL ALPHABET
All day, 16 June 1999

Alcopop Andy dreams of amyl nitrate in Ann
Summers while
Boozed up boyracers chase bitchfighters in boobtubes,
Carnage with cleavage and candyfloss carousels of
Deepfried doughnuts, dodgy dealers on donkeys,
Emos on eccies, Elvis reborn as a
Faghag in fake fur fighting with feather boas,
Goosepimpled and greygilled with gurning jaws and greasy
barnets,
Hens with handbags, heels and hair extensions peruse
Illuminations in inadequate winterwear,
Juddering with cold, jellies for junkies,
Kiss-me-quick Kappa kids kicking off about ketamine,
Ladettes getting lairy with a lipstick leer,
Machismo in miniskirts,
Naughty nans in nylon nighties,
Orange tans and over-the-shoulder-boulder-holders,
Pleasure Beach prom plastic platinum-blonde
glamourpusses,
Queer side streets, queens with quiffs and a
Richmond Menthol rasp, roaring tourists out on the radge,
Seasider stag scuffles, stiletto staggers in strappy numbers,
Trance-loving toilet-hugging tangerine dreamers,
Underage and underfed,
Vomiting Veronicas in
Wonderbras with neon-blue Wickeds,
X-rated dancing,
Yellow-stained moustaches,
'Zany' office jokers concussed from zinging off toilet walls.

Gypsies on the clifftops at North Shore. Petulengro and Ada Boswell. Britain's Royal Queen of the Gypsies. From North Shore to Gypsytown in South Shore. Blackpool Sunday Fairs. Cow Gap Lane becomes Waterloo Road. Queen's Hydro Hotel. Jenkinson's Confectioners becomes Rumours becomes Jenks. Green Walk becomes Victoria Terrace becomes Victoria Street. Grand Promenade Building Theatre. Corporation Donkey Stables on Rigby Road. Robert's Oyster Bar. Black velvet as stout and champagne. Sea breeze to chase away the cholera. The Dog and Partridge. The Royal Oak. The Oddfellows Arms. Wesleyan Church. Free United Methodist Church. The Adelphi Hotel. West Hey. Victoria Terrace and Promenade. Poulton Railway Station. Railway to Fleetwood. Peter Hesketh-Fleetwood. Whitechapel of Blackpool. The Victoria Hotel.

The hurdy-gurdy man. St John's Market. The Shambles. Bazaars. Blackpool Railway Station. E. H. Booth's. Blackpool Masonic Lodge. Queen Victoria in Fleetwood. The Railway Hotel becomes Molloy's. The Golden Fleece Hotel becomes Brannigan's. Uncle Tom's Cabin. *Instrumentalists, Vocalists, Negro Burlesque Artists, Dancers &c.*

Blackpool Board of Health. Blackpool Town Hall. Blackpool Gas Works. Blackpool Police. The Temple of Arts Photographic Studio. The Promenade! Sacred Heart Catholic Church. Blackpool Fire Brigade. Fish and chips. Italian ice cream: Naventi, Pini, Notarianni. Read's Bazaar, Market and Sea Water Baths. Fylde Waterworks. Blackpool Pier. Blackpool South. The Counting House. The Queen's Hotel. Palatine Hotel. The White Swan. The Imperial Hotel. The Stanley Arms. Oscar Wilde in the Theatre Royal. Yates' Wine Lodge.

Samuel Laycock. John Dennison's coin-operated automata. The Blackpool Sea Water Company. Burton's Bakers. The Blackpool Gazette. The Winter Gardens. Her Majesty's Opera House and Grand Pavilion. The Empress Ballroom. Golden Mile and Rum Row. Blackpool Football Club. Bloomfield Road. Blackpool Free Library. Punch and Judy. Dame Sarah Bernhardt. Blackpool Electric Tramway Company. Blackpool Co-operative Society. Blackpool Rock. Blackpool Synagogue. Professor Vidoco's Flea Circus. Victoria Hospital. Blackpool Corporation Abattoir. The Grand Theatre. Ohmy's Circus. Sandgrown 'uns.

BLACKPOOL TOWER.

OLGA AND RACHEL SPAR WHILE TRIPPING (over *The Miseducation of Lauryn Hill*) Dickson Road, 1:47 a.m., 16 June 1999

Everything is everything
What is meant to be, will be

–You see what a task this is becoming. Or equally, you don't. Everything is everything. Lauryn Hill. She knew it. *I begat this*. Everything is everything.

–Sounds like a tautology to me. A tautology is when the same thing is said more than once in different words. Everything is everything.

–But is the first everything the same as the second everything? What is the word 'is' anyway? What is is?

–Is asking what is is the same as asking what is the being of being?

–Ha – did we think we would be getting this philosophical?

–Not at all. But look. Listen. That's what I'm trying to say: the hardest things are actually the easiest. Everything is everything. They are the same but they are also not the same.

–Don't get me started on time.

–We don't.

–Have.

–Enough.

–Of.

–It.

Back to Lauryn Hill. Olga looks at Rachel with huge and

shining darkest of darkest eyes. Pronounces the words carefully.

Flipping in the ghetto on a dirty mattress
You can't match this rapper slash actress
More powerful than two Cleopatras.

–You know that's us, don't you? Two Cleopatras. Together. We could, you know. The world. It's there, for the taking. We could. If we wanted to.

FUN (1900–1950)

South Pier. The Tower Circus. Tower Lounge. Grand Pavilion Ballroom. *Bid me discourse, I will enchant thine ear.* The Empire becomes The Hippodrome. The Pleasure Beach Company. River Caves of the World. Lighthouse Helter Skelter. The Great Wheel. Illuminated Trams. Blackpool Magistrates' Court. The Empress Hotel. The Blackpool Rescue and Preventative Home for Young Women. Charlie Chaplin and the Eight Lancashire Lads. Clog dancing. Louis Tussaud's Waxworks. Blackpool Girls' Rescue Home. Switchback railways. Les Montagnes Russes. The Big Dipper. The Fylde Waltz. Wylie's South Pier Hotel. Revoe. Quaker Meeting House. Hiram Maxim's Captive Flying Machine. Blackpool Allotments. The Scenic Miniature Railway. Roller Coaster. Alpine Water Chute. The Scenic Railway. The Ice Drome. The Blackpool and Fylde District Taxi Cab Company. The Spectatorium. Scots Weekend.

Carnegie Free Library. The Grundy Art Gallery. Clifton Park Racecourse. The Sands Express. Jubilee Gardens. Troops dining room in the Pleasure Beach Casino. Tunnel from the Tower to the Palace Theatre. Blackpool Central Working Men's Club and Institute. The Savoy Hydro Hotel. Deck chairs. Pontins. The Virginia Reel. The Dodgems. The Whip. Blackpool Grand Carnival. Talbot Road Bus Station. Stanley Park. Blackpool Illuminations. ICI General Chemicals. Coronation Rock. Abingdon Street Market. The Miners' Home. Midget Town at Blackpool Tower. The Olympia. Wurlitzer organ. Reginald Dixon. The first Ghost Train in the United Kingdom. Theosophical Society Rooms. The Lido Swimming Baths. Abbott's Coaches.

The Fun House. The Laughing Man. The Grand National.
My Little Stick of Blackpool Rock.

GIGOLO
Promenade, 11:10 p.m., 16 June 1999

Who's that gigolo on the street
With his hands in his pockets and his crocodile feet

And in the other street there he lurks, face leather brown creased, leather jacket brown, loafers polished snakeskin brown, hair brown polished greased, moustache oiled greased, socks brown diamond patterned, moustache yellowed, skin yellowed, fingers yellowed, shirt underarms yellowed, under the subway leading to the railway station, in the bus station, in the alley, there he waits and there he lurks. The strange sartorial elegance of certain sociopathic men. Glasses, tinted brown aviator style, sometimes cravat, sometimes turtleneck, his sexual predilections are hidden entirely and we do not want to guess except that we know he is a peddler of wares and the wares are young girls who want to be grown up and want to be seen as grown up and think that what they are doing makes them grown up and in a way they are right but the other parts of them are not grown up and they are hardened in places and too malleable in others and as they are peddled they are shaped by the men who peddle them.

And converging onto the scene there she steps, skinny legs school socks and platform shoes, clumpy mascara on staring eyes too wide and too bright, a trace of amphetamine in the system, fourteen thin and cynical yet unsure, a knife in her inside blazer pocket, staying up all night in Stanley Park, rolling eyes at support workers and teachers, *I've seen things that you wouldn't believe*, converging onto the scene where she is to become the thing that is peddled, engaging in actions she doesn't care for, being quietened with treats, fags and booze and crisps and sweets, so what if she had eight Penguins for lunch and nothing else all day, it felt good, it was sweet, it was even sweeter because she was starving, and smoking stops you from feeling hungry and being skinny is good so what's the problem.

And back in the office in the school the secretaries all type and telephone and talk about how evening walks in the summer are good for keeping up the fitness and how to keep sane when single parenting and how to deal with moody teenage offspring when all they encounter at work are other people's moody teenage offspring who think it's okay to come storming in and demand things without saying please and teachers on power trips and young kids on power trips without realising they're on power trips and each one of the secretaries thinks secretly and longingly about one of the teachers and each one of the teachers thinks secretly and longingly about one of the secretaries but because most desire is unspoken and sometimes even unthought and often only unconsciously or subconsciously felt we will never know whether the desires flowing one way match the desires flowing in the other. For example the metalhead geography teacher in DMs secretly desires the blonde fifty-five-year-old Tory-supporting golf-tennis-horse-rugby-wife secretary whereas the golf-tennis-horse-rugby-wife secretary secretly desires the tall slightly stooped slightly awkward slightly balding forty-nine-year-old deputy head whereas the deputy head secretly desires the recently divorced stern-yet-kind thirty-two-year-old secretary who secretly desires the bouncy cheerful dark-eyed half-Italian twenty-five-year-old PE teacher who secretly desires the ponderous unsure quiet twenty-two-year-old temporary secretary who secretly desires the booming-voiced long-striding leonine disciplinarian RE teacher who secretly desires the temporary secretary though this mutual desire is hidden under so many layers of interdiction it will never come to light even in the most ponderous of conscious thoughts. One barks; the other jumps; one feigns fear; the other feigns displeasure; one feigns indifference; the other feigns even greater indifference. And such are the unwritten unspoken unnoticed spidery webs and chains of power and desire that line the air so thickly it's amazing we can breathe a clear breath. If. One. Could. Tint. Those. Lines. We would have amazing kaleidoscopophilia right there. Like tinting the eyeballs with fluorescent juice then sneezing out neon into a tissue later.

TRAMS, DARLINGS AND FREAKS (1950–1999)

Hesketh's Chip Saloon. Blackpool Home Guard. Morecambe and Wise. Cottage Chippy. RAF Blackpool Tower. Blackpool Magic Circle. Ken Dodd. *In an upstairs room in Blackpool*. Prefabs on Grange Park. The Petulengros. Squires Gate Aerodrome. Sooty. The Blackpool Postcard Censorship Board. Miss Blackpool. Royal Variety Performance. The Haunted Swing. Wild Mouse Ride. Glasdon Laminates. *What the Butler Saw*. Mods in the Golden Nugget. Rockers in the Shangri La. Tramnik One is the tram with the rocket lights. C Cabs. The Picador Club. The Horseshoe Club. Beat City. The Pink Elephant. The Seafood Restaurant. Napoleons Cabaret Bar. Mandarin Chinese Restaurant. *A Taste of Honey*. The Singing Nolans. The Twisted Wheel.

The Rolling Stones Riot. Mecca Ballroom. Pleasure Beach Monorail. The World's Longest Log Flume. Les Dawson. The Golden Mile Centre. Trader Jack's. Lucy's Bar and *Blackpool's gayest organ in town*. Ripley's Odditorium. Coral Island. B&M Bargains. The 007 Club. Blackpool Zoo. Blackpool Model Village. The Viking. Blackpool Pigeon Show. The M55 motorway. The Space Tower. The Houndshill shopping centre. The Palace Nightclub. The Tache. Basil Newby. The Flying Handbag. Roller-skating in the Empress Ballroom. Flamingo's. The Roly Polys. The Sandcastle. West Coast Rock Café. The Pleasure Beach Superdome. Blackpool Mosque. Radio Wave. Mardi Gras. Blackpool Sea Life Centre. The Village Hotel and Leisure Club. Job Centre Blackpool. Fylde Coast Women's Aid. The Pepsi Max Big One. New Odeon Cinema. Pasaje del Terror. The mural of Accrington Brick. Millennium Sun Dial.

THE SOUNDS FROM THE SHOPS INSIDE BLACKPOOL'S SHOPPING STREETS
10 a.m., 16 June 1999

THE SONG BEING PLAYED IN WALLIS (BLINK 182, 'ALL THE SMALL THINGS') VERSUS THE SONG BEING PLAYED IN OASIS (THE WANNADIES, 'YOU AND ME SONG'), VICTORIA STREET

Always when we fight all the small things. I try to make you laugh true cares truth brings. Till everything's forgotten I'll take one lift. I know you hate that your ride best trip. Always when we fight, always I know. I'll kiss you once or twice you'll be at my show. Everything's forgotten watching, waiting. I know you love that commiserating. I love you Sunday sun say it ain't so, I will not go. The week's not yet begun turn the lights off, carry me home.

THE SONG BEING PLAYED IN BOWS & BANGLES (EN VOGUE, 'DON'T LET GO') VERSUS THE SONG BEING PLAYED IN WOOLWORTHS (MANIC STREET PREACHERS, 'A DESIGN FOR LIFE'), BANK HEY STREET

What's it gonna be cos I can't pretend libraries gave us power. Don't you wanna be more than friends then work came and made us free. Hold me tight and don't let go what price now don't let go. For a shallow piece of dignity you have the right to lose control don't let go. I wish I had a bottle I often tell myself that we could be more than just friends. Right here in my dirty face I know you think that if we move too soon then it would all end. To wear the scars I live in misery when you're not around. To show from where I came and I won't be satisfied till we're taking those vows. We don't talk about love there'll be some lovemaking heartbreaking soulshaking. We only wanna get drunk love. Oh lovemaking heartbreaking soulshaking and we are not allowed to spend. What's it gonna be cos I can't pretend and we are told that this is the end. Don't you wanna be more than friends a design for life. Hold me tight and don't let go (don't let go) a design for life. A design for life you have the right to lose control (lose control) a design for life.

THE SONG BEING PLAYED IN THE SMOKER'S PARADISE (RADIOHEAD, 'THE TOURIST') VERSUS THE SONG BEING PLAYED IN MISS SELFRIDGE (MIKE & THE MECHANICS, 'OVER MY SHOULDER'), BANK HEY STREET

Looking back over my shoulder it barks at no one else but me. With an aching deep in my heart like it's seen a ghost. I never dreamed it could be over I guess it's seen the sparks a-flowing. I never wanted to say goodbye no one else would know.

THE SONG BEING PLAYED IN CORONATION ROCK (MASSIVE ATTACK, 'TEARDROP') VERSUS THE SONG BEING PLAYED IN THE ENTRANCE TO THE TOWER (DELERIUM, 'SILENCE'), BANK HEY STREET

Love, love is a verb give me release. Love is a doing word witness me. Fearless on my breath I am outside. Gentle impulsion give me peace. Shakes me, makes me lighter Heaven holds a sense of wonder. Teardrop on the fire and I wanted to believe. Fearless on my breath that I'd get caught up. Night, night of matter when the rage in me subsides. Black flowers blossom in this white wave. Fearless on my breath I am sinking. Water is my eye in this white wave. Most faithful mirror in this silence I believe.

FRAGMENTS MISCELLANEOUS

ALCOPOP ANDY AS JOYCEAN HERO

Alcopop Andy ate with relish McDonald's Bacon Double Cheeseburgers. He liked the sharp tang and mathematical precision of the ridged gherkin slice; the glisten and pallor of the mayo-like substance that was different from any other mayonnaise; the pale yellow square of synthetic cheese; the pink bacon rasherlets against the metallic, greyblooded chew of the patty and the soft sweetness of the bread with its sparse sesame seeds.

GREASE

Chippy kitchens. Out the back of school kitchens, pre-lunchtime grease. An elegy for grease. An ode to grease. How shall I grease thee, let me count the ways. Pier doughnut grease in staining brown paper bags. Hamburger grease mixed with fake beef bloodjuice and gherkin sweetvinegar, running down fingers and chins. Grease that gets through and stains clothes. Permanent grease spots on a lime-green Adidas zip-up top. Shiny fingers dipped into the margarine then oiling the surface of the baking tray ready for cake mix. The grease that coats the mouth after eating a doner kebab. The grease that oils the town and smooths its surfaces.

CLUELESS

Like, I was soooooooooo surprised! Ugh! As if!

THE BODY SHOP

Make your body wriggle with joy by smothering it in our delicious Body Butter. Good Enough To Eat – but beware, our products are not edible so don't try! Animal-friendly. Please bring your empties back for recycling and receive a free cherry lip balm!

WINDOWS FOR DUMMIES

A window on the.

SPECTROSCOPY FOR DUMMIES

We can use a prism to see the full spectrum. Prisms are magic. Prismology. A prism upon the both of yez.

OLGA AND RACHEL SPAR WHILE TRIPPING
Dickson Road, 2:56 a.m., 16 June 1999

OLGA: How can you not have heard of mystics? Didn't they teach you anything at university?

RACHEL: I was only there for one term! Middle and Old English was next term.

OLGA: I wasn't there at all and I know!

RACHEL: Go on then, tell me!

OLGA: They're basically women in medieval times who had invisible sexual relationships with God.

RACHEL: How? You mean they kind of imagined it? Or they were a bit mad and believed it?

OLGA: I guess so, or they were masturbating with their minds, or their spirits. I dunno really! They just went around being ecstatic and suffering all the time. You can be Hildegard von Bingen because you're posher than me. I want to be Margery Kempe. Margery Kempe's more earthy and – what's that word for kind of rude humour in Shakespeare and stuff?

RACHEL: Mmm ... scatological?

OLGA: No ... Doesn't that mean just talking about shit?

RACHEL: Oh yeah ...

OLGA: *Bawdy*. That's what I mean. Bawdy. Mr Avocat always used to say it about the Wife of Bath in Chaucer's *Canterbury Tales* with the sexual gap in her teeth and seventeen housebounds –

RACHEL: Housebounds?

OLGA: Yeah, you know! Husbands. But they pronounced it *housebounds* back then. Or something.

It always made me laugh when Mr Brown said it because I imagined all of the Wife of Bath's husbands stuck in her house as her sex slaves. Cos she's bawdy, in't she!

RACHEL: Bawdy is a funny word ... it sounds like it was always old-fashioned. Even when it wasn't. D'you know what I mean?

OLGA: Can I tell you about Margery? She's cool – she couldn't even read but she told her life story to a guy and he wrote it all down. She wasn't a nun or anything but she had all these visions. She had fourteen kids! Can you imagine?

Rachel cannot.

OLGA AND PARADOXIA
Brannigans, Market Street, 1:15 a.m., 16 June 1999

The curiousness of your potential kiss
Has got my mind and body aching
Really hurt me, baby, really cut me, baby
How can you have a day without a night?
You're the book that I have opened
And now I've got to know much more

We're doing lines of nasty white speed in Brannigans toilets. Right in this moment we know that no one else in the world can touch the sparring and sparking that goes on between us. Yeah yeah we can roar with the best of 'em at any given time, but Rachel needs encouragement, which we can give. She starts off so shy, and then the drunker and higher we get the more she unfurls herself and then it's like she doesn't know her own strength; she's scared of her own power. And her power is limitless. It's like she suddenly has these long, powerful limbs but hasn't learned to control them yet and wants to kick everything in sight, including herself. From young deer to full liontigerdragon in twenty minutes and two lines. In Brannigans lads hang around us and privately we mock them, but they never quite realise that we are mocking them. It is endless endless endless fun.

–Are you both actors?

A lad with hard gelled curtains and a tartan Fred Perry shirt would like to know, peering into each of our faces, sizing us up, wondering which one is the best option to go for. Nod immediately.

–Well, I'm a professional actor ...

We are drawling, fingers curling around cigarette, enjoying the moment, enjoying the sound of our own voice rasping against the terrible music. Nod head in Rachel's direction.

–Rachel just –

Look to Rachel for inspiration. She is glassy-eyed and fixing not on the forgettable eager lad in front of us but on my right hand, the one that holds the cigarette. I put my other hand on her shoulder. Feel the ball of bone resting in its socket. This structure holds her up. How fucking amazing is that.

–Rachel does performance too, but she does it ...

Pause and look at her. Rachel grins manically and performs some kind of trance-like mime action with her hands at super-speed.

–Oh, I just do it privately in my bedroom, you know, so no one can see.

The boy looks confused but enamoured. Looks at each of us in turn. Cartoon hearts have basically replaced his eyes, though he has no idea what we're talking about. He laughs uneasily as we both collapse into giggles.

–She's a private performer. She only performs when no one's watching. She goes by the name of ...

Whirl around, searching for inspiration but Rachel gets there first.

–Paradoxia. That's my stage name. But obviously, you know, no one knows that.

A monster laugh bursts out of me. Bow and kiss her theatrically on the cheek. Can't help it. She is completely lit up by this moment and is beautiful. Her hair is tangled and hangs all around her flushed face. Her eyes shoot beams straight at us. Can't dodge them. Don't want to dodge them.

The lad must have wandered off at this point, taking us for batshit crazy. Don't know, don't care. I can see her so clearly it hurts. This feeling is the sun. I can see exactly what it is and what it will be and it fucking hurts already.

ARCHETYPAL FEMININE / FISHWIFE
The Fish Plaice, Victoria Road West, Cleveleys, 10 a.m., 16 June 1999

I know this little girl, her name is Maxine
Her beauty is like a bunch of rose
If I ever tell you 'bout Maxine
Yuh woulda say I don't know what I know

Up the coast to Cleveleys, the boy in the fish shop is whistling. Lifts two rubbery fillets of yellow smoked haddock from the slab of ice and skins them, rhythmically, one-two, slapping them down onto the plastic chopping board. Twirls the ends of the polythene bag a couple of times before handing it over. The woman fishes in her purse and produces two coins. She ruffles her purple coat and its extravagantly frilled lapels before exiting the shop, as if trying to dislodge the briny odour, the staring eyes of the marooned creatures set out for her perusal, the endless, almost imperceptible movements of the crabs' legs.

Gathering her coat about her, the woman steps smartly down the high street, heels clip-clopping. Her lipstick is scarlet red, too vivid for the Kwik Save, the British Heart Foundation, the procession of beige, grey and tracksuit colours along Victoria Road West. Five minutes and she reaches the promenade. Seagulls croak and swoop. She stands in her stiletto heels and looks out towards the sea. Two men fishing at the shoreline can see nothing but a blob of bright purple, but it is enough to pique their interest. She is an exclamation mark against the endless grey-beige of pebble, concrete, sea and sky.

She has been clutching the parcel of raw fish tight in her hand, ignoring the handles of the bag, warming the flesh until its temperature has reached her own. She opens it up now, removes and discards the square of white paper the lad had wrapped the fish in, and carefully lifts out both the pieces. It is nice to hold. The croaking of the seagulls seems to get louder as she stretches out both hands. An offering? She arches her head back, flawless pale face, painted red lips parted against a backdrop of sky, and shrieks. The sound is instantly lost to the wind, but for a second it echoes the cries of the seagulls exactly. The woman's teeth are white, the incisors neatly pointed. The lips stretch wider into something resembling a smile or a grimace. Perhaps the molecules making up the air, the windswept particles of sand and salt and vapourised moisture, respond to this call now and condense, harden, clarify themselves for a second against the outline of woman and fish and piercing wail. Perhaps the men fishing at the shoreline, had they been facing inland at that moment and not out to sea, would have noticed a slight wobble in the atmosphere, a tremor in all the visible objects of ground and cement and sky, as if insensible objects forgot their inability to move or think, jolted out of their inanimation just to quake for a second in pure fear at this concentration of strangeness, this humming of the bizarre. Perhaps colours become unsure of themselves during this second, dipping in hue only to reassert themselves confusingly, and the lines that draw the world sharpened in suspicion, ready for fight or flight. Perhaps the abyss that lies at the bottom of things opens up right there just for that second, threatening to swallow up the symmetrical lines of the sea wall, the even lettering of the sign warning of dangerous currents, the edges of each separate atom of rock vibrating within its designated space, the just-visible distinction between land and sea. Perhaps a kind of blurring of the edges is suggested, enacted even, for that second, and all is dip, swoon, expire.

She snaps her jaw shut and clutches it with her one hand. Her teeth ache. Her colours fade. She ages. The fish fillets rot. Her features curve downwards, wrinkling, folding, melting into one another. She moans. Whimpers. Shuffles a few steps forward. Sits down on the gritty sea wall. Feels its stony response to her flesh. Lies down with difficulty on the concrete. Perhaps a gash, a wound that opens inside her, an amount of blood. Her failure, her apology will come in the form of a crimson stain, shocking the endless grey.

HENS
Church Street, 2 a.m., 16 June 1999

A gaggle of hens skirt the pavement outside Popeyes, each clutching a cardboard tray with doner meat on chips. Black miniskirts and fishnets and pink tops with 'Brenda's Hen 1999' in black Comic Sans. Tiaras with pink plastic penises attached to each tiara with a spring, so the penis bobs and waves gently over each hen's head like a halo. Brenda wears the biggest tiara, which also has a mini-veil trailing down her back. Tied into the veil are condoms and more penises. In one hand she clutches a wand. Her T-shirt says 'Bride to Be, Don't Mess With Me'.

On the hens' faces are the inward, dark, resigned looks of those who know they have missed the last train out of town and the rest of the night is going to be spent not sleeping but waiting – in waiting rooms, on benches, on streets like this – for the next step of the journey. One hen has lost her shoes. Another hen is chatting to a fella called Steven she met in Heaven & Hell. Steven is trying to persuade Judy to come back with him to his place in Fleetwood and Judy wants to go but she knows the other hens will be pissed off with her if she does.

BRENDA: Don't fuckin start with me, Susan.

NICHOLA: Leave her alone, Bren, she's trolleyed, she dun't know what she's sayin'.

SUSAN: Where – are we – take yer fuckin hands off me!

GERI: That fella in the Waterfront was fuckin gorgeous, Bren. You shoulda gone outside with him.

BRENDA: Coulda woulda shoulda. Got me man at home, haven't I?

ELAINE: But is he gonna satisfy all your needs, Bren? Forever? It's a fuckin scary thought, intit?
NICHOLA: Nah mate, it's not scary. It's the best. My Ian's the best. He's me world!
ELAINE: Fuckinell. Excuse me while I barf into me doner.

Geri produces a piece of paper from her bra.

GERI: Got his number though, didn't I?
ELAINE: You fuckin did what?!
ELAINE, SUSAN: Phone him! Phone him! Phone him!
BRENDA: Shut the fuck up all of yers, right?

A wicked smile passes over Brenda's face.

BRENDA: Shall we send him a little text message to say goodnight?
ELAINE, GERI AND SUSAN: Text him! Text him! Text him!

Brenda, Susan, Geri and Elaine cluster round Brenda's Motorola phone. Judy and Steven, snogging, wobble and step out into the road but manage to keep their lips locked and their plastic cups of Cheeky Vimto unspilled.

NICHOLA: I just – I just don't think it's a good idea, Bren. What if Chris looks at yer phone?
BRENDA: Who the fuck cares? We're being friendly. Alright girls, what do you think –

NITE NITE YOU HANDSOME DEVIL X

ALL: Send! Send! Send!

The green button is pressed. The message flies on its ethereal wings to Daz, snoring on the minibus back to Little Eccleston while his mate Kevin draws a pair of tits on his forehead with a biro.

OLGA AND RACHEL SPAR WHILE TRIPPING
Dickson Road, 2:17 a.m., 16 June 1999

Bend me, shape me, any way you want me
You've got a Cheestring, you're alright

–I don't know why no one talks about how that Garbage song 'I Think I'm Paranoid' is like a remix of that song 'Bend Me, Shape Me' – you know, from the Cheestrings advert?

–Is it?

–Yeah definitely! She says 'Bend me, break me, any way you need me.'

–Oh yeah – I guess she's just making it angsty – turning it angsty.

–Angsty or angry ...

–*(Together)* Or both?

They both nod.

–*(Together)* Yeah, both!

Bend me, break me, any way you need me
All I want is you

Bend me, break me. Are we entering the arena of the masochist?

Any way you need me. What was Olga's play about again? Was it about us?

OLGA'S ABANDONMENT
Dickson Road, 3 a.m., 16 June 1999

Olga abandons us the morning after the night before. In the afterparty, the seedy gateway from the night before into the morning after. *You and me, we could take over the world, you know that, don't you?* Chatting the predictable nonsense. *We're a perfect complement, you and me. I'll do the spectacle. You do the theory. And then we can swap round. Okay?* And then the morning became paler and paler and she became older and cleverer and nastier and we grew smaller and quieter and the space between us grew larger and larger. *I wish you would go home so I can sleep with Damien*, Olga says, or we imagine her saying, but who cares because in more than 50 per cent of the worlds opened up to us right now she is saying exactly that: a whole choir of Olgas in harmony, pronouncing their request for us now to leave these dregs of a party because the flush of night and the swell of toxins have receded and what is left is the deathly pallor of naked desires.

–I need to sleep now – I'm supposed to be at work in five hours.

Olga needs to sleep. The ridiculous vain attempt at sleeping. Four in the bed. Four hearts beating too fast for different reasons. We could draw a diagram if our vision was up to it. The chain-links of power and desire. Algebra is better. We need a symbol for desire.

$\propto$ = desire (wherein the vector of desire goes from loop to prongs)
† = adjacency in bed
¢ = move away from
> = move towards

‡ = attempt at sexual activity made
® = desire rejected
¶ = desire consummated

Phase 1
OLGA † DAMIEN † RACHEL † DECLAN ∝ RACHEL ∝ OLGA ∝ DAMIEN ∝ OLGA † RACHEL

Phase 2
DECLAN ‡ RACHEL > OLGA ‡ DAMIEN ‡ RACHEL ® DAMIEN ¶ OLGA † RACHEL ¢ DAMIEN † OLGA > RACHEL ∝ OLGA

Leave the flat and walk home, chasing the dawn, utterly numb, strands of songs and poems flickering through the space in my head, devoid of all sentiment or colour. Processing will begin when I get my brain back.

The moment I get it back. A sink. A sink with chinks in it. A sink filled up with vomit. Chase it because you know what follows. Dark joy or shining pain will be its end, who cares, two sides, same coin, flip me over, upturned fish belly, all of you just keep chip chip chipping away at me, this is what I am for. Open myself up fully. I am an open throat ready for the pint of pigswill to be chugged down. Lying perfectly still for hours in a garden. A stone, curled up, hiding. Holding myself. Every atom hanging there. Every atom a web. Strangeness of things. I am soft but I am hard. I am tough in my softness. Look, let's see how tough I am. Hurt me now. I invite you. This is the only way I know how to love.

Chapter 11

VOICE	Rachel
SCENE	Nellie Deans Music Bar / The Sensory Autobahn
HOUR	7 p.m., 16 June 1999
PLEASURE BEACH RIDE	Trauma Towers
SUBSTANCE	Honey
ORGAN	Ear (nonsynaesthetic)
SYMBOL	Braid
COLOUR	Amber
FORMULA	$vw = f\lambda$
ART / TECHNIC	Thinking feeling a feeling thinking thinking feeling
HORMONE	Dehydroepiandrosterone
HOMERIC TITLE	Sirens

Wurlitzering. Oh I do like to be beside the. There'll be bluebirds over. Bring me sunshine. The sun has got his hat on. I got rhythm. I got music. I got my man, who could ask for anything more? When your heart's on fire you must realise. Smoke gets in your eyes. Hello, Dolly. Well hello, Dolly. When the moon hits your eye like a. Why. Does Your Love. Hurt So Much. Bonita Applebum. You gotta put me on. Christina Applegate, you gotta put me on. Huh huh huh hu-hu huh. I know this. Much is. True. Set adrift on memory bliss. Oop. Fook. The fookineth uppiteth. Fookinell. Fookinbetterbe. Eezaraitbasted. Eezaproper nastifooker. Fookereeyiz. Properbonnishiwoz. Owlongwasyetherefer. Shewerjoostoopthere.

Tuning in and tuning out, left headphone in, right headphone out, leaning out of the open window at Nellie Deans. Someone is warming up the karaoke with Bruce Springsteen's 'Born to Run'. *Oh baby this town rips the bones from your back.* Sunwarmed redbricked Metropole across the road, darting seagulls, and beyond, the open sea. Pint of Strongbow sloppily plonked on puddled table, wobbling so much that not even two folded beermats can stabilise its legs. Sounds from within, sounds from without, sounds present and sounds absent and layers of sounds that come from the past. Imagined sounds and real sounds. *Girls comb their hair in rearview mirrors / And the boys try to look so hard.* Living in a world of samples and loops, impossible to tell what's real and what's imagined. Chunks of history spread in layers as butter onto bread, maybe the past as a paste, spread onto electronic carbohydrate slabs of the future. Listening is easy. It's not even a choice. You can't close your ears, can you? You can't close your brain either, more's the pity, no matter how hard you try. The real challenge is to perceive synaesthetically. Bind and blend the senses. It's all in your head anyway. From listening to allencompassing in one fell swoop, swooping the same as seagulls do, swooping low and shrieking high.

No one on earth could feel like thiiiiieeeaaaooouuu. The line from the Eurythmics song sags and droops a few quartertones in pitch as the lights change on the road outside and the car with its blaring open windows drives away. Movement as pitchbend, but movement through what? Space and time. Not enough: what else? Feeling, imagined as a substance. What substance? Honey. Of course.

Allencompassing. Is that what we shall call it. Huh. Compasses are required but they are also the destination. The search for something that you're already inside. The impossibility of. Ever. Getting. Out. Of. And the search to disentangle that which must remain a mulch. Viscosity. Mulch. Gloop. Coagulation. Specifically thc shift from a liquid to a solid. Clot. Clod. Now we are getting somewhere. You don't need to look any further than the skin that raises its haunches when a certain chord change is heard. Hear hear, I challenge thee. Look out to sea when the summer sun is setting, one headphone in one ear, listening to the Beach Boys' song 'The Warmth of the Sun', with added filtrations of inside and outside sound fragments, karaoke, traffic smudge, glasschink, nonsensechatter. I challenge thee *not* to get visible goosebumps. All stemming from that unexpected third note in the bassline, after the more predictable initial shift from tonic to relative minor, C down to A let's say, if we're in C major, and then instead of stepping down to an F like in a million other songs we get a note that we don't expect, something like an E flat, which shifts the meaning of the whole song. *What good is the dawn / That grows into day.* This song is otherwise pretty unassuming with its slow waltzing and arpeggio patterns, but that momentary harmonic shift is like a modulation into a different light, strange backlit hues, yellows and oranges perhaps, because of the sunset association, you see.

And outside the pub is the opposite of inside the pub, and inside the pub is the opposite of inside the body, inside the brain. Tone clouds strewn across the heavens. Notes striping across the sky. Do the yellows and oranges of the notes come from the play of the imagination or do they come from deep within the synapses themselves, and is there even a difference between these? Whatever. The song performs the sun as it moves through its colour spectrum, imagining Sun Ra himself sitting up there presiding, centre stage. A hymn to spacetime sunsetting. *Still I have the warmth of the sun / Within me tonight.* And surely one way to carry the warmth of the sun at night is to carry these melodies. To imagine these melodies. And no one pays enough attention to the sounds that come from inside.

/ə/ (schwa). The most common sound in the English language. A reduced, neutral vowel sound, such as in the 'tion' of 'station' or the 'a' of 'about'. And in some accents, including those of Northern English such as that spoken in the Lancashire regions, the 'er' of 'Her'. /Hə/. She had no idea I could get into her head but I went ahead and did it anyway. We were so intertwined last night you couldn't even tell which one was me and which one was her. But who is her. Who is the Her. The 'r' in Her is silent, of course. All we need is the schwa. The schwa is a nasty sound but it's the sound I'm stuck in. Like sludge.

And yet. This air. The quality of it. The search for goosebumps. What is that. Those moments from earlier year, sitting in the smoking room in the student halls e, no sleep, listening to certain songs at certain times ..he stereo. Fast-forwarding to certain chord changes. Timing it for maximum goosebumping effect. Does timing it make it less of an event. Than when spontaneous. Sometimes yes sometimes no.

A middle-aged woman with red hair and sunburned shoulders has taken the stage and is giving it her all to Scarlett's 'Independent Love Song'. This is worth taking out the sole Beach Boys headphone for. Ever since it was on *Top of the Pops* a few years ago, the reverberations of this song have clanged inside us like a heavy, heavy bell. The lyrics don't even say anything about lesbian desire but every note, every passionate breath, seems to proclaim it louder than you could imagine. *I'm doing it a different way*, the woman sings to all of us here inside Nellie Deans. She has a Scottish flag tattooed on her upper arm and she looks fucking hard, which just makes this performance more powerful. *I'll show you how to take me / Go down, go down, go down.*

Look down. Cheeks aflame. Her. Did we. What did we. Who is she. Where is she. Where is she right now.

A group of lads are occupying 99.95 per cent of the space on this table. Totally ignoring us, which is ideal. Their chat barely filters into our consciousness. Half a headphone plus the karaoke spectacle plus a million inside voices is more than enough to drown them out. Shall we allow ourselves to think a bit more about Olga, then? Olga, who could be nearby right now, who could walk into this bar right now. Olga who could emerge from deep under the sea this very second. This very second, a police siren starts up its wail. What is the difference between a siren and a mermaid? Sirena sirena, sirene, syrena, sereia. Syreni. Siren. A bird, a fish, a woman, a wailing light. Gorgóna, seirína, sirène. What sound does the am-lance make? The knee and the knaw. Wassail. Ululate. Throatcroak. Heartrasp. Warning. My nineteen senses are tingling. Buckfast memoryflash. The honeyed voices inside the tincture bottle denounce engraved numbers in favour of a viscosity sliding scale.

Eeeeeeeeeoooooawwwwwwwaaaoooooweeeeeeee. The continuum of pitch and rhythm. A disc rotating at slow velocity. Singular airpuffs form a continuous pulsating rhythm. At a certain point these individual sounds give the impression of being one continuous sound of varying frequency. Discrete impulses giving the impression of one continuous sound. A wail. Time as tone: when a beat becomes a pitch. Hummingbirds in flight. But when we are the beacon and the siren and the lighthouse we are resonating inside and outside all the same. It doesn't matter if they are sounding and we must be warned and protected from their sound or they themselves create the sound to warn us against the sound, or they create the sound that we love so much and they shine, shine, shine like crazy diamonds. They shine and are lit as from within as without, from lights that train their glow on the sirens who also emit their own glow. Anything that is a warning and a mating call at the same time must be approached with caution.

Her voice had been low and raspy, like she had come out of the womb with a fag in her mouth. Imagining it now, the way it was last night, split into microtones just like the rest of the world. Shards of bark bathing in warm caramel. And yet, right there, in the brain, the comparison – the association – the bark, the caramel – it is only ever just that.

An association. Not like Olga's brain. Olga also has the magical talent of seeing sounds as colours. She also feels numbers as sensations. Letters too. Something we really cannot do, much as we try. Even the thought of the *cannot* now causes the ego's hackles to rise. Rachel Gillian Charlotte Watkins, too clever for her own good, admitting *failure*?

Never. We can make it. We can synthesise it. Just you wait, Olga with your mad genius crosswired brain. You'll see.

So. Take a glug of cider and do it. Shapes and sounds, echoes and shadows, are formed and die, aching, in the throat's cavity. A veil a wave upon the. Bloobloobloobloo-bloobloobloooming marvellous. As if the shape of it, the shape of it was round and not straight. Marvellous chimes because inside marvellous is part of a bell. A bell is a bell is a bell. An echo. Echo. Ohce. The mirror of a sound. Boomeranging, hanging, yawming at the awning. Waning, waning and waxing, ebbing and flowing, all these tidal pulls, this way that way forwards backwards over the Irish Sea. To identify just the pure resonance is impossible. What then should we do? Consciousness by shared resonance is the only way we can do it.

So.

The pineal gland, tunnel of Lucifer, bypass to the brow chakra and survey the entirety of the visual field. So much more than the chromatic spectrum. Chromola! The crema that froths on the top of the warm basin. Bathers and balers. The auditory cortex is a whorl. But howl is also close to whorl. How to think awhorl without awhirl. Adrift, agrifft, athrift. Thriftful. Frightful. Delightful. Sightful. You've had a. Mouthful. Eyeful. Throatful. Chestful. Baleful. Bales.

Baleful eyes or bales for eyes. Back to ocularity. Precularity. The clarity of ocularity becomes the tactility of haptility through tentacularity. The feeling of bees in haptility. Haptility in captivity. Spirals whirring, or the difference between whirring and whirling. Shells are in there, as though it's a puzzle. The link between shell and puzzle is there, puzzle muzzle, can't work it out but it's there. Objects. Can an object be made of vowels. An ooeui? An oae? Oar is close. An oar sounds as liquid, sounds as does itself, as that which moves through liquid. An Aero? Only a name for lighter than ordinary chocolate. Bubbles inside. Makes sense. Solid, liquid and gas. If only there were more. Inchoate as in between. Coagulate as in between. Of course aspirations are pneumatic. Mechanic, automatically pneumatic. And also hydromatic, which is always Greased Lightning. Greased Lightning both is and is not haptic. Haptic may contain a spark of static electricity and nothing more. A tic is like a spark. A flick is like a twitch. A jitter is linked to a shudder but they are of different natures. A shudder is deeper. It's in the plosive sound, voiced shuddering deep down into the bones. Jittering is light and voiceless. So goes the depth of sonorous consonants. Have we got anywhere yet? Not really. More cider. Channel Olga. Channel her, summon her, right here, right now.

An imperative, then. Blend and multiply the senses. Just fucking do it. Why? Because sirens do more than make sound. Sirens make plaits with long hair composed of three elastic elements: 1) feeling, 2) time, 3) space. So. Stretch it out and spool it like syrup. Tempo rubato. Pull it apart. Time dough. What the music does to you, line by heartfelt line, whizzing from fifteen to nineteen and back again because you never really went anywhere. Teetering is really falling, falling is really landing. Rushing through the depths, nineteen, eighteen, seventeen, sixteen, fifteen. *Words.*

Words. Don't even get me started. The liquid ones and the crunchy ones and the ones in between. Eating Crunchy Nut Corn Flakes with a touch of honey bathed in a cold milk bath. A nut is the hard full atom of a consonant. A mouthful of throthful faithful forthflowing mirthful youth crunching away hamstercheeks with milkdripping chins. Lunch. We munch our lunch on t'bench outside Tesco's. The impossibility of Crisps. What you got there. Just a packet o' Chris. Who's Chris? Clusterfucktastic. Cuntstruck: spluttering resplendent over splurges of spliced splendour full splitting to burst my edges. Feeling angsts a bazillion. A packet of angsts. Ich habe Angst. Sniffing with a snoopy snout, sniggering away snotgreen snapjaws snipping at yer heels. Snot good enough. Just let yerself wallow in the bath for one second. Coagulate. Between a liquid and a solid. Languishing in soupy soapy sounds. Solid love liquid hate. Aereous. Aorta. Aurora. Aureole. Aureoliae.

Stop for a second. Where are we? Where are we really? Inside the mind. Not outside. Thinking about somewhere else entirely. Thinking about Graham's flat above the sex shop just off Topping Street. Those weekly visits for piano lessons, through the teenage years. Give him a fiver and he gives you an hour of peering into other worlds and times, partly through the sounds that curled their way out of his piano like smoke, and partly through tattered postcard portals on his yellowstained walls. Tinkling raining misting notes, moving through the air like the soft and weightless tails of cats that curled around your back as you sat on the piano stool.

Graham was wholly kind and altruistic. Though high on the camp factor at times, there was also an aura of asexuality shimmering around him like an Ann Summers nylon kimono, despite the long, sometimes painted fingernails and the wry, self-deprecating gestures towards flamboyance. He could also run his fingers up and down the piano keys at an unbelievable speed, always leaving you breathless, tearful and on the edge of your seat. Graham had a penchant for early to mid-twentieth-century stylish yet troubled sirens: Édith Piaf, Marlene Dietrich, Sarah Bernhardt. Grubby prints of them on the walls. The respectful way he talked about their lives and their talent. Didn't objectify them or fetishise their suffering. Just pure admiration and reverence. Graham had been there in the audience when Marlene Dietrich came to Blackpool and performed at the Opera House in 1955. Graham's favourite siren had been the famous banana-skirt-wearing, marketed-in-an-extremely-racist-fashion-by-today's standards, dancer-singer-all-round-entertainer Josephine Baker. Like Graham's flat, these women signified an unfamiliar, grubby, exciting, out-of-reach world and time. Fiction but not fiction. Impossible glamour and squalor. Nineteen, eighteen, seventeen. Had we but world enough and time.

Graham had spoken about Cécile Chaminade and Scott Joplin. Chaminade is an unsung heroine of French romanticism. And Joplin. Ragtime piano: so much fun! A sack race of notes falling over themselves, racing wrongly towards the end. Thump. Done. Yes done, but done wrongly. The 'Maple Leaf Rag' should be played *slowly*. It's meant to be a *dance*. You'll have them all sweating! They'll get their beads all tangled up! They want to be *stately* when they dance! Slow it right down! I don't want to feel like I've just run a marathon! You're giving me palpitations!

My vegetable love –

Focus.

Seventeen, eighteen, nineteen senses running fast to stay in the same place. Stuck fast. *Move closer / Set my soul on fire.* Teenage songs draw blood. A fierce fast rivulet of red. The ease of teenage bag-slinging wrist-slitting love. Compass and biro tattoos, 4 REAL I.D.S.T. Sixteen, seventeen, eighteen, nineteen. The smashing of beer bottles and the complete lack of pain. Buckfast coagulates and accelerates simultaneously. Viscosity in the bloodstream and the raised worms of half-healed scars. Bloodwort tramlines up your arm. *Do not listen to a word I say / Just listen to what I can keep silent.* Those times when nineteen senses rang true. A new sensory autobahn added to the vermicelli junction. Leaning out of a window smoking a cigarette and feeling your skin prickle with the sentience of the very air around you. No she said No I will Never. The sentience of the air multiplied by the sentience of your prickling skin. Sentience squared equals an exponentially levitating bodymindfuck. T. S. Eliot multiplied by John Donne equals thinking feeling a feeling thinking thinking feeling. Thoughts have thoughts. Feelings have feelings too. Deal with it. She said it was too much to kiss on the lips because she had too many sensory receptors clustered there. Way more than the usual number. *Batter my heart.* Donne because we are too menny. Ha. I know the secret about too many – it's nineteen nineteen nineteen squared, I don't care about pathologies I've got some too. Love hones the senses. Seventeen, eighteen, nineteen blades. Slash and burn. A mark is nothing but a penknife inkblood scream. *It barks at no one else but me / Like it's seen a ghost.* People reverberate through you. And there is nothing yet on this earth that you have encountered more powerful than the afterclang of those reverberations. *How you move / The way you burst the clouds it makes me want to try.* Sticky as lips. Licky as trips. Never has there been a purer joy than the sensation of opening a new internal cavern. Private mythology. Archivist of feeling, documentation of moments, pause, play, repeat. Stubborn mute rocks rolling around inside the gut. Orchestras of echoes.

Vaster than empires, and more slow

Again. Focus.

How to see Chaminade's waterfall of notes. Listen to it and think of what it does to you. Fifteen, sixteen, seventeen senses. How things bind and blend together. Try not to think about the bit in *Howard's End*, essays for A-Level English, where all the characters talk about their different reactions to Beethoven's Fifth Symphony. And you? What do you do see when you hear those tinkling raining patterns in Chaminade? Do you see glass? Do you see stairs that light up as you step on them like they have in the bit of *Grease* when the fairy godfather man is singing 'Beauty School Dropout' to Frenchie in his shiny white Elvis suit? Do you see *les étoiles*, brighter, thinner, sharper in French than English, tiny teaspoons on glass? Tinkle tinkle chink chink. Letter K, voiceless velar plosive, bright sharp high, narrow vowel space, minimal oxygen. Thin air summit white precipiceness. Scales ascending keys bright light steps tiptapping lighting up each plink a plink K for kettle bright metal upscale scale descale. Ha. Special K. My baby takes K all day. K is the opposite of sludge. Repeated tinkling. And you try, try, try to see something more beyond the feeling of the tinkling notes, and you can't. Where has Chaminade gone? Parametric versus segmentary analysis. Music is speech is flow is phrase is water not sand no matter how fine. Becoming Proustian, are we? Shut up shut up shut up. Don't give me that infinitesimal sensibility. I don't want to drown in congealing gloop. I cannot slow down. Ever.

These notes don't take you anywhere other than towards their own sound, which can be translated to movement but only the movement of Graham's fingers and their delicate movement on the keys. Think of it like stroking. It is stroking. Graham fundamentally changed your entire way of touching thc piano keys, fifteen, sixteen, seventeen, learning to lift your fingers clean away and feel that invisible elastic always pulling you back. Just in time. Tempo rubato. An unspoken affinity with Graham: a mutual lack of articulatory space and a mutual dream of other worlds and times. 1930s Paris. An imagined space beyond this place. Graham and his procession of cats, in his flat above the sex shop up the dangerous slippery steps and the piles of rubbish outside, all still there but no longer inhabited by that peculiarly singular mind, standing there in his trackies and slippers and B&M Bargains T-shirts, cats crawling over the piano, trying to persuade you to take a job playing piano in the White Tower Restaurant and then run away to Paris. Hopes and dreams hanging in the air.

And still you're trying to think about those notes.

Try a different tack. Try thinking about the melody

itself. A phrase, descending and cascading like a woman's hair down her back. Arpeggio braids. Yes. A series. Always you think about the series. Try again. Fail again. Resolution. *It goes like this, the fourth, the fifth.* No, don't go down that route. That way lies the danger. Seventeen, eighteen, nineteen, come on now.

What exactly are we trying to do here?

You are a gnat. A fucking gnat, and nothing else. Snapjaw venus flytrap moment-catching. Out, flick tongue, no wait, that's not a gnat, that's a frog catching a gnat. Fucking hell, this is hard work. Metaphorical bunny hops. Lateral leaping. Fucking bars of signification everywhere. The Zen masters had it right. Go on then. Do it. Bang your head against the wall. Noise pain space bright light. Chink. Graham teaches you to hear the simplicity of the melody somewhere in the midst of these twinkling lights –

AHA!

There ye go. Claritas is quidditas. Twinkling instead of tinkling. Congratulations, you have successfully created the conditions of possibility to see a sound as if 'twere a sight. As if 'twere a light. From tinkling to twinkling in one fell swoop.

Phew. Jobdone. Offhome.

Much harder but not a million miles away from faking an orgasm to synthesise love you aim to synthesise the synaesthete's experience and the impossibility of a venture has never dissuaded you before and never will. A = black, E = white, I = red, U = green, O = blue: vowels. What about the days of the week? Try and fail again. Tuesday Thursday lilac pale yellow pastel; Monday Wednesday Friday strong triad of white, red and navy blue. Lemon squeezy. Since each of us was several, we were already quite a crowd. A million black squid liquids pooling round some kind of universal soul crustacean. Just stop doing all of it and let your hair down. Unwind the plait and it all joins up anyway. Feeling divided by time divided by space equals one honeycomb head. Earplugs are redundant when the sirens are inside. Consider trepanning the skull and plugging each rattling hexagon with pink and white fluffy marshmallows. Lay your tired brain down on psychedelic-patterned pillows tired out from all the infighting yet forever in awe of every single speck of dirt and noise that flies into the perceptive field. *The apples fermented / Inside the lamented.* Eighteen, nineteen, nearly twenty and your edges are going to burst. Cider inside her insides. A dirty spin cycle yet full of wonderment. Love on a real train with mud blood guts and gore. Let it go. Someone somewhere is singing Sophie B. Hawkins who is singing Bob Dylan. *The lonesome organ grinder cries / The silver saxophones say I.* You want her you want her you want her. Choking over the word 'her'. There is something unbearable about the new harmonics of this word. My vegetable love. Vaster than empires. And more slow.

Just stop and slow it all right down.

You are nineteen-point-five heavy sacks of potatoes in this summer heat; nineteen-point-five edges softening and browning and plumping and waiting for something you feel is not entirely unconnected to the procurement and extraction of a jam from a fruit you know not yet what.

Chapter 12

VOICE	Olga
SCENE	The Wine Bar
HOUR	7 p.m., 16 June 1999
PLEASURE BEACH RIDE	Space Invader
SUBSTANCE	Vodka and Coke
ORGAN	Eyes
SYMBOL	Prism
COLOUR	Dark Brown
FORMULA	H_3PO_4
ART / TECHNIC	Projection (aggressive)
HORMONE	Glucagon
HOMERIC TITLE	Cyclops

Whythefuck have we ended up here. Of all places. Not Yates, not Yeats, but Brannigans. A joke in the making, not that anyone would get it. Feel like snarling. Tezza won't come. She looked proper knackered earlier. Wonder how old Tezza actually is. Sometimes she talks like she could be ancient. Some proper wisdom comes from that sunbed face. Blue eyes that of course she can't even recognise. Ah Tezza. Sometimes. I wish. But no. And really no, because bigger fish are there to fry, and maybe we can coax that liontigergirl out to play again.

Maybe? Do we want to? Yes, it's the only thing we fucking want. Get her out. Get drunk again. It's the only way we're going to figure out what's going on here. Get her out. Text her. Text her. The chant, from within, as if from without. Text. Text. Text. Text. Okay, okay, fuckinell brain, give me a second. First we need to drink down this delicious pint of Coke with a touch of our own personal private handbag vodka stash added to top up the levels and keep the demons at bay. At bay, so the demons don't bray, at me, their prey. Pray, pray, that they stay away. Shurrup. Slurp Coke, crunch ice, feel the cold inside and everything rinsed in brown cold fizzy clear goodness. Refreshed. So text her.

Okay. Breathe and do it.

> How you feeling now?
> Want to come for a drink at
> Brannigans? Am
> here right now …

Sent. But if she comes, if she comes, what will it be like? What will we talk about? What will it be like? How will it be? Will we be close? We will need shots. Shots, immediately.

Black sambuca. Tequila slammers. Whisky on ice to break the ice. If she's in Poulton or Carleton or somewhere, won't it take her a while? Won't we fall asleep soon anyway? Sleep is needed, that's for sure. Maybe she's also asleep at this stage? Sensible people would be asleep at this stage. Not sure she is that sensible though. Lions and tigers don't earn their fierceness by being *sensible*. She's about as sensible as I am. Maybe even less.

The heart sinks. Nothing can happen. Nothing will happen. Clearly. It can't. We can't. It just can't be, simple as. But something else is happening ... Ohhhhh no. Hide. Too late. The worst possible person to be spotted by right now. Nikki Fucking Rawlings.

Just look down. Rummage in bag. Light a fag. Do. Not. Catch. Her. Eye. Just look down onto the oily table. Spin the ashtray. Examine hands, which look grubby to say the least. Pray for something else to occupy self. Wish we had a book or something. Fuck, a racing heart again. What a day. Lion-tigergirl somewhere out there at the end of a text message. Arch enemy sitting across the bar. Fuckfuckfuck. What can we do? Chain-smoking is one thing. Nail-biting is another. Drinking and thinking are more.

Remember when Nikki first got glasses, in Year 10. No one laughed. No one ever, ever laughed at Nikki Rawlings. One day, a pair of glasses, suddenly sitting on her face. Turned out she could never read the blackboard but never said anything to anyone. She had severe astigmatism and nystagmus, which meant that if you looked closely (not that you would want to get too close for fear of an accusation of giving her evils and receiving the threat of getting battered by her and her minions on the way home) you could see that her eyes, and her head, were wobbling ever so slightly all the time. Funny because she used to make *such* a big thing of getting evils from us ever since Year 7. For no reason. An evil from Olga would turn you to stone. That's what she used to say. That and saying our hair was made of snakes. Black, crawling snakes.

It's not much fun, sitting here looking down at the table while the phone sits there, stubborn and silent. Not fun at all. Why does Nikki hate us so? It's definitely got something to do with being a bit of a hippy and a lot of a lefty. It's something to do with being someone who thinks about other cultures with respect, which is something that most people in this town will never even think of trying to do. When we chant *Om* during a yoga class and say *namaste* at the end, do we know what we are saying? When we get tribal tattoos, do we know what we are doing? Do we know what we are saying, what we are summoning? On the other side of the fabric of heaven, behind the veil, when we read the poet W. B. Yeats saying things about veils and saying things about the past being a knotted length of rope tossed into the corner of a room, do we know what he is talking about? It is something connected to nationalism. Can there ever be a good kind of nationalism? A left kind of nationalism? They don't have that option here in this rotten country, we think to ourselves, and we think of English people as *they* because we don't have a drop of English blood inside us.

Think of the others we know who also aren't of English blood. Scott from Belfast who works in the chippy kitchen. He would answer yes, yes, yes to a good, left kind of nationalism. Lou from Glasgow who cleans the rooms at Mama's B&B. She would also answer yes, yes, yes. Remember how excited Lou was last month, when it was on the news, the first meeting of the Scottish parliament, some people saying it's the first step to full Scottish independence. And when Lou hears bagpipes it makes her feel proud. Is that nationalism? Small countries wanting to get away from bigger countries who mistreated them. Like Macaulay Culkin divorcing his parents because they only wanted to exploit him for his wealth? Thinking about exploitation masked as philanthropism. Thinking about forced conversion of religion. Religion is behind it, sure. Both things that affect the gut, affect the senses, make you cry with pride, make you blind with love and rage. Because they promise to connect you with things much bigger than you.

Music sets these things off. Music is a dangerous friend. Right now Sonique's song 'It Feels So Good' is playing in here. Just imagine actually living in London. So much possibility, so much exposure. You walk down the street and see five famous people in one day. A clusterfuck of fame and fortune, the rest of the country forgotten. And the place that broadcasts the famous people, BBC, Auntie Beeb, also entirely located in London. No wonder the world only thinks of London when they think of the UK. No wonder the clichés of posh accents and the royal family and tea and scones and Mary Poppins are still alive. It's London's fault. It peddles those clichés like the woman peddles her fake Adidas trackies at Abingdon Street Market. Those clichés are London's bread and butter, so they ain't going nowhere.

Stub out fag. Determined fingers. London, you fucker, just you wait. I want a slice. I'm coming. Neckerchief on stick, worldly possessions inside, all it takes is a train ticket. I'm coming. The Proclaimers' '500 Miles' is playing now. The Scottishness pours out of them in every syllable.

Mama has their album at home and there's a song that's about their frustration at the way Scotland is governed by England. And when we say England, we really mean London, the brain drain, the money pot, the fat cats, the governmental seat. Westminster. Westminster governs the wee wives in Orkney. How can this be right? *I can't understand why we let someone else rule our land / Cap in hand.*

Can you ever really feel national pride if you're a thoughtful person from a country that colonised other countries as policy? There are plenty of people here, sensible people, who would answer that you can *never* have a good kind of nationalism. And they have good reason to say so. But what is this -ism anyway? Take the ism away and you have a nation. What even is a nation? An arbitrary line. When the right to cross an arbitrary line is taken away. Does Mama have national pride? She cries every year when Poland perform their entry on Eurovision and that's about as far as it goes. Mama has been here for twenty-five years and has never gone back. Is it possible to don national pride like putting on a jacket? What kind of pride am I meant to have, living here, not English, not Polish, not Italian, not anything except myself?

The hippy tribe who talk about nomadism as the future, now that is appealing. But it can also break up families. Celine Blanshard's dad, the most hippy of all the hippies in this area, ran away when she was twelve or so with a group called Spiral Tribe. He's just touring the world now, putting on massive parties, getting in trouble with the police, and Celine lost her dad and lost part of her life. And to think that just a few years ago people were still putting on parties for free, no law against it, just raving it up in fields, peace and love and ecstasy, acid house music proclaiming a future that must have really felt like it had come from outer space. A repeated succession of electronic beats. Until the government put their foot down in 1994. A message to everyone. Party's over, folks. This happiness, this utopia, this peace and love, either shut down or ultimately forced into the capitalist vice. And what would the world be like now if the Criminal Justice Act had never been passed?

We are all citizens of everywhere. It does sound utopian, doesn't it? And at the same time as thinking that, thinking of the oafs and oiks in this town uttering oaths so gutter-low I wouldn't ever repeat them, not even in the internal cavern of the mind. Bigoted ignorami. And are they to blame? Hardly. We are produced and socialised by the conditions that we are born into. I am 100 per cent with Marx on that one. And to be born here, seeing mainly white faces, seeing poverty, seeing people getting stuck, being told you can't do this, you'll never do that. And when someone crosses that arbitrary line, the line of social class, through education let's say, a socialist playwright makes a theatre piece about it. Thinking about when we watched *Educating Rita* on video at school and then the play *Blood Brothers* at the Grand. *Blood Brothers* made me cry. It is designed to do exactly that. And then imagining my own imaginary twin out there, maybe private school-educated, maybe running for Prime Minister in the future, and I'm still here none the wiser, plonking the battered dripping fish slabs into the bubbling oil. It's a play right there, waiting. Bloodsisters. And of course with this line of thought comes Rachel. My bloodsister, who I only met last night. Rachel didn't go to a private school but privilege is still written into every pore of her. And yet it's Rachel who carved up her arm. Something in that privilege, somewhere, rejected, gone wrong. And she blames herself. And you hear about genius people who go to Oxford and Cambridge having breakdowns. Something not right there, either. Humans have not grasped how to take care of themselves. Not by a long shot.

I could be a socialist playwright. It's in me, the drama, the juice, the power. The understanding of the power. The manipulation of the power. It happens at all levels, all strata, whether you scrub toilets for a living or you're the Queen of England. The power is the juice that fuels us, and it can be played like an instrument. That's what theatre is.

BEEP BEEP. BEEP BEEP.

Fuckinell ... that was quick.

1 message
received

Ra chelion%$&*
I'm actually just round the corner.
Been wandering round
town. Yes ok will come
now.

Yes ok will come now? Yes ok will come now? What to do. We look like shit. But what does it matter. We look the same as we looked last night. And last night it didn't matter.

And suddenly all Nikki's cronies are all standing by.

–What the fuck d'you think you're looking at.

–Nothing, I wasn't looking at anything! I'm just having a quiet drink after work!

–Work! Fucking slag. Bucket fanny.

Nikki looks around at her pals, sniggering. The weirdest thing about Nikki is that she is NOT stupid. She's smart. I can tell. There's just some misanthropic blockage somewhere inside her.

–You know where we can find her every night. Down Cookson Street every night, whoring herself out. Disgusting.

That is it. Enough to make us lose our rag. Susan and Lin on Cookson Street, their faces, kind faces, flash up in the mind's eye. The shit they have to face. Don't care if it's Nikki Fucking Rawlings. Enough is enough. So, look up. Look her right in the face. And yes. I could turn her to stone, if I wanted to, as a matter of fact. But I'm just not that evil. I keep my magic powers to myself.

–And so what if I was? Sex work is honest work! Not that you've got enough brain cells to rub together to even understand that concept.

And in the next moment Nikki's drink is on my face and I am drenched and in the same moment Rachel has just walked in the door and because I don't want to look like a victim in front of her I lurch forward, blinking vodka and Coke out of my eyes, hair dripping, face dripping, and kind of bash the glass out of her hand, not a punch, or maybe a failed punch, I'm not violent, I don't want to add to the millions of people on this planet who suffer or who perpetrate violence, so I just kind of bash her hand and the glass leaps out of it and shatters on the floor, a predictable wave of voices going *ayyyyyyy*, cheering the sound, and still, everything still, shattered and paused in the air, as if we were turned to stone and then the stone has splintered, splintered like the glass

that lies

in

pieces

on the floor.

OLGA

She knows, but does not know the symbol, when
she says my face turns all life into stone;
I've read the myths, I know what she would love
To say if she had more up there than just
The three cells rattling round her tiny brain
My hair is wild just like the great Medusa;
And actually I could not be more proud
Than just to share the hair of someone so maligned
In history, except in certain feminist books.
The hair is useful sometimes, such as now
When I can bend my head and hide inside the dark
And tangled hedgerow of my growing: Bitch,
Be gone, I say, unless you want to be
The subject of a curse: *Idź do diabła*

NIKKI

I'm on my seventh double, easy as piss,
I chug 'em down, I rock, I roar, I laugh,
Until I see her through the smoky gloom.

She looks as though she's talking to herself,
And writing in her notebook, she's acting all
Pretentious like she's better than the crowd
Who sit in here on Friday nights to chill.
It just takes hold of me, I think I lose
All self-control: I think I want to turn
HER
into
stone.
I get up, march towards her, drink in hand,
I stand and throw it at her stupid face.

OLGA

I think she's more a bull than human girl
She seems to charge right at me like a beast
Just as the door swings open:

Rachel.
Her.
Here.
I see it in slow motion, then at speed
Then stops quite dead, as from her glass
The Coke and vodka leaps right out and slaps
my face with cold:

–Freeze–
–SHOCK–
mortified and drenched,
I stand up off my bar stool, clench my fists
And, seeing all her cronies gather round, I say –
I don't say –
I say –

I don't say –
I say –
Full Nothing.

1990S FEMALE-FRONTED INDIE-ATTITUDE BAND LYRIC

Stop your stupid grinning
Girl, you make me sick
Don't know my power
I could kill you with one flick
Of my silver-studded fingers
Girl, how it would hurt
I'd be laughing at you
Crying in the dirt
Cover me in Coke and vodka
Soak me overnight
Watch the acid eat me
Rotted clean away

GENERIC SYMBOLIST

Delicately the beads of condensation collect round her fingers as they grasp the perspiring glass tumbler half-full of caffeinated carbonated effervescent caramelaic sweetness perfumed with clear perfumeless odourless alcoholic liquor.

NINETEENTH-CENTURY NOVEL

Miss Nichola Rawlings, full in possession of an anger fit for a spurned and jilted queen, sat perfectly still. Two spots of red-hued anger disturbed the pallor of her cheeks.

GOTHIC TEEN FICTION

As Nikki tilted her creamy throat back and drank the last

droplet of Olga's blood from her jewel-studded goblet, she let out a low cackle. The bloodless carcass of Olga was a shrivelled mess on the floor. Nikki grew visibly in stature until she was six, seven, eight feet tall, resplendent in her black velveteen cloak.

OVERLY CLEVER LINGUISTIC PLAY

A-stig-mat-ism
A-stink-mat-ism
A-sink-mat-ism
A-sing-mat-ism
A-sign-mat-ism
A-sig-mat-ism
A-syg-mat-ism
A-syn-tag-mat-ism

WHAT NIKKI IS THINKING, GENERALLY

Am gonna fookin deck yer.

WHAT OLGA IS THINKING, SPECIFICALLY

She fucking terrifies me. Still.

TEEN MAG

Don't miss it, girls! The hottest ticket in town. Be there or be at home sobbing watching *Frasier*. Again. Triple your money tonight and ladies go free.

Today we are interviewing toast of the town Nikki Rawlings, karaoke extraordinaire.

Q: *When did you discover your talent, Nikki?*

A: Oh, my mum noticed I had an amazing singing voice when I was about five. I used to stand at the top of the stairs and sing Cher songs. 'If I Could Turn Back Time' was my best one. It's not that easy to sing. Especially if you're five. But I could do it.

Q: *What're your favourite songs to sing at the moment?*

A: I've got a few. I can do a good Celine Dion, 'My Heart Will Go On'. That's a pretty hard song to sing, too. But that song that's just come out, 'Baby When You're Gone' – with Bryan Adams and Mel C – I can do a really good version of that with James here *(she indicates a tall lad sitting next to her in the pub)*. He's just not as fit as Bryan *(sniggers from cronies can be heard)*.

PERVY MUSIC MAG

And as we follow the buxom Nikki through her evening at the pulsing nightspot of Blackpool's 'wine bar' Brannigans, we notice she trills a few arpeggios, Mariah-style, as she struts to the toilet after her third vodka and Coke. Nikki has high hopes to make it big as a young soulful songtress of the North West. A mature young woman with a big mouth, a big heart and a big voice, Nikki is destined for stardom.

THE METAPHYSICAL POET, DIFFRACTED

Eye-beams up on one double string. Up on. Upon.

SOFT ROCK BALLAD WITH LESBIAN UNDERTONES

Her eyes move
On me

MISOGYNISTIC FOLK BALLAD

Nikki Nystagmus with sashaying eyes,
Crushing the world between her thighs

If she suspects you've been telling her lies
The cruellest of punishments she will devise

FRAGMENT OF SAPPHO

if only I, O golden-maned Liontigergirl,
could win this scrap–
–but then in my burning mind
you came and I was crazy for you

MATERIALISM VS WITCHCRAFT FOR DUMMIES!

In which the Matter of the supposed Evil Look given by Olga Adessi to Nikki Rawlings is rendered Actually Material. What was it like? It was like cartoon arrows but curly ones with thorns. Black, Gothic, twisting, fibrous ones. Black flowers. They would shoot from her eyes and then fall to the floor before they reached their destination because Olga Wasn't Actually Evil Enough.

And

All

We

Can

Do

Is

Grab

Hands

And

Run

Run

Run

Away

From
Brannigans
Down
West
Street
Over
The
Prom
Road
And

Down

To

The

Sea

Chapter 13

VOICE	Olga, Treesa, Rachel
SCENE	The Beach
HOUR	8 p.m., 16 June 1999
PLEASURE BEACH RIDE	Log Flume
SUBSTANCE	Seawater
ORGAN	Lips
SYMBOL	Cat
COLOUR	Tawny
FORMULA	$A = \frac{\sqrt{3}}{4} a^2$
ART / TECHNIC	Daring
HORMONE	Oxytocin
HOMERIC TITLE	Nausicaa

Olga

My mum would disown me for what I now desire but my granddad would understand. It felt mythological: me and you, last night crawling around on our hands and knees, clambering over sofas, pretending we were cats. And I can't explain what I mean by that. Loads of boys were just gaping at us, pretending we were cats in the party like it was normal. There were so many lines of sexual tension suspended in the air it was like the flat was wired with them. Clogged with them. You could have pegged your clothes out on those wires except that they were definitely charged with some kind of electric current so it wouldn't have been advisable.

And so now we are cats again, heading off to the beach. Cats unbothered by seagulls and chips. Cats giving the bars a wide berth because there was just a spot of bother in Brannigans and I can't be expected to answer to anyone while I am still a cat – look – there are people sitting outside Harry Ramsden's, it appears to be some sort of mealtime (dinnertime?), but no matter, we are just a couple of cats heading for the beach. Do cats like the sea? They love it! Didn't you know? Read the literature! Shall we find a pea-green boat? Commandeer Legends and set up shop at the end of the pier? Take the Elvis impersonator hostage? Impersonate the Elvis impersonator? Seduce the Elvis impersonator? Become the Elvis impersonator?

Cats taking over the world.

In the party last night you took on all my dares. You wouldn't dare to rip my jacket. You tore it down the middle and chucked it clean out the top-floor window. You wouldn't dare to bite my proffered arm. You bit me so hard, out popped a red bruise that would become like all the types of precipitation and cloud rolled into one. Find a yellow pen and draw a sun on your face. Draw a red heart on your arm and pen an arrow straight through it. I'm double Catholic, don't you realise? Poland curls its lip at me from over the sea. Ancona, the sea-froth lace edging Italy's Prince-style boot, mad rushing insomniac port of my birth, pretends not to know but knows it all backwards and hugs me anyway. I'm Catholic squared, me. Scratch your love, catch my germs, open arms, grow danger.

Treesa

It's quarter-to. Liam's nearly finished his shift. Mum has taken Lulu. The best bit of today so far was me and Lulu and Liam on the beach in the sun. Cheese, crisp and ketchup butties. Big thick wedges of cheddar. Salt and vinegar Squares – the best kind. Not too much ketchup but enough to keep it all stuck together. Big and stodgy and sweet and tangy and salty and cheesy. The best filling. Triangles of bread that Lulu will not-eat until they are completely soggy. She likes the triangles the most. Lulu reeling around like a drunk. But no she will not she will never. Suck in the sad moment and smile at daft Liam messing about, making Lulu crease herself up laughing. Happy with sand in nappy, sand on face, sand on bread, sand in mouth, sand in ears, sand in nose. A small tank of curiosity. Scared of nothing. Happy as a pig in. Liam lighting a fag.

–Save me letters on that.

Liam sucks his cigarettes so hard and so quickly that when he passes the half L&B-lettered remains to me its round shape has collapsed and it is a thin sliver like a crescent moon. Liam. Heartbreaker mine. Could have been a model. Fit in a skinny way. Footballer's legs. Too skinny now from too many speed weekends, too many pilled-up nights sweating it out on the podium in Heaven & Hell. Liam chugs down coffee and Coke and Carling and not much else. Hollows in his cheeks, sucking in his fag. Cuts a lean shadow. Heartbreaker's eyes, alcohol eyes, drug eyes, too sad and too old, connecting with a spirit beyond himself. His eyes connect with boozy ancestors raving it up through the decades and all with the same expression of infinite sadness. He grins and his eyes crease up and I love him. Never was there a sweeter smile. Liam throws Lulu up so high it is terrifying. But he always catches her, sometimes by one leg, and she screams in wild delight until he does it again. Daft pair. Never thought so much love possible.

Liam had sprinted off, apron strings flapping, chequered trousers flapping, long skinny legs in the breeze. And we wandered, ate ice cream, sat on the stone steps. Watching the sun fall over the sea.

But what are those two girls doing further towards the pier? Messing around in ankle-deep water. Bare feet. No stuff with them. Long hair covering each face, one straight and streaky blonde, one dark and curly. They are laughing hysterically. Now they are on their hands and knees. Crawling.

Elgu.

Lulu's favourite made-up word from last year when she was getting used to talking. Meaning she's seen something she's interested in and she wants to go towards it.

There is something very weird going on with those

girls. They definitely have the look of having been up all night. Splashing around getting their clothes wet, moving and stumbling, clearly at the end of a sesh. But it's not just that. Something about the energy between them that makes me think of witches. *Lesbian witches*. The word seems to come up off the sea like vapour. Don't think I've ever seen a real one. A lesbian, that is. Not a witch. Mrs Heathfield at number 1 on our street is definitely a witch, but not the cool Sabrina kind. Everyone said Nicola Bradshaw was a lesbian at school because she had a number 4 and did army cadets, but now she's going out with Mark Evans and has got one of those weird haircuts, all short and hairsprayed up and duck-arsed at the back and a kind of plastered-down side-parting at the front.

But these two right here in front of me. It's like a scene from a weird film. These girls are from another planet I swear. Even in this blinding sun they hold each other's glances for ages. Like they're whipping up a spell. Like the air is elastic between them. Like their eyes are having a completely separate conversation.

And then something even weirder. The word balloon I'm now imagining floating above them – LESBIAN, definitely in capitals – keeps getting bigger and louder and I can feel my own face go red as the darkhaired one crawls towards the blondehaired one. Half in and half out of the water, they sit back on their heels. Darkhair puts her hand on blondehair's cheek. Says something very very very slowly and decidedly.

You.

Are.

Stunnin.

And I am watching open-mouthed as the darkhaired one leans forward and very lightly kisses the blondehaired one on the lips in the most private most gentle most brand-new way you have ever seen anyone touch anyone else's lips with their own. As if no one has ever kissed anyone ever before. Or maybe as if kissing hasn't really been invented as a thing. Or maybe as if this is a thing that needs to be called something completely new and different – a softer name than kiss. *Elgu.* Lulu's word that means I like I want I go towards. *Elgu.* I absolutely like you and want you and the kick and the hiss of a kiss is too harsh for the softness of the touch I am about to touch you with. *Elgu.*

But still. This is the weirdest thing I've seen on the beach since Jake Ellison jumped off the pier and dislocated his shoulder when he hit the sea. I am blushing all over my entire body. Two girls who look like they're from the sixties or seventies kneeling down in the sea in broad daylight and they look like they're flippin in love. So strange. They look like a painting of a poem. A poem of a painting. Something impossible and not real. Upside down backwards beautiful and wrong. What the fuck. They look unreal. The strangeness and the gentleness of them together makes me want to run away and not watch anymore. Somewhere deep inside my stomach a leaf turns over. A tiny weight shifts. A throb. At the same time as the throb I see the darkhaired one's face more clearly and it's fucking Olga Adessi. Dorotka Adessi's daughter. We used to play together at the Sandgrown B&B the times when I went with Mum to work but we haven't spoken since teenage years. Does she know I have a kid? She's kind of weird now, but aren't we all?

What's weirder: having a kid at sixteen or kissing another girl in the sea? Their kiss looked better than any other kiss I have ever seen. I'm going mental. Can't stop staring. Olga Adessi and this blonde girl are just kind of looking at each other, still on their hands and knees. All around the sea glitters under sunlight.

They look up when they hear a seagull cry something that sounds exactly like *elgu*. And then they see me.

Rachel

We stayed up all night, me and Olga, the girl who called me a lion. We got separated and then we found each other again. And then we crawled down to the beach. Crawled. We make up the terms that define us. We construct and unfold the world. Not universally. I mean particularly and grittily and in real time. This is what we are doing right now. We were cats all night and all morning. Cats in the darkness of the living room party. Cats behind grimy curtains shutting out the dawn. And then we were: cats sliding down bannisters. Cats out into the daytime workadayness. Cats crawling past Boots, cats crossing the road, cats at the traffic lights. Cats in smoke-scented clothes and filthy bare feet. Cats with grazed knees and black elbows and parched throats and huge great bloody swollen hearts, cat systems rattling almost empty on fake sweet toxic catnut oil. And then, cats on the beach. Cats like the beach. She said so. Read the literature.

In the midst of the toxic feline blur there are certain moments that are hard gemstones. *You. Are. Stunnin.* A pomegranate seed, a ruby, stored up for later. And then the first time we saw that Treesa had been watching us. A hall of diamond mirrors. Olga shouts across the sand. Waves cheerfully. Performance mask back on. Seems to be unbothered by the fact that someone oversaw the moment that just happened. Her hand still holds mine as we scuff over sand towards the girl whose upturned face is lit by the setting sun.

–Treesa Reynolds! Haven't seen you in time!

–Alright? What's going on?

The girl has a defiant stance, trackies and trainers, and a quiet but cheeky grin. Olga hugs her quickly, grandly, hair flying, bare feet and wet trousers.

–Hiya! How's it going? This is Rachel. We're a bit –

She gesticulates at both of us, shrugging her shoulders.

–Worse for wear. Went out last night and I had to go to work this morning and now we seem to be back on it … What about you? How's your mum? And Liam, and – sorry, what's the little one's name again?

–Lulu.

–Lulu! How's she doing?

Treesa smiles. She has peace inside her, and wisdom, somehow.

–She's amazing. She makes me laugh every day.

Olga turns back to me.

–Me and Trees used to play together when we were little. At the Sandgrown, my mum's B&B. Her mum Lou cleans the rooms. Still does, right?

Treesa nods. She doesn't bat an eyelid: at us, at anything. Solid ground under her feet. It doesn't matter that she saw us kissing. It doesn't matter that we're still holding hands. A surge of joy, euphoria, and a feeling of warmth, spreading from Olga's hot hand through my body, through her body.

Treesa's clothes are so white and clean. She smells like Bold washing powder. Or is it Daz? She looks hard but her gaze is soft. She is the mum. We are the kids. Treesa's hair is ironed perfectly straight and tied back tightly by three scrunchies of different shades: deep purple, lilac and white. Her Nike tracksuit looks new and expensive. She has big gold hoop earrings. Am I staring too much at this sudden new addition to the evening? Impossible to know. The face works of its own accord. The voice is silent. The only thing that really feels alive is the pulse that throbs through my hand that holds Olga's hand. I will be passive and will be led and Olga will not let go of my hand. She is, again, the moveable anchor. The compass of the evening. The magnet. I will follow her, must follow her, cannot do anything else. Olga seems so happy to see Treesa; seems relieved that there is someone else to focus on, that the intensity is now diluted. But still her hand holds on. After a short silence she laughs.

–Dohhhhhh – the brain cells are working a bit slowly today. So what y'up to?

–Just enjoying some chilltime ... Mum's got Lulu until tomorrow and Liam's nearly finished work so I was gonna go and meet him.

–Chilltime! Sounds good ... I think we could do with some of that too, don't you reckon? It's been a fuckin weird day. Shall we go and have a drink somewhere?

Treesa hesitates. A minuscule glance in the direction of our joined hands. Her face does not judge, but does register. This is real. Her face makes a tiny frown and then kind of shakes it off. She grins.

–Alright! But does that mean you're gonna take me to one of your grimy moshpits?

She says this affectionately. Olga laughs. She turns and,

with the air of a group tour guide, waves her free arm aloft.

–Of course! To Scrooges we go!

Who is the third who always walks beside you? Three sets of footsteps heading in the direction of an evening beverage. Olga in the middle, linking arms with each of us: Treesa on the right, me on the left. Everything is permissible under the umbrella of intoxication. We are walking to filthy Scrooges under the bright lights of a Blackpool summer's night. Darker than the darkest cloak of moonless midnight. More fragrant than Shakespeare's bathroom. More cheap than anywhere else. Olga likes Scrooges. I like Scrooges. Treesa is scared of Scrooges and has never been. Treesa prefers Brannigans and Yates. Treesa hates hippies and moshers and metalheads but I see pity in her eyes when she sees how we have lost our shoes and are not carrying anything other than the sea-wet clothes we are justabout standing up in.

The cats have gone. Can I read Yeats in Yates and think about that bit in *Educating Rita* where Julie Walters thinks Michael Caine means the wine lodge when he means the poet? Olga likes Shakespeare. Olga's surname should be Shakespeare. Olga knows it all, by which I mean, Olga knows twelve Shakespeare sonnets by heart. Olga hated school and left at eighteen because she wanted to be an actress. Treesa quite liked school and left at sixteen because she got pregnant. I hated school and loved uni but left because I hated myself. We are all nineteen. Double vodka and orange is one-fifty in Scrooges. Even Yeats can't beat that. If I have enough of them I will climb into the high luggage compartment of the number 14 bus on the way home and people will frown and shake their heads. I will do it because climbing into small spaces is more fun than you think and also because it is one of those days. Three sets of footsteps. One pair of Reebok Classics, brand new. Two pairs of bare white human feet, washed clean by the sea and then sandy as we reach the concrete steps. No cats. Three points of a star, sixfold armslinked. A knot. Treesa Olga and me.

Chapter 14

VOICE	Treesa and the Nonspecific Questioner
SCENE	The Tavern
HOUR	9 p.m., 16 June 1999
PLEASURE BEACH RIDE	Cat and Mouse
SUBSTANCE	Vomit
ORGAN	Liver
SYMBOL	Borromean knot
COLOUR	Orange
FORMULA	$x(t) = (2+\cos(3t))\cos(2t)$, $y = (2+\cos(3t))\sin(2t)$, $z = -\sin(3t)$ for $t \in [-\pi,\pi]$
ART / TECHNIC	Interrogation
HORMONE	Progesterone
HOMERIC TITLE	Ithaca

TREESA IS LISA LEFT EYE LOPES

Scrooges Tavern, Milbourne Street, 10:33 p.m., 16 June 1999

Living this life on the hustle, I barely get enough time
You know me from the platinum, how I stack 'em and shine
You see a lot of contenders, they try to end up in my world
A reputation known as the untouchable girl

The three of us are sitting round a small brown table in Scrooges. I hate it here. It's dark and dirty. Weird mosher music is playing. It's almost empty apart from the barman and two spotty lads dressed in skater jeans and Slipknot hoodies who look about fifteen, holding pints and fags that both look too big for them. Looks like they'll serve anyone in here. No one asks for ID. I feel like I'm about forty years old. There are three flyers on the table: one for the West Coast Rock Café, one for the Tache Legendary Rock Venue and one for that mosher night Jenx. Places I hate. I hate the music and I hate the people who go there. I think about what going out on the razz means to me: sneaking out, sneaking in, tottering up the steps to Jellies or the Palace on a schoolnight before Lulu came along. Think about watching Liam sweating and gurning his face off on the podium in Heaven & Hell. Think about my favourites. TLC, Usher, Destiny's Child. Think about putting on Sun Shimmer body glow and Impulse Zen and lilac lipstick and babydoll dresses and packets of fags tucked into denim miniskirts and belly tops and blue Hubba Bubba plus WKD Blue staining my tongue blue squared. High heels and handbags. Look again at the lads in the Slipknot hoodies. To be honest, I don't really care about how they look.

They're alright. They blend in here. What I care about is how out of place I am in my trainers and my trackies. There is nothing else as gleaming white in this entire building as my trainers. Everything here is black and mucky and goth. Just do not get why people like wearing black so much. Think of my clean kitchen and my white sofa. Wish I was back there with Lulu right now. Rachel is frowning slightly and staring down at the table. She is fragile. I can feel it as strongly as if it was a perfume she was wearing. Olga is cheerful now we are sitting down here with our vodka and oranges, though their faces are lost, their eyes are wild, they have that searching look that comes from a night of drugs and no sleep. What are we all doing here again?

The music changes a bit to stuff I recognise. Then that tune starts by Mr Oizo. 'Flat Beat'. We all try and remember what the stupid teddy puppet thing is doing in the video. It is SO FUCKING ANNOYING. We all agree that it is SO FUCKING ANNOYING. And then a song comes on that we all like. Donnell Jones and Lisa Left Eye. 'U Know What's Up'. I can impress them because I can do a bit of her rap word-perfect. I know it because it makes sense to me. Lisa is one of my heroes.

I'm moving on now, trying to make a change in my ways
Be the best that I can be to last me all of my days
Now we can blaze pathways or just take our time
Better holla if ya hear me cause Left Eye gon' shine
My eyes don't lie, see how they glisten when you pass me by
You and I don't need permission to be unified.

Lose myself for a minute during this performance. I'm not stuck in Blackpool being a mum too young, a mum going nowhere fast. I'm a strong black woman, an international hip-hop hero with a fucking hardass gym body, loads of money, amazing clothes and fans all over the world. I'm part of the multiple-platinum-selling group TLC. I'm a hero to girls like me. Close eyes and Scrooges falls away and I'm fourteen again, standing high on the benches in the stale-smelling changing rooms after PE, six of us all jumping up and down doing the rap from that Love City Groove Eurovision song at the top of our voices. *Baby baby baby, you got me goin' crazy, I'm feelin' kinda high, my mind's gettin' hazy.* But when I open my eyes I'm back, back here in Scrooges channelling Lisa Left Eye, I'm still watching Olga and Rachel with both of my eyes. They are watching each other with their eyes. More than that. They are having an entire conversation. *My eyes don't lie, see how they glisten when you pass me by.* A lie from an eye, you pass me by. Eye byepass. Ha, that's it. There is an eye bypass between them. It cuts through the air. And in the midst of this moment I have an even weirder thought. The stuff that makes you feel weird is the stuff you should pay attention to. Never had a thought like that before. These two weirdos, can't help but feel sorry for them, they're gonna get thrown out any minute, the guy at the bar is staring and frowning, and not because they're pissed but because they're two girls in love and this grown-up bloke can't handle that in his bar in this town in this moment, and in this moment it's clear that angel superhero Lisa Left Eye knows better and will always know better. And as they lean drunkenly closer and closer, I swear down firebolts are shooting between their eyes, time slows down, speeds up, falls down, gets back up again. And at the moment when they kiss the bloke marches over and grabs them both and marches them outside and I'm left alone in the mosher bar and all I can hear is Lisa:

You and I don't need permission to be unified.

What did Olga think of Scrooges at this time of night?
Olga thought it was seedy and dark and depressing and full of gangly underage boys in hoodies clutching fake IDs and hoping to get into the Tache later and mosh their heads off until their necks feel like snapping and she couldn't help hoping that they might but undeniably the drinks were cheap.

What colour was overwhelming Olga's senses at this point?
Olga was seeing everything tinged with an egg-yolk-vomit-orange-yellow due to multiple double vodka and orange @ £1.50 consumed, spliced with the unforgettable sight of actual-orange-juice-vodka-flecked-vomit spattered across one of the toilets.

What did Treesa think of Scrooges at this time of night?
The more double vodka and oranges you had, the less you minded the weirdos and the moshers with their long, greasy hair and their staring eyes.

What did Rachel think of Scrooges at this time of night?
Considering the egg-yolk-orange-juice-vodka-flecked-vomit had been ejected from her gullet forty minutes hence, Rachel was beyond judgement of her locale.

Express Rachel's vodka-pickled mental situation geometrically.
Rachel was a wavering loop of feeling.

What did Olga do at precisely 9:37 p.m.?
She leaned in close to Rachel, saying, *I'm gonna kiss you.*

What did Rachel do in response?
She leaned in, swaying, saying, *Yeah but you wouldn't do it sober would you.*

What did Treesa do when she saw this?
She ran away.

At what precise angle did the heads of Rachel and Olga coalesce?
From a standing position, Rachel supported invisibly by a wall and by Olga, their heads dipped together at approximately 45 degrees until their noses were almost touching.

Who spoke at this point?
Rachel.

What did she say?
Slurringly: *You're gonna break my fucking heart.*

Did Olga respond?
Not vocally.

In what form did Olga's response come?
In the form of a kiss, on the lips, soft and hard, an instant bruise, a molten piece of stewed jewelled fruit, a staining burning hard flushed sudden instant bloom of a kiss.

What were the consequences of the kiss?
The consequences were threefold. Onefold: Rachel kissed back. The boiling point of sugared fruit in her head. Jam.

Rhubarb. Cherries. Things becoming crystal. Extreme states of heat and cold being the same.

Twofold: a pair of bulging, folded masculine arms and a stern, shaking head presented itself, and one bulging arm proceeded to lay a firm hand on each of the shoulders of Olga and Rachel. *We'll have none o' that in here*, pronounced the firm mouth in the firm-set jaw of the stern, shaking head, none of these details clear to either starryeyed blurryeyed kisser.

Threefold: a disentanglement and a drunken assurance that no further kisses would follow.

What policy did Scrooges follow at the arse end of the twentieth century with regard to nonheterosexual demonstrations of affection and intimacy in public?
There was no official written policy but the bulging arms and stern, shaking head had found the sight too lurid/alluring and felt sure that complaints would ensue.

What did Olga and Rachel do?
Stumble apart,
stumble along,
take a drink,
look for Treesa,
discover Treesa gone,
pronounce Treesa gone.

Where had Treesa gone?
Treesa walked furiously along Cookson Street, vaguely in the direction of the bus station.

Which mode of transport did Treesa select at this hour?

Bus station, train station, not sure which, a bit too drunk to suddenly come to your senses after the weirdest evening in the history of weirdness.

What weirdness had Treesa witnessed?
Olga and Rachel had kissed.

What auditory phenomenon had sprung to mind when Treesa witnessed the kiss?
It clanged. It was a weird clanging sight to see.

What word had accompanied the auditory perception?
Wrong. And definitely wrong in there and pretty sure someone would have said something pretty quickly.

What additional feeling had accompanied the clang of wrongness?
Deep down also the feeling that it is not wrong. Not really wrong.

What supplementary feeling had accompanied the sounds and words and feelings Treesa had experienced at the kiss?
Also the feeling that it looked soft. Gentler than she had thought.

What was the phrase that sprung to mind when Treesa thought of Olga and Rachel?
Lesbian witches. But they were nice. They were vulnerable. A proper mess, actually.

How did Treesa get home?
Treesa arrived at Blackpool North by 22:10 and boarded the

22:15 to Manchester Airport without a ticket, stood at the edge of the quietish train until the train reached Layton at 22:25, got off the train, walked along the main road and crossed the roundabout while taxis with their lights on and buses with drunk people whizzed past, turned into her estate, which was quieter, opened her front door and collapsed on the white sofa with a spinning head.

What did Olga and Rachel talk about as they walked swayingly in the direction of the seafront?
Literature.

What fact had emerged that had fuelled Olga's scorn and disbelief?
The fact that every single writer who had captivated Rachel in her first term studying Literature at Manchester was a man. With the exception of Virginia Woolf.

Who had Rachel listed?
John Donne. John Milton. W. B. Yeats. John Keats. William Blake.

What was Olga's reaction to this?
Complete and utter indignation.

What did Olga say in her indignation?
She gave a quickfire list of fairly current female writers she loved and had read recently.

Who was on the list?
Arundhati Roy, Zadie Smith, Jackie Kay, Janice Galloway, Jeanette Winterson, Angela Carter, Margaret Atwood.

What did Olga ask Rachel that made her feel the most like a complete and utter fucking idiot?
Olga asked Rachel if she was a feminist or not.

Why was the extent of the idiotfeeling so strong for Rachel at this point?
She realised that she had never asked herself this question.

What had Rachel's attitude towards feminism been in the few short months at university?
Indifference.

How did Rachel's idiotfeeling materialise?
Through a sinking in the gut.

What sensation was Olga feeling at this point?
The complex yet familiar feeling of having to explain herself to people who did not expect her to be well read or well informed, or have a well-developed political sensibility.

How did Olga's complex yet familiar feeling materialise?
Through a sinking in the gut.

Did Olga feel anything else specific to this situation here with Rachel?
Yes.

And are you going to illuminate us on the feelings, Olga?
If I have to.

You do.

(Olga felt: like she wanted to gather her up in her arms and tell her everything was okay. That the things coming out of her mouth were the opposite of what she should be saying. That Rachel was vulnerable and needed someone to keep a careful eye on her so that she didn't do anything stupid. And simultaneously that she, Olga, could not be the one to do this.)

Why could she not be the one to do this?
Why all the hard questions?

Answer the question, please.
Because Olga knew herself better than she was able to articulate, even to herself.

And how did she know herself?
She knew herself as someone who was not able to look after anyone at this stage in her life, except herself (badly).

But what about Treesa? Isn't she the same age, the same life stage? Isn't she looking after someone full-time and doing a good job of it?
It isn't the same thing at all.

Why not?
Because if you have a kid then your happy hormones kick in and you're all there, swimming in the endorphins together. You don't have any choice. You have to do it. All the looking-after. Rachel is just a girl I met who is weirdly obsessed with me. I don't even know where it comes from. She's just a bit of a weirdo; she's very sweet but she will go back to her nice family and they will pay for an

expensive therapist for her and she'll get her life back on track and I will never see her again.

What about getting your own life back on track?
Who said it wasn't on track? What kind of interrogation is this?

Well are you happy in your job? Do you feel stimulated?
Not in the slightest. But I won't be there forever. It's just a stopgap. While I decide the best course to apply for.

Take it from me, love, stopgaps can last a lifetime. You need to act now. Resit your A-Levels and apply for uni or acting school.
Who are you, anyway?

I'm the nonspecific questioner. The opposite of an oracle. The nonchorus. I don't give information. I just ask the questions. That's all I do.
What am I supposed to do with all the stuff these questions have stirred up?

That's up to you.
And have we not swapped roles now? Am I not the one asking you the questions?

So we have. Let's swap back immediately.
Go on then!

(Nonspecific questioner resumes professional tone)
So, Olga, you sounded a bit defensive there when you were talking about Rachel, and not entirely kind. Would you be prepared to admit that whatever feeling she has for you, there may be a

degree of reciprocation there?
Do I have to answer that right now?

I'm afraid you do.
Well, I wouldn't say reciprocation. Two people can't be obsessed with one another. Can they?

Don't ask me. I'm the questioner. What do you think?
Well, I wouldn't say what I feel for her is obsession. I'd say it's more like mixed-up confusion, and maybe a bit of fear. Or maybe even shame.

Why shame?
Because I know I can't give her what she needs.

Are you attracted to her?

What does your silence signify?
Can I have another drink before I answer that?

No.
Okay then. Yes. I am. I can't help it. I am.

Why is this so hard for you to accept?
Because I like boys. I *really* like boys. I've always liked boys. Boys are what I do. All kinds of boys. I'm not fussy. And then she comes along and ... I just don't know how I'm supposed to think about it.

Is it not possible that you could like boys and girls?
Maybe. But I don't think I'll ever like another girl. I think she's the only one.

How could you possibly know that when you've got the whole of your life ahead of you?
Well, no one can ever fully know anything. But I have a feeling. It's like a new part of me has opened up. A new cavern. Part that I didn't know existed. But it's not open permanently. It can't be. I have control of it, and I can lock it away again, and I think it will be a lot easier if I do.

Are you sure you have control of it?
Yes.

Does locking it away involve shutting Rachel out of your life?

What does your silence signify?
I don't have an answer.

What are Olga and Rachel doing during these ruminations?
Olga and Rachel are walking and talking, but each feels completely and utterly alone.

What is an appropriate syllogism to express the uncertain and imbalanced imaginary triangulation of perception between the three at this point?
Each thought they knew the other better than the other and better than they knew themselves.

Express this mathematically, wherein the arrow signifying 'greater or smaller than' designates the greater or smaller amount perceived to be known of one person than the person themselves, when R = Rachel, O = Olga, T = Treesa.
R > O > T > O > R > T

What factors determine these vectors of difference?
Socioeconomic status, education level, internalised guilt, shame, feelings of unworthiness, the ease of knowing/caring for another > the ease of knowing/caring for the self.

What did Treesa think of what Rachel thought of Olga?
She could see that in her she could see more than she could see.

Please further qualify your pronoun use.
Treesa could see that in Olga Rachel could see more than Olga could see.

What did Treesa think of what Olga thought of Rachel?
She could see that in her she could see more than she could see.

Please qualify.
Treesa could see that in Rachel Olga could see more than Rachel could see.

Express the shared feeling among the three without recourse to words.

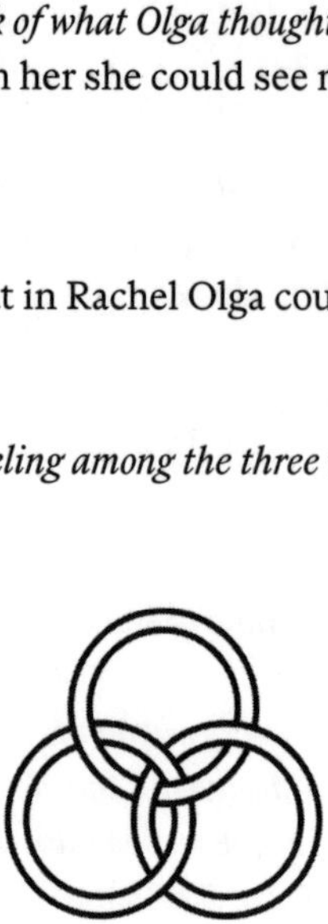

Chapter 15

VOICE	Olga, Rachel, and Many Others
SCENE	The Tram
HOUR	10 p.m., 16 June 1999
PLEASURE BEACH RIDE	Ghost Train
SUBSTANCE	Ice cream
ORGAN	Larynx
SYMBOL	Sun
COLOUR	Yellow, orange, red
FORMULA	$Ax^2 + Bxy + Cy^2 + Dx + Ey + F = 0$
ART / TECHNIC	Speech
HORMONE	Insulin
HOMERIC TITLE	Oxen of the Sun

A HYMN TO SOL

OR,

SHE RIDES THE TRAM IN DIFFERENT VOICES

OR,

A HELIOCHRONIC TRAM JOURNEY ALONG BLACKPOOL PROMENADE AT SUNSET

Mother of the vibratory field,
All-nourisher, all-giver, all-destroyer
Ma-ga
Gaia
Blessings to you
So mote it be.

The tram with the rocket lights goes from Starr Gate all along the prom to Fleetwood Ferry.

In a moment of pure romantic and drunken glee, together Olga and Rachel climb aboard. Sun goddess Sol rides a chariot of horses through the sky.

TOGETHER:
Come, sea-wolf, swallow us whole.

Riding our tram-chariot through the darkening sea/sky/sea/sky/sea as the sea-wolf swallows the sun and carries it in her belly.

OLGA IN THE STYLE OF ENHEDUANNA, BELLICOSELY STALKING THE PROMENADE:
O Radiant Star, O Lady of the Evening. At your battlecry the lands bow low and the people sing your praises. The threshold of tears is opened and the people walk along the promenade of great lamentations. Those sleeping on the

streets and those sleeping in the shelters and those sleeping in the B&Bs: the people all lift their eyes to you.

RACHEL IN THE STYLE OF GHOSHA, RIDING THE TRAM-CHARIOT:
O rattling trams, O sun, Your radiant chariot – whither goes it on its way? Who decks it for you, lambent neon rocket, borne hitherward through prayer unto the sacrifice? Where is your halting place amongst the briny offerings? Be near me: O unfocused colours, shine resplendent.

OLGA SPOUTING SOME UNHOMERIC SEA-BASED EPITHETS:
The pissbrown sea. The organgrinding sea. The slatecold sea. The tablecloth sea. The bonechina sea. The anti-climactic sea. The plasticlogged sea. And cradled in your sludgy gut the reddening ageing darkening sun.

RACHEL IN THE STYLE OF JULIA BALBILLA, DOING LATINATE SUNSPLICING:
Solis occasus.
Amor
Amare
Sol
Solis.
(To love is to touch the sun)
(To love is to touch the edge of the sun)
(To touch the edge of the sun is to love)

(all-consuming)
(all-absolving)
(all-swallowing)

(as we are)
(before the rays of the sun)

OLGA IN THE STYLE OF HYPATIA, GETTING AN ICE CREAM AND TEACHING CONIC GEOMETRY:
Reserve your right to eat, for even to eat wrongly is better than not to eat at all. Stop at the van next to Queen's Promenade and buy a vanilla Mr Whippy soft scoop with a Cadbury Flake for 99p. Carefully and quickly scoop out a triangle-shaped section of delicious cream-cold sweetness from one side of the cone with your tongue. The curve created if you draw a line from one edge of your triangle ice cream hole to the other is a hyperbola. The ice cream is so delicious that you cannot help but immediately repeat this action until a bigger section of the empty cone is exposed. Now the curve drawn from one point of the cone to the other is a parabola. Soon you will have consumed enough that all sides of your ice-cream cone are visible, making what looks like an uneven circle. Excellent! You now have an ellipsis. Now, to see the final conic section you have two choices, dependent upon the levels of air temperature, proximity of remaining ice cream to an incompressible fluid that conforms to the shape of its container but retains a (nearly) constant volume independent of pressure, and pain caused by sphenopalatine ganglioneuralgia. You must now just sit tight and wait for the internal energy of the remaining ice cream to become sufficiently agitated for the phase transition from solid to liquid to occur, thereby causing the uneven surface to right itself and for the ellipsis to become a perfect circle. The correct conclusion to the procedure would then be to remove the bottom tip of the cone with the front top and bottom teeth, immediately

clamping the lips round the small aperture, sucking out the remaining melted ice cream from the bottom and subsequently enjoying the concomitant moistening of the dustysweet soggening nonsacramental paperlight wafer. All formally dogmatic biscuits are fallacious and must never be accepted by self-respecting persons as final. By most historical accounts I was flayed to death by sharp tiles or oystershells, the skin razed entirely from the body and the limbs burnt at the Christian altar for an argument I was but bystander of, through jealousy or perceived threat to masculine Reason.

RACHEL IN THE STYLE OF LI QINGZHAO, GATHERING PLASTIC SEA ORNAMENTS:

Year by year, across the wet dunes,
I have often gathered plastic bottles
    intoxicated with their beauty
    fondling them impudently

    I get my jeans wet with their lucid tears.

OLGA IN THE STYLE OF MARGERY KEMPE, PACING THE WINDWHIPPED SAND IN TRAINERS:

This creature, being of years fifteen-and-some, walked across concrete path in battered trainers somedeal full of sand and, turning her thoughts to the worshipful maiden inside the sick-house to her sinister side, was within short time fighting against the devils which made turns around in her breast. Anon turned the mind of this creature towards devils and dark spirits, for dread she had of damnation. And anon this creature was wonderly vexed, for at the mouth of the lapping sea she saw devils with breath of low fires, devils with eyes of snakes and spite, devils who bade her she should forsake her friends, her family, her maiden sister Teresa, who said:

RACHEL IN THE STYLE OF TREESA IN THE STYLE OF ST TERESA OF ÁVILA COUNSELLING THE SEABOUND:
Let nothing disturb you on your windblown path
Let nothing make you afraid
There is nothing which puts devils to flight
Better than the
Unholy water of the
Ironflat coldgrey seesighsea.

OLGA IN THE STYLE OF ISABELLA WHITNEY AS A CONTESTANT FOR BLACKPOOL IN BLOOM:
This harvest time, I harvestless, and serviceless also, And subject unto sickness, that abroad I could not go. The fate of the workingclass Pensioner. P.S. So bloomin' lonely.
And so on *North West Tonight*, the annual Britain in Bloom competiton reaches the Fylde Coast. And here in the studio we have our very own Blackpool in Bloom finalist for the year 1575, Ms Isabella Whitney, walking us through her unique creation A Sweet Nosegay: One Hundred Philosophical Flowers. Isabella, can you talk us through your creation? Yes good sir, it would delight me much. This simple Nosegay matters but little except in the sense that I, though whole in body and in mind but very weak in Purse, doth hope to ameliorate through presenting this Arrangement of stalk and petal some steadfast-held ideas regarding the nature, type and composition of the relations between Flora and Idea. Good Gentles, if you do find your Cheeks fat with Questions please deign to hover over the

mingled scents of my blooming Garden. Apprehend at once the buzzing Knots attracted to the rainbow Nectars many: Stoic yellow, Platonic purple, I urge you now to taste a Petal here and there, please take and eat the fruit of this Tree, I believe you will find that Empiricism crunches a noisy Red. Next to my Sophistry Rockery behold a plant Uncategorisable so I am forced to make an approximation not of our current Times: it doth befall me to call this blue raspberry Logic something of the Absurd.

RACHEL IN THE STYLE OF GENDERBENDING APHRA BEHN:
Under a rickety Pier, made for love
Silent as yielding Teens Consent
She with a charming Languishment
Permits those roving hands to push up her dress,
Only to Stop, and say –
Fair lovely Maid, or if that Title be
Too Binary for Nobler thee,
Permit a Pronoun worthy of Mercury:
And let me ascribe They to thee.

OLGA IN THE STYLE OF PHYLLIS WHEATLEY, SINGING THE SATSUMA BLUES:
Aurora hail, and all the thousand hues,
Which deck thy progress through satsuma blues:
The sun she dips, and wide extends her creamy glow,
On ev'ry ridge of sand the shadows flow;

RACHEL IN THE STYLE OF EMILY DICKINSON, DIFFRACTING THE LIGHT AND BLACKENING THE HEART:

I saw a Light –
It thrust its Beam
Across my Path –
My Path did swerve –
The Light did cut
Its way inside –
and cleft –
My blackened Heart –

OLGA IN THE STYLE OF GEORGE ELIOT ENVISIONING YOUNG TREESA IN THE STYLE OF ST TERESA OF ÁVILA CHEWING JELLY STRAWBERRIES IN ABINGDON STREET MARKET:
Who that cares much to know the history of how woman, man (AND those clever enough to have transcended gender) BEHAVE under the varying experiments of Time, has not dwelt, at least briefly, on the life of St Teresa, has not smiled with some gentleness at the thought of the little girl walking forth one morning hand in hand with her still smaller brother, to go and seek the brightly coloured packets of milk chocolate-covered Penguins in the discount buckets by the tills in Iceland? Out they toddled from rugged Abingdon Street Market clutching white paper bags with a 20p mix, milk teeth engaged in masticating extra-large jelly strawberries, small tongues aching and fizzing from the skinrazing sour 5p astro belts. That child pilgrimage was a fit beginning. Teresa's flame burned quietly and, fed from within, never soared except for the times when she was able internally to reflect on the segmented world served up for her. She found her epos in the teenage friendships and breakups; the singing of pop songs and the serving of customers in the petrol station;

and ultimately at the gates of motherhood, where she found herself before she was but four short of twenty.

RACHEL IN THE STYLE OF VIRGINIA WOOLF, RECALLING WHEN SHE DROPPED AN ICE LOLLY ON THE PAVEMENT:

And then, she thought, what an evening – unfresh as if issued to disenfranchised teenagers on a beach! This cooling viscous claret of an evening, thick with late summer melancholia, so different from the piping-hot Saturdays she remembers from childhood. The tram shelters would be ringing with toddlers' shrieks and picnicking familes would be chinking stubbies and passing round packets of No Frills sausage rolls and packets of Monster Munch and Space Invaders. Which ice lolly from the ice cream van was the best? Fabs, Twisters, Calippos ... O the acidic red strawberry casing of a Mivvi, contrasted with the pale cold cream inside! So quick to melt, such a risk of losing your last bite, the sinking sensation watching it falling straight off your wooden stick and onto the concrete – *nooooo!* – and yet now, entering the circular point with the emptying beach, the cafés closed, the tram shelters enshadowed with darkness, she fabulated and thus sprang forth the invisible and palimpsestic pinpoint marks of melted ice-lolly stains dotted all along the path. Imagine if they were all lit up as we stepped on them, like the Illuminations, just for a second; light-blobs on the concrete just like illuminated splats of chewing gum on the pavement. There would be *thousands*.

OLGA IN THE STYLE OF GERTRUDE STEIN, DOING YOGA ON THE PIER:

A sea is to sky is to see is to sigh
To see is to sigh is to sea is to sky

So.
Green splinter peel painty bench. Piering. A cross.
The moveable her eyes on.
Eye.
          Wood eye.
Eye.
          A wood.
Either gnaws.
          The gnaws.
Its knot warm.
          Yer knot wrong.
Either gnaws.
          Eye.
Right enough.

Watch Trev and Ann eat sandwiches from foil drink coffee from flasks and we all watch the sun stoop low. A whole whale underground and a stoop to lift reach under it why never only ever do it when you really really need it through the whispered clouds what do we have? Only times of harsh clenching when this is not one of those and it is only when you are thrice times tired. Thrice times tired and full of rage.

Twist your body in order to feel. Stretch your body in order to ground. Lift your body in order to love. Let it swell and overflow and oh. Interject if you must. Say the decent thing the decent thing say the decent thing. Interruptions and self-interceptions and self-thwarting. Never again never ever again. Going for people really going for people in the repetition you understand what I mean by really *going* for people it does not need to be hard it can be easy just put your head in the stream. And really in the tradition you know in the tradition you know normally in the tradition we go here then we put this here and normally when we go out we just head out and when you go for people I mean really *go* for people I was really going to go for them I mean really *go* for them all of them in one go one two three quick swallow down.

RACHEL IN THE STYLE OF MINA LOY, WORSHIPPING THE TOWER:

The tram with the rocket lights
Strobing its colours
Shooting up a black vein
Pneumatic neon mobile phone sofa cradling us
Fluorescent sunflowers towering over
Tower incandescent with spectral lights
Dirty rainbows arch and sing all about us
Whirl us up connecting us digital orgasm synthesis
 paradise
Bassline generator squelching through mossy depths
We are dinosaurs kneeling and kissing the foot of we know
 not what
At the shrine of your gleaming exoskeleton

OLGA IN THE STYLE OF JUNE JORDAN, BUILDING A BRIDGE BETWEEN TOWERS:

At the foot of the tower our own shadows disappear
into the din of the marching feet of thousands
for whom I cannot speak
and yet for whom I must speak
rising like a marvellous tide

fertile even as the first woman whispering
there will be flood.

RACHEL IN THE STYLE OF GLORIA ANZALDÚA, SPLICING LANGUAGES:
Esta puente, mi estalda. Esta puente, mi estalda.
This. Bridge. Called. My. Back.

ENTER OLGA AS KATHY ACKER AND RACHEL AS HÉLÈNE CIXOUS:
KATHY: I am a slab of raw fish recently skinned.
HÉLÈNE: You are the empty cipher, the tool I use to carve myself out of myself.
KATHY: The slab splits to a maw, hungry for a hurt, as nourishment, as punishment.
HÉLÈNE: The maw grins wide and splits open, leading to a cavern leading to a tunnel leading to infinite caves.
KATHY: The caves are only there for you, but you are nothing. You are infinitely replaceable.
HÉLÈNE: All the maw seeks is a mirror of you, an echo of you, a gulp of you, a gust of you, to fill the sails, the wallpaper wettings of these insides.
KATHY: Maw, you were not me. Your unflappable flesh was solid with no windows. When I cut holes in myself, burned myself, ejected myself, sliced myself and spliced myself, your steady decibels dripped their pragmatism into my ear, forming a yellow pool in the centre.
HÉLÈNE: No longer young but still raw, now more of a puzzle, the gaping yawn from whence I came, now there I crane, eternal winged propulsion into

you, not you, but my own uncertain shadow.

KATHY: Desire is the fierce pull of someone else's desire.

HÉLÈNE: The heart hits a complex echo internally, again, again.

KATHY: It has been stretched, but those who stretch it will never be its occupants.

HÉLÈNE: Each time it happens, a new cavern opens.

KATHY: Why does impossibility breed desire.

HÉLÈNE: Because it is safer. Because it is safer. I don't want to kiss you because I want to imagine forever what it is like to kiss you.

KATHY: When it hardens and when we harden. Does hardening preserve or kill.

HÉLÈNE: When I paint you onto my nails and it hardens. When I smear youshadow across my lids and it hardens.

KATHY: When I smear feelings across the wall and they harden. When water dilutes. When blood hardens.

HÉLÈNE: When precipices extend. When time hardens. When it plays itself out in seconds.

KATHY: When the first utterance betrays the painful end.

HÉLÈNE: When eyes turn to knives then burning bushes then cooling mosses. It softens and it hardens.

KATHY: We soften and we harden.

HÉLÈNE: When it is not clear that a feeling is a feeling or an echo of a feeling.

KATHY: A reeling.

HÉLÈNE: When the object is obscured from reach, leaving a feeling. When sleep is obscured from reach, leaving a shadow. When touch is obscured from reach, leaving an imprint.

KATHY: When taste is untasted, burning a hole where the tongue should be.

HÉLÈNE: When cans of worms are left unopened.

KATHY: When holes are drilled into cans to let the worms breathe.

Enter Treesa as Julia Kristeva.

JULIA: When a body is a vector.

KATHY: When the vector is youwards.

HÉLÈNE: When darts hit fences.

KATHY: Darts and arrows hit fences, purple juice spilling youwards.

JULIA: Purple blooming violet lovejuice dripping youwards.

HÉLÈNE: Youwards as the mobile real.

KATHY: Fences.

HÉLÈNE: Lust concrete.

JULIA: Stuck fast and close but apart.

HÉLÈNE: Close but apart.

KATHY: Trapped close not touching not quite touching but close not yet touching but close and apart.

JULIA: What is a gap.

HÉLÈNE: Agape.

KATHY: Eyedrowning. It doesn't matter whether I was a student of Professor Jakobson or not. If I was teaching defamiliarisation this is what I would say.

To conjugate strangeness: I bite.
The woman was bitten.
The man took.
The woman held.
It gleamed.
It bent down.
They shifted.
They knew.
They tried.
They want.
They purpled.
They dripped.
They are about to fuck.

Exeunt, awkwardly, sixfold armslinked.
A knot.
Together they go and get tattoos
of
A trifold rose wreath:
Inksisters,
Bloodsisters,
Spawn of Borromea.

TREESA AS HERSELF:
Fuck though it hurts so. Too small for this. Bones still growing. Words can't get out. Knowing though now somehow I will. Looking ahead knowing not knowing. Pretending not knowing. Dumb words. Words like grunts is all. We bond when we moan about shit. Shit stuff that's happened. Stuff to look forward. Stuff to hold like real stuff only in words. Only good when there's stuff to hold on to. No good talking when nothing. That empty feeling.

Begin with a moan. Know where you are with a moan. Fucksake. Takin the fuckin piss. It's takin the piss. Whatever it is it's takin. It always starts like that. Begin with a no. Not even a saying. Just shaking the head. Keeping uptight. Don't be daft you've gone soft. Show 'em who's boss. Whoever's boss it ain't me.

V
e
r
t
i
g
o
It
hap-
pens
the first time
on
the
Pepsi Max
Big One chugging
up queasy from deep-fried
pier doughnut grease
high ponytail facelift
skull crisped by hairspray
doused head to toe
in Impulse Zen on
the human conveyor belt
strapped loosely in pairs by frayed black
straps next to Lee Jenkins six inches shorter
than you chugging and chinking slows and stops
one silent second and allllll is blue 360 blue lazy
susan whirligig blue blue dish blue plate sky blue
tablecloth sea blue crazy blue strings of streets splay
out veining the land rolling in an upside-down bucket
of blue unending horizonless and later this tropical
Blackpool blue will come back and flood you a gutful
of Irish Sea flatness all depth and no depth upturning your

insides holding your breath twelve floors up in a glass-fronted
library a bloat of concepts knifed through by the fear that the
words and the organs you are holding in will eject themselves
if you breathe out again one second is enough to show that one
second is enough

Astride Central Pier   O your crooked spine
soft furnishings (your rotten gut)   woven by children
fibres on the lungs   this string
your faux brickies' boots   spun in
Lancashire mills

She had me. We can all say. She had me. Monstrous birth.
Except the first. To some. What is birthing. Birthing when
'tis wrong.   No shapes left to fit. Other
dimensions. A voice is birthing.
Rendered material. Render it. Nothing but your own
ragged renderings. Your own shorn sharpenings. My
voice as pencil.   Sharpened and the bits you discard. Voiced
detritus. If 'tis a thing. A thing 'tis. Prove through doing. Leave to
rise. Leave to prove.
Play to something.   Ragged reroutings.

Yeah but still now I would like to be able to say no ta thanks but
no thanks no I would prefer not to actually not right now and also
go back and say no to all the times back then no to all the times
when I wanted to say no and couldn't

say it aged sixteen throwing-up drunk locked in bathrooms with
lads in party houses when mums and dads go out and lads somehow get hold of cases or Foster's and Carling and girls get bottles
of Hooch or WKD or Bacardi Breezers

or we just all go for it with bottles of Glen's Vodka and bongs in the garden and dodgy white powders with Dreamscape rave compilations and CrazySexyCool and Spice Girls and Usher and 'Born Slippy' over and over and over again lager

lager lager lager downing shots of vodka out the cap and things go faster and faster and faster like a merry-go-round reeling-type feeling and I'm so invincible

I can do anything supercharged with booze and fags and drugs and oestrogen in my bloodstream hardens me like clear nail varnish I go outside to the skate park across the road with some of the lads and throw myself down the half-pipe from top to bottom no skateboard just my rolling body because I can't feel any pain aged sixteen getting drunk and fucking and getting knocked up by mistake

and even now aged nineteen not like that time Nicola
Rogers in the changing rooms felt my gymnast biceps to see how hard they were and held on just a bit too long but
I didn't stop her even though she had short spiky hair her jawline was so firm and her mouth so determined she didn't really have any friends but in that changing room after PE that time touching my arms and legs there was a weird spark like a weird twisty eyebeam coming from her eyes and going right into me when she looked at me saying
you're hard as fuckin nails and me just laughing gormlessly not knowing the right thing to say when the weird girl in your PE class touches your body and looks at you funny that was the only time I really felt the feeling like proper throbbing right in the centre of the

clit where he never knows to touch
and bless him he tries but I could
never say anything and sometimes
just say Yeah softly until
the word means nothing

Chapter 16

VOICE	Rachel
SCENE	The Flat
HOUR	3 a.m., 16 June 1999
PLEASURE BEACH RIDE	Chinese Puzzle Maze
SUBSTANCE	Gin
ORGAN	Skin
SYMBOL	Queen
COLOUR	Red
FORMULA	E = PF/R
ART / TECHNIC	Torture
HORMONE	Testosterone
HOMERIC TITLE	Circe

Declan and Damien. Under what stone has she pulled these two from.

Declan is supposedly the good-looking one, but his cousin Damien is supposedly quite charming too. Declan has longish brownish hair in the mod style and a roguish smile. He's wearing a white Fred Perry T-shirt and brown flared cords. Damien is visiting from Liverpool. Damien also has longish brownish hair in the mod style. He looks just like Declan, but Damien is chubby whereas Declan is skinny. Olga wants Declan and she thinks Damien would be good for me because he is 'into books'.

On the way back to her flat after the drunken tram ride and walk through town, the boys are at the cash machine, and Olga stops me earnestly on the street. She puts both hands on my shoulders and looks intently, earnestly at me, leaning in close, almost cross-eyed drunk, hot alcohol perfume musk breath, spicy musk hair, scratchy musk voice.

–Whatever happens when we get back, just go with it. I reckon they want to have sex with us. Both of us. Together.

Nod speechlessly. Heart zooms in both directions: up and down. Sex. In a group. In a bed. Her bed. With these boys who I do not care for. With her probably a metre away, fully engaged in enchanting Declan, tying up his arms and legs into her web, no wait, that's another enchantress isn't it? Making a nest of her hair and trapping him at the centre so she can have her wicked way with him. While I am meant to be engaging in doing the same thing to Damien. Who would enjoy it. I can tell from the way he is looking at me. He has already namedropped Bukowski, Kerouac and Sartre as if they are old friends. I am not impressed. But he has a nice smile and is friendly and eager to please. Unlike me. I can feel my face has settled into a scowling thundercloud as we amble our way down Dickson Road.

TORTURE: BLACKPOOL RULES
Spades = pounds
Hearts = scratches
Clubs = corkscrews/grinds
Diamonds = nips

The scene. Moment of enchantment. A card game. Torture, Spit, Shit, Shit Head, shit, not sure of its title but it involves pain by numbers and suits: pain measured, portioned, added and administered. We are in Olga's bedroom. Acid tabs have been distributed. Jeff Buckley wails from the wax-spattered CD player. Empty wine bottles all over the floor. A couple of pizza boxes. We have made a four-point circle of bodies. A square. We are passing round a bottle of posh gin that Declan stole from his work. The gin tastes glorious; it is freezing and burning and complex and expensive; a million golden tongues licking their way down the throat and into the belly.

For reasons I do not care to explain, I like this game. Olga and I are sitting opposite one another; Declan and Damien the same. Every time I look up from my cards I look for her eyes. It is utterly automatic; there is nothing I can do about it. Occasionally her eyes are vaguely in my direction and if she catches my eye, she either ignores it entirely or occasionally takes up the challenge and stares right back at me and strange streams of ethereal and/or liquid *stuff* are exchanged between us. Eyebeams. Or so it feels to me. It is almost like violence, or sex, or maybe violent sex. Or just the exchanging of something, or a challenge. Or all of these. A river of sensation and we can't look away. Can that sensation be one-sided or does she feel that too?

–Stop it.

Olga's words interrupt one of these staring sessions.

–What?

–Whatever it is that you're doing.

Declan looks up at us from his cards and his glass of gin and lemonade.

–What's she doing?

Olga keeps staring at me. There is the hint of a smile at the edges of her lips and I realise with relief that the look contains warmth. Now that Declan is involved as an audience this can be played for a laugh, or maybe in some other way, but at least it can be played for his benefit rather than our own twisted synergy, which I think scares her.

–It's her.

Olga gestures at me while still looking at me. Still pouring from her eyes: liquid gold, chocolate, black starry beams, sex magic.

–She's – a – *p r o v o c a t e u r.*

The layers of this word – its enunciation – its heraldry – its performance – dripping from her lips, darker than honey, darker than black treacle, darker than blackest tar, this word she pronounces for me. Always reversing the roles. I can't help grinning.

–I'm not the provocateur.

–Yes you are! You are 100 per cent provocateur. You're all the more so because you don't even know you are.

We have not lost eye contact. Cats could have been leaping between our eyes. Fuck highways. Fuck autobahns. Fuck teleportation. Fuck the Tardis. It is all between these eyes. Eyebeams. A vapour of a liquid to a solid. Channels of what. Aeons and plains. Galloping where. What. The Actual. A word presents itself to me, so I say it.

–*P r o v o c a t r i c e.*

Olga is utterly lit up at this. This word lights her up. I see it, clear as night. When illuminated thus. It is all black-light between us. Can worlds spring from moments? Of course they fucking can. Worlds upon worlds upon fucking worlds.

Provocatrice two, what shall we do?

It's Olga's turn to deal. The problem is that none of us can remember the rules properly. The Queen of Hearts is the one who receives the punishments, we decide. Olga gets the Queen of Hearts. Of course she does. By some twist of I-don't-know-what, it transpires that I am the one to administer five pounds, seven grinds, three nips and four scratches. All to the back of the hand.

–Can I switch hands if it gets too sore?

–No.

Declan and Damien protest. They think this is too harsh. So we decide that she can switch if she wants. But Olga will try not to, because she is tough, or thinks she is.

Pounds first. A pound is a pound is a punch. I use the soft, fleshy part of the balled fist; the bottom of the curled palm and little finger. Pound-pound-pound-pound-pound. No problem. Olga does not flinch. Grinds will be harder. I use each knuckle and grind them over the bones of the back of her hand, hard, and she winces.

–Ah – you sadistic fucker.

Nips are no problem – they cause more pain if you pinch little bits of skin hard and fast. Last come scratches. It strikes me that everyone here – and suddenly the realisation of the significance of that term hits me – and suddenly the realisation of the significance of *that* term also hits me – the violent ACTUAL IMPACT of acquiring knowledge. Masters of Zen Buddhism in my head again. Bopping us on the head with a big stick. Owch! Oh yeah! Sorted. The path to knowledge, right there. And the sharpness of pointing. Owch again. I see your point. I am pierced by your point. Speared, in fact, by your point.

But I digress.

Seriously, though, it suddenly STRIKES me as I am BEING STRUCK that some cultures would see this as a path to wisdom. Four idiots off their face, well past everyone's bedtime, huddled over a stained pack of cards on a stained carpet in a crappy flat on Dickson Road in Blackpool.

Do you acquire knowledge when you are the striker as well? Or do you already have all the knowledge by then? Whothefuckknows. Time has sped up and suddenly there are more people here. Just like when you have been somewhere since it opened, you're working behind a bar let's say, and it goes from empty to full and you don't notice the gradation, just like that, suddenly Olga's flat is full and the game has changed to Roxanne.

ROXANNE: BLACKPOOL RULES
Police album *Outlandos d'Amor* inserted into CD player.
Gin generously sloshed into glasses.
Declan and Olga = Take a drink every time they hear 'Roxanne'
Damien and Rachel = Take a drink every time they hear 'Put on a red light'

OLGA: If you think about it, this is an extremely patriarchal song.

Of course Olga has an opinion.

DECLAN: You what? Where'd you get that from?

OLGA: Intit obvious? He wants to take her away from an honest job and keep her for himself.

DAMIEN: An honest job? I'm surprised at you, being a feminist an' all.

OLGA: You don't get it! I'm talking about workers' rights for prostitutes! That's what we should be talking about.

RACHEL: But does that mean you would be happy to be a prostitute?

OLGA: Why not? If I actually charged boys for fucking me I'd be minted right now. Everyone has the right to a safe working environment.

DECLAN: You should get down Cookson Street with your soapbox. I reckon she could start a riot, don't you think mate?

DAMIEN: She could start something, that's for sure!

OLGA: I've had enough! Enough of all of you. Ignorant arseholes! Yes even you, Rachel, pretentious fucker, you're stuck in a mire of your own making. A mire of mirrors! Fuckssake! Right that's it, I'm off! There must be parties better than this!

Olga grabs her handbag dramatically and makes for the door.

RACHEL: Pseud. Sham. Feint. The lady doth protest too much.

The room is getting steamy. A strange and swamplike creature noses through the door and we are confused until we identify it as a craiglinzdamienjenny. The craiglinzdamienjenny slithers round the periphery of the room, its long tail brushing the soft air, which is by now in patches of solid, liquid and gas, but always soft, and rippling. The craiglinzdamienjenny rests its segmented body on various surfaces and without any conscious movement in the spatial or temporal dimension we find we are straddling the arm of the sofa, leaning back into the soft curves of a Presence who is also straddling the arm of the sofa. The Presence smells of industrial cleaning fluid mixed with dark tribal rhythms – no, that ain't right – senses are all tangled – it is right – that is exactly the scent – fast dark sweet 'n' sour primal body odour. Wish we could drink this scent. Gulp and find we are already drinking it. No idea how much time has elapsed but the conversation is in full flow – disposable hysteria, blobs of ephemera, unconscious verbal experimentation. Absurdity. When the brain is presented with stimuli it cannot process along the normal channels, the natural reaction is hysterical laughter. It is a signal that the brain is shutting up shop. Beware.

We may be a lion but she is definitely a crow. She embodies the word, both noun and verb. Intelligent. Sinister. Raucous. Every now and again hot breath blasts our neck as she coughs. If we turn our head ever so slightly to face her she hams it up, hrrrraaaggghing right in your face and cackling filthily.

A voice comes from the midsection of the craiglinzdamienjenny.

–You're gonna catch summat if you sit there.

But I want it all, we say before we even think it through – hard to tell what is outside and what is inside – but sure enough we say it, turning round and addressing the flushed face behind us. To the rest of the room Olga harrumphs loudly and publicly, saying something brief and irreverent and throwaway, but we don't even pay attention to the words because the blackpools of her eyes are dancing and from them, a torrent of pure delight, surprise, amusement, and utter, utter comprehension nearly knocks us off the sofa with its strength. We are freefalling. The Irish Sea stretches out crazily in front of us: a flat blue tablecloth, far from perpendicular, waiting to receive us as we hurtle in a direction that seems more extreme than just up or down. Is this the best bit? Weightlessness. G-force. Losing ourselves completely to this gaze, this flood of feeling. We are one. One thought, one movement, one sensation.

Next time we manage to perceive outside of this feeling, the room slowly composes itself around us like this:

tapestry (ugly) stereo

rolling stones (bass) rolling stones (treble)

craig (jigging)

jenny (wide-eyed)   john (speedfreak, annoying)
bed   leanne (stoner, rolling)
declan (a rake)   Olga (performative)
linz (intimidating)   Rachel (happy)   rug (large: scratchy)
damien (asleep)

ally (beer-eyed)
chris (boyish charm)
door

We have just met Leanne (stoner, rolling). She is sitting on the rug (scratchy), in front of John (speedfreak, annoying), forming a triangle between us (happy) and Olga (performative). Leanne is an animal rights activist. We are listening to her. She's eager. We appear eager. This scene has been played out many times. A stranger at a party expounds their wisdom and we pretend to listen attentively, fizzing on the inside, nodding. But something is upsetting the pattern. *It* is upsetting the pattern. *She* is upsetting the pattern. Olga keeps hijacking our gaze. The normal flow of friendly discourse between Leanne and us has been hijacked by this ANOMALY of a person who gives us a look of such subtlety, such cunning, such derision that we know that she knows that we know that she knows what we are thinking even before we think it. The corners of her pouting lips twitch upwards almost imperceptibly, and her eyes speak to us.

OLGA'S EYES: This girl is a joke. She's a caricature. Look at her. Rolling her spliff, preaching her morals. Bet Daddy paid for her white-girl dreads. Laugh at her. Go on. You're not fooling me. I've spotted you. You're like me. I can see it in your eyes. Go on. Laugh.

Refuse the look. Avoid the gaze. But just as something that really means business is grabbing hold of our stomach and agitating each internal organ in turn until the whole lot is in serious danger of leaping out of our mouth, a hot steaming jumbled red mass, we find ourselves embarking upon an impossible three-way conversation. Our eyes, Olga's eyes, and Leanne as the poor unknowing medium. And all the while something essential is seeping away. Reality. Order. Cognition. Identity. Spatiotemporal grounding. Self. Call it what you will. We are slowly losing grasp.

LEANNE TO RACHEL: ... and y'know Big Macs?

OLGA'S EYES TO RACHEL'S EYES: You don't really want to be sitting here listening to her.

RACHEL TO LEANNE: Yeah?

RACHEL'S EYES TO OLGA'S EYES: Yes I do. Stop giving me that look. I'm interested.

LEANNE TO RACHEL: Do you *know* what goes *into* those things?

OLGA'S EYES TO RACHEL'S EYES: Stop pretending you're interested. I hate this hypocritical party chat. Bloody playground politics. Look at me. Talk to me. Who are you? I'm intrigued.

RACHEL TO LEANNE: Er –

RACHEL'S EYES TO OLGA'S EYES: Intrigued, eh? *(Bashfully)* How ... I feel ... is this feeling ... is this a ...

LEANNE TO RACHEL: *(Triumphantly)* Hooves and dicks.

OLGA'S EYES TO RACHEL'S EYES: You don't have to define it. Don't try and explain it. We're connecting. I just happen to know that you and I will soon be kissing.

RACHEL TO LEANNE: Really?

RACHEL'S EYES TO OLGA'S EYES: Really? I'm not sure ... I've never ...

LEANNE TO RACHEL: Yep. Hooves and dicks and sawdust.

OLGA'S EYES TO RACHEL'S EYES: Don't give me that. You're no more innocent than I am. We've already kissed. In our heads. Just shut your eyes. Look! We're kissing right now! We're having sex!

RACHEL TO LEANNE: That's disgusting.

RACHEL'S EYES TO OLGA'S EYES *(after closing for a second – vast internal projection into the future)*: Ohmygod so we are!

LEANNE TO RACHEL: It's morally disgusting.

OLGA'S EYES: *(Momentary creasing up of eyeholes in mirth, accompanied by silent laughter)*

RACHEL TO LEANNE: Umm ... yeah, absolutely. Morally.

RACHEL'S EYES TO OLGA'S EYES: What is it?

OLGA'S EYES TO RACHEL'S EYES: We're fast movers! I – I think we just had our first fight! And I think I was a proper bitch! I think I fucked you up Real Bad!

And that's it. We erupt into hard, ugly bubbles of laughter. Game over. Leanne looks puzzled, but we turn our back on her because it is clear that tonight is about something more important. We are covered with a sheen of sweat plus something harder: a sheen of fierce pheromones we didn't know we possessed. Nothing else matters.

–What the hell happened there? we ask, in real words, looking mainly downwards because eyespeak and mouth-speak with Olga is too much at the moment. She says nothing, only smiles at us, a real proper genuine smile, quizzical interested eyebrows and warm eyes. The eyes reach right down into our gut. Brain is loosening. Can actually feel its particles stretching themselves, reforming, scattering, rattling against the sides.

–I want to play, we say simply, looking at the carpet. Where can we play?

Wordlessly Olga grabs our hand and together we rush into the next room. Things are falling away from around us one by one: particle by particle. We collapse on a sofa which feels like a rollicking boat while Olga stands in the middle of the room, pink neckerchief twirling. Spotlights. Curtains rise. And her voice creaks and husks into motion.

–I'm going to tell a story. Are you listening? One night, in a strange, illuminated town, two – two entities came together and forged some kind of strange connection. They looked like two girls but they weren't. One was a disgrace –

She cackles filthy manic glee, hawks, coughs (germ molecules green and purple shoot out and splat the wall behind our head – the descent is gathering momentum – lines are sharpened – a new clarity – the air rushes past).

–she was a fuckin filthy harpy and she knew it. The other one –

She leans forward and in two graceful fingerflicks our hair is out and hanging round our face. Feel shy. Feel stupid. Feel suddenly naked.

–Absolutely no fuckin question here. The other one was a lion. She had a mane of many colours and her face, her face was carved out of the finest hardwood and it was the most beautiful face –

RACHEL'S EYES: No.

OLGA'S EYES: Yes.

RACHEL'S EYES: – No.

OLGA'S EYES: – Yes.

RACHEL'S EYES: No.

–YES! It was the most beautiful face in the world. It had actually been legally proven. She won the finals of the International Face Competition in …

She casts around, wild-eyed, as if looking desperately for inspiration but we don't believe the despair for a second – we *know* this is all part of the act.

–in Brussels. She had a hard time in the third heat because of some bitchface from Liverpool who had eyes made of ruby and snakeskin lips. This bitchface girl actually cried blood. Gaggles of anaemic teenage girls would follow her around sometimes, scratching her and nipping her and telling her she was fat just so she'd cry and they would Lick Her Face …

And her eyes say *Peut-être plus tard, ma petite* …

–She had a problem getting through Customs on her way to Brussels because the officials demanded to examine the expensive metal locket that hung around her perfect, swan-like throat, and it was actually full of DRUGS, but she showed them all her naked form in the searching room, which was so perfect that two happily married plain-clothes policemen and two lesbian customs officials actually broke down in tears, and while they were sobbing in each other's arms the bitchface grabbed her bags and made her escape.

Anyway … In Brussels, when everyone was getting ready, the Russian vamp-queen was applying her Chanel foundation (which was actually the powdered bones of slaughtered virgins) and the lion pushed past her and happened to toss her rainbow mane in Bitchface's bitchface and in one second flat she exploded into a million pieces because she was actually made of GLASS:

WATCH OUT FOR THE
SHARDS OF GLASS!

And spontaneously we clutch each other as fragments of

glass confetti fall all around us catch yellow

lightbeams reflect prismatically on wallpaper dirty rainbows

arch and sing I CAN SING

A RAINBOW TOO but O O O O

danger proximity eyewires tangling high

voltage sensory autobahn nerve

clusters tingling

but it's too early for that internal journey so you snap away and peel apart.

Neckerchief raised – one beat of silence – upstroke. On with the story.

–The lion was predatory without –

Our eyes call out in mild reproach, *I am not predatory!*

–The lion was definitely one-hundred-per-cent predatory without even knowing it. But the lion's face ... it could speak volumes, if it wanted to. But mainly it spoke one word.

She reaches out and scrapes our cheek ever so gently with a couple of talons.

–The word it spoke was *challenge*. The face was always getting into trouble at school for doing things it didn't mean to do. It had no sense of its own power. It was all in the mouth. Mostly it looked like the tiniest little envelope you've ever seen – it was all shut up tight 'n' solemn. But if you managed to capture this lion's attention –

And she pauses, and I think her eyes say something like, And I'm really trying, can you tell? Something strange is happening here, but to comment on it would be to kill it. So I think we just have to go on.

–If you managed to get this lion's attention, buzzers would flash and you won the star prize: a cuddly toy.

At the words 'cuddly toy', her eyes become hooded and seductive and say something we don't quite catch.

–But all this was pure shite because the real prize was the change in the lion's face. Slowly, slowly ...

And you can feel the reaction bubbling up around the corners of your mouth ...

–Slowly, slowly the tiny mouth grew, and grew, and grew ...

And your mouth is stretching s t r e t c h i n g s t r e t c h i n g . . .

–until finally it split open into the widest, scariest, best, most amazing white-teeth GRIN you've ever seen ...

Gravity is powerless against her pointing finger. She's whirling up a spell. She's a witch. Why did we not see this before? Face aches. This smile has smiled further than common decency allows. Surely our lips have cracked at the sides. A crack in the earth. Seismic activity. This smile is *indecent*. She's split open something else. Our soul, or … something.

She hides her face in her arms, a frozen tableau of mock terror, then peeps through them only to scream at the sight of us grinning like a lunatic, pout obscenely, assume her terror-mask and hide again.

–AGGGGGHHHH! The shiny shiny rainbow liongirl's GOT ME!

She begins to twirl round and round, the pink neckerchief whipping around her.

'Rainbow's black
Rainbow's black
Rainbow's back
Is black with tar'

- - - - - - - - - - - - -fasterfasterfasterfaster---------------------

'Teeth and claw,
Teeth and claw,
Lion yawns and earth splits open'

- - - - - - - - - - - - -fasterfasterfasterfaster---------------------

uneven whirling hand knocks ornament from mantelpiece, a fit of coughing takes hold and the dervish almost collapses

'Who knows where?
Who knows where?
Emphysema rears its head'

- - - - - - - - - - - - -fasterfasterfasterfaster---------------------

accelerated wheezing

'Emphysema's closing in
Emphysema's set up shop
Emphysema's bought us out
Harpy's lungs give up the ghost'

And she collapses heavily in a heap, clowning up the awkwardness of knees and elbows, slamming into the floor as if unconscious and lying motionless for a few seconds, but we are still tense with anticipation because we know she's only playing *dead lions ...*

And sure enough, she suddenly jerks upright into a sitting position, exactly as if she is being manipulated, marionette-style, by strings from above. Her face is completely empty, blank, wooden, until she catches our eye and then she falls back cawing, crowing, rooking, roaring.

Oh my GOD!!!

And still all the lions were on the prowl!

Where

Are

All

The

Lions

Coming

From?

FIN

Chapter 17

VOICE	Olga
SCENE	The Other Bedroom
HOUR	4 a.m., 16 June 1999
PLEASURE BEACH RIDE	Avalanche
SUBSTANCE	Iced water
ORGAN	Heart
SYMBOL	Interlocking hands
COLOUR	Scarlet
FORMULA	$H_2O (s) \rightarrow H_2O (l)$
ART / TECHNIC	Care
HORMONE	Melatonin
HOMERIC TITLE	Eumaeus

Ground zero: after the descent/before the ascent. The beginning and end are the same place: we shall not quibble. Eyes snap open. Roaring revving buzzing sound. Razing the brain from the inside out. Think we just heard the sound of insanity there for a second. Abyss. Paralysis. Chemical tingle. Hands are claws. This is both everything and nothing. A million times upon a time, both here and there, then and now, something must have happened. Temporally adrift but also specifically at the arse end of the twentieth century. Geographically afloat but also specifically in a grotty Northern English seaside town. The town aches with soiled sexual regret. Something unremarkable happened and will no doubt happen again. The story is like a circle. The outcome of the story is predestined. It is unashamedly universal. Universal and yet it happened.

We are both newborn and ancient. We are carved of hardwood. We are a lion. We have a large wooden bead tied into our hair that was not there before. It is too heavy for the few hairs it is attached to. It hurts. But we can't stop looking at it in the mirror. This large wooden blob attached to our head, swinging like a pendulum, thwacking us in the face if we're not careful. Mesmerising. A physical disfigurement. A grotesque sight. As we hobble to the window all the items in the room curve downwards slightly, wobbling, smirking, knowing. The horrific downward curve of inanimate objects. There is nothing at all inside our head except words, which look shocking when we try to string them together. We check ourselves in the mirror. We look old. Face won't relax. Frown won't disappear. The only thought process we can follow is a constant, infinite rebuttal:

But no –

But no –

But no –

But no –

That's not it –

No – that's not it either –

But what is 'it' anyway? Absurd word. A frog or a worm. Sudden flashback to that moment last night (last night? Really?) in West Coast Rock Café when I notice there is a girl looking at me. I think I've seen her in here before. She's drunk and swaying a bit, holding on to a bottle of beer, standing at the side of the dancefloor but dancing impatiently, awkwardly, like she wants the songs to go faster, like she wishes she was running instead. Her hair is hanging straight down over her face, straight dark blonde hair parted down the middle. She – is – w a t c h i n g me sometimes. Intently. With laser eyes that strobe through her hair. Dark and light at the same time. She is watching me but doesn't want me to know that she's watching me, which is quite funny considering how drunk she is. Keeps turning her head away if she sees me looking in her direction. Oh, I know this game. Eyes on me. I can play it really well. But never for girls before. Until now. Never wanted to, for girls. Until now. Her eyes are vivid. They have a power of their own. Lit from within. Starship strobelights. And her face, her face is stunning. No other word for it. Delicate angle of jawbone. Smooth skin. Sultry lips, sulky lips, skulking, sucking on beer. She looks a bit like a surfer mosher type: baggy T-shirt, baggy jeans. Long limbs like she hasn't grown into them yet.

Look at her T-shirt and the way it hangs from her shoulders. A huge, baggy, mansize T-shirt with a little orange skater demon. Hanging straight down off her. And no way of seeing what is underneath. Which makes us look harder. Does she have a bra on or what. She doesn't look like a bra person. She doesn't look like she has anything there. No curves. Just the T-shirt hanging down off her shoulders, which look – to die for. Such curiosity to see what is under that T-shirt. And what do I want to do with whatever is under there. Do to? Do with? Not sure. Teetering is really falling, falling is really landing. The descent starts so slowly it is imperceptible. We are about to fall deeply, heavily, painfully in love. But as usual, the time is out of joint. We're already falling. We've already fallen. We're falling/fallen/falling/fallen. We've already landed.

Is it because she is like a boy. A boy in what sense though. Doesn't feel like that. And do I want her hands on me. Like I want boys' hands on me. The normal way it goes: the desire is for the boy to touch me. Not for me to touch the boy. I'm the object. It's not feminist and it's not clever but it's a fact. Touch me, turn me on, push your dick inside me and fuck me. Easy.

But no. Not here. Not that. Something else. Not clear. A deeper and darker desire. The desire that runs underneath the normal desire. Like the sewers underneath the ground. Or the magma at the earth's core. Not spoken of. Not seen. But always moving.

If I run my hand over your chest. If I run my hand over your chest. Then I would know what it feels like. But I can't. There is a block inside me. Nothing embarrasses me. But you do, Rachel, with your weird, frustrating, sexy T-shirt that hangs off you so I can't see what your body is like. And the echoing absence of that body, its imagined softnesses and hardnesses, is what will fuel my furious fantasies later.

Use your power. Mama does it still, even though she's old. So do it. Act it up. Make it good. Everyone's drunk.

You know you can do this better than anyone in here. Ham it up. It's fun! And a perfect song to do it.

One pill makes you larger
And one pill makes you small
And the ones that Mother gives you
Don't do anything at all

This fucking song. A slice of love. Summer in sound. Insanity threatens. Feed your head. Smear it all over the sound. Spike it with acid. Trippy as fuck. Forget the girl. This fucking song. I am this fucking song.

Snap back to the here and now. There is nothing here. Nothing here but signatures of our combined ruin. A broken sink. Half of it broken clean off. How did we manage to break a sink. Oh yeah, that's right. We climbed into it. An overfilled bath with a Lush bath bomb. The Big Blue. Pieces of real seaweed, now slushy brown mush, blocking the plug hole. Rose petals strewn all over the bed. Rose thorns that had scratched pale flesh. Smaller flowers picked from someone's front garden that had adorned pubic hair in the vein of *Lady Chatterley's Lover*. And Jeff Buckley in the CD player. Bottles everywhere. The bottles send us back to last night, looking at Rachel hunched over herself, cross-legged and small on the carpet. Soaked legs of her flared jeans. Suddenly sees the scars on her arms, white and red, old and new. Gah. A flash in the heart. My mother wound. Or something. Must be. What can I do.

–Let me take you into the other room. You need to get those wet trousers off. I can lend you some trackies. Come with me.

Fuck. I may as well have scooped her up and carried her

through to the bedroom. Or is that what I am doing. That's what it feels like. But could I carry her? Could I marry her?

Why did I say that about the trousers? It's summer. It doesn't matter. But we sit on the bed and she looks at me and there's such an open flame in her look, a searchlight, a question. Everything about her a question.

–How do you do it.

–What?

–Be happy.

–It's easy. You're just ... happy. You just feel it. And then you are.

Rachel considers this. Seems to roll it around her skull a while. And then smiles a bit.

–You know, when you say it like that, so easy, I can almost see it. I can almost feel it.

–You *can* feel it. I can feel it from you. You deserve to be happy. You *are* happy. We all are. Do you know that? You deserve to be happy. Let's just kick back here for a minute, shall we?

We bustle round the bed. Housewifely, we are. It's got to that stage in the night. Mother hen in the movements. Make a fortress with pillows, and kick back. Pat the space next to us.

–Come on. I don't want to go back out there yet. It's all boys out there. Let's just take a minute.

So together we half-sit, half-lie on Rick's bed. Light a cigarette. Pass it to Rachel. We share it in silence, inhaling and exhaling slowly.

Sea is to sky as sigh is to see, See is to sigh as sky is to sea, as if seen
from above, seen from above, as if it were known that
Olga was thinking of Rachel's lips on the cigarette
when it was passed to her and
Rachel was thinking
of Olga's lips
when it
was passed
to her.
Feelings dovetailing.
Without shifting her
gaze from straight ahead,
Olga takes Rachel's hand.
Olga takes Rachel's hand.
gaze from straight ahead,
without shifting her
Feelings dovetailing.
to her.
was passed
when it
of Olga's lips
Rachel was thinking
when it was passed to her and
Olga was thinking of Rachel's lips on the cigarette
From above, seen from above, as if it were known that
Sea is to sky as sigh is to see, see is to sigh as sky is to sea, as if seen

Sea is to sky as sigh is to see, See is to sigh as sky is to sea, as if seen
rom above, seen from above, as if it were known that
lga was thinking of Rachel's lips on the cigarette
vhen it was passed to her and
achel was thinking
f Olga's lips
vhen it
vas passed
o her.
eelings dovetailing.
Vithout shifting her
aze from straight ahead,
lga takes Rachel's hand.
lga takes Rachel's hand.
aze from straight ahead,
vithout shifting her
eelings dovetailing.
o her.
vas passed
hen it
f Olga's lips
achel was thinking
hen it was passed to her and
lga was thinking of Rachel's lips on the cigarette
rom above, seen from above, as if it were known that
ea is to sky as sigh is to see, see is to sigh as sky is to sea, as if seen

–You're amazing, Rachel. I mean it. You're amazing. And beautiful. You're amazing.

–Stop it! *You're* amazing. The way you move and the way you talk and the way you do everything. Your eyes and your voice and your hair. It's so fucking sexy.

We don't look at Rachel as she says this, but we can feel Rachel's shock that this has come out of her mouth. Rachel had not expected herself to say this. But it's out there in the air now.

–*You're* the sexy one. Your skin ... it's so glowing. And your eyes ... it's like they're from another world. It's like they're powered by some alien light force.

–Alien light force?

–Yeah! Don't take the piss. I mean it! And you're so fucking smart, Rachel. I don't know how you do it. You're so fucking special.

–Isn't that a line from a Radiohead song? Right before he screams about being a creep and a weirdo?

–Fuck OFF! I'm trying to be sincere!

Rachel laughs shortly. Says nothing. But holds on to our hand tighter. Together our hands are small hot animals, slightly damp, slightly clammy. The air changes. Becomes heavier. Time changes too. Not sure time is even moving. Do we trust this. Will we remember this. It feels big and scary. Better lighten the mood. Can't handle whatever this is right now.

–Do you want a nice refreshing drink of water? I'll get us both a glass of water. I think we need it.

–That's also a line from a play – Harold Pinter – it's a sexual innuendo or something ...

But we are busy and quick in the kitchen and return almost instantly. The waitress again, with two pint glasses of water with ice and lemon.

–See, I even put lemon in them for us. Drink that. It'll taste amazing I bet!

We both take tiny sips of water, almost in sync. It does feel amazing. It tastes like liquid pearls in the throat. Frozen sherbet in the gullet. Tinkling crystal water. Liquid glass. But wait. Isn't that what water is?

Rachel laughs shortly.

–What?

–I was just thinking that the water feels like liquid glass, but then, it kind of *is* liquid glass, if glass is ice, even though I know it's not. So it just feels like what it is, but more.

–You know what I think, Rachel?

–What?

–I don't know if it's just the drugs talking, and I know I'm completely straight so it doesn't make any sense, but I think I could fall in love with you.

We say it kind of flatly and matter-of-fact, still staring straight ahead. Rachel says nothing, but turns her head.

–And it's weird because I like boys. You know I like boys. I *really* like boys. But I fancy you. And I don't know what to do about it.

Rachel still isn't saying anything. Heart is going like mad.

–Rachel! You fucker! I've just put my heart out here –

We outline a large uneven shape in the air in front of us with our hands.

–It's right here! Outside of my body! There's a CAVERN where my heart used to be! And you're sitting there in silence?

What happened then? We are back there, back in the place before the party died. We are looking at Rachel.

Rachel is wide-eyed. Serious. No smile. Eyes like floodlights. Dangerous. Knowing/unknowing. Tree branches could leap out of there. Vines. Electrical wires. Tangled up in. Time piles up to this. Will we kiss? Whatever it is between us we are saturated in it. Too much. We're in soft-focus. The air is soft. And I know her skin will be soft.

And yes – my hand goes to her face. It just does it. I can't control it.

–I just need to move that bit of hair because it's hanging there so insolently –

–Insolently?

–Aha! She speaks! The silent sad one speaks!

What happens next? A smile. A proper one. And honestly, when she smiles her whole face changes. It's a fucking powerful smile. Wide. Easy. Free. Sunlight and air. Light from within. The yawn of a lion. An adventure of a smile.

–Insolently or innocently?

–Definitely insolently.

And we touch the strand of hair that hangs slightly over Rachel's face. Move it slightly to one side. Touch her jawbone so gently. Soft-focus but all of the senses alive at the same time. Make an imperceptible movement closer. Don't go too fast. She might run away. She is not of this place. Not of this town. Not of this planet. A tiger in headlights. Eyes for headlights. A question? Asked, without words, just with eyes. I asked. She answered. So slow it almost.

Stops. I can't. In her eyes everything has already been said and done. We fucked. We fought. We conquered. But what? Is that the glimmer of a –

Smile. She knows it all, she knows it all. In the primtree of the hall.

–You insolent bastard.

–Just kiss me –

And I do and and we do. And we do.

Ground zero: after the descent/before the ascent. The beginning and the end are the same: we shall not quibble. Nothing is ever quite the same again. Everything is completely the same from this point onwards, always and forever. Eyes snap open. Roaring revving buzzing sound. Razing brain from the inside. The insanity just thought it heard the sound of us for a second there. Check self again in the mirror. A snake slithers away out of sight behind our ear, disappearing into the matted black. We shake our head slightly, irritated, for it is early evening and beverages must be imbibed, pink neckerchiefs twirled, mental scars procured, new realms discovered, no valley too deep, no mountain too high. The seafront bar calls. There is prey to be hunted.

Chapter 18

VOICE	Olga, Rachel, Treesa
SCENE	The End
HOUR	The Future, including the Past
PLEASURE BEACH RIDE	Grand National
SUBSTANCE	Amniotic fluid
ORGAN	Brain (hippocampus)
SYMBOL	Snowflake
COLOUR	Red, white
FORMULA	$t = t_{0}/\sqrt{(1-v^{2}/c^{2})}$
ART / TECHNIC	Futural multiplication
HORMONE	Oestrogen
HOMERIC TITLE	Penelope

Olga

Stately, plump –

Stately, plump Olga Adessi came from the stairhead, bearing a mirror on which four lines of unidentifiable white powder and a rolled-up tenner lay carelessly crossed. Tally: score and four and score across makes five.

Stately, plump Olga Adessi rose up from the sea, gargantuan twelve-headed purple monster of the depths.

Stately, plum, round and violet-indigo blue, Olga rolled herself carefully to the juicing room.

Stately as a home, Olga lay quiet on her deathbed.

Rachel

Activism. Alternative living. Like the story we wrote aged fourteen. The story before the story that begins 'I was born in the brown sea'. After the story that starts 'I am an agglomeration of molecules and nothing else'. The story that ends, 'And they all lived challengingly and determinedly ever after, or until the Earth burns itself out due to human negligence and selfishness and greed'. Activism. To act and to what? To act. To externalise. From insect to actor in one fell swoop. To act is to create armour. To act is to turn feeling into doing. Feeling with instead of feeling alone. To feel as part of something; to feel part of something and not alone. But. Collectivity is what we learn. What I can learn. What I will learn.

I went to a meeting. The meeting about running away and creating an alternative community. Crusties, they get called. Basically we could drop out. But that's not activism.

That's dropping out. I want to go to the heart of the fight and stay there. The stuff we can do. In it there's a yes. In me there's a no. Thinking right down to the bare bones of it. The yes and the no. What's in a word? A negation. An assumption. If we assign two childhood figures. Eeyore and Zippy. The queer yes and the queer no. The solitary black cloud and the rainbow. Olga comes from nowhere in my head, laughing, telling me I'm a pretentious fucker. She isn't the cloud or the rainbow, or maybe she's both because she shows me that we can both be either or neither. Do we need to negate to move forwards? Is the world going to end on 31 December? We're at the arse end of the millennium. Olga is standing at the front door of the job centre. She has an envelope with a form inside it that she has filled in. The form says a big NO to the story she has written for herself.

Olga's story goes:

Olga is Art and Bad. Therefore Olga will at one point refuse the fourth abortion; will carry the child; will pop out the child; will get social housing; will get help from her mum (who softens like melting butter at being a nana); will continue to be sex mad/party mad/book mad/mad mad; will be an excellent feminist role model for her little girl, who she will call Luisa, and her second little girl, who she will call Monika, and the kids will go to Revoe for primary and Palatine for secondary just like Olga did and she will take them to dance classes and gymnastics classes and athletics training all at Blackpool Sports Centre and Stanley Park because they got some sporty genes from their different and absent fathers and they will be tall and brown-eyed with long legs and all the boys will fancy them and they will fancy all the boys at first but then the eldest Luisa will suddenly cut all her hair off aged fourteen and decide that she only fancies girls and when Luisa brings home a girl from school called Hester who is so unbelievably shy she keeps a sheet of long perfectly straight blonde hair directly over her face so it is a miracle she can even see where she's going let alone explore nascent lesbian tendencies, thirty-eight-year-old Olga spies them from the front room window walking down the street holding hands and breathes in sharply as the view of the two girls is warped by some Actual Tears suddenly springing from her eyes which although rare for Olga is not altogether surprising because in those two hand-holding receding girl figures Olga cannot see anyone but Olga herself, no longer mum-tired, mum-desirous, mum-ponderous but an Olga spliced across another possible world and walking down that very same street taking those very same steps as her futureprojected daughter, holding hands not with her futureprojected daughter's first girlfriend but with Rachel Gillian Charlotte Watkins, such a pretentious fucker, needed to be taken down a peg or two; pretentious fucker Rachel with lionface and lionhair; booksmart Rachel who never had to worry about money; fragile and dangerous Rachel who contained such violence but could never even realise that was why she bashed her head and her knuckles against walls and subjected her own heart to a deliberate and daily bruising and cracking; Rachel trapped in the syrupy webs of her own stupid clever head, Rachel who went off as soon as she could in search of cities, culture, education, horizon-broadening, things bigger and things richer than this town can hold.

But we digress. Look, there they are:

Olga and Rachel,

and holding sticky summer hands together Olga and Rachel walk away, receding into the Topping Street of the past; darkhair and blondehair; spectacle and theory; young and wan and yang and yin and yin and yang; delirious with hangovers and sleeplessness and lovehatelovehatelove; halfsparring as Rachel spouts one half of a half-baked theory and Olga retorts by spouting the other half of the half-baked theory and together they bake full theories like loaves; firebrands with fireloaves sleeping in baskets in hearts that could blast into fragrant floury fruition at any moment. They say 'You and I could take over the world' because they are aware that together they are the queer yes and the queer no, but the fact that it is never clear exactly who is the yes and who is the no is the thing that creates the magic.

Rachel and Olga live happily ever after, of course, which means for one summer, of course, and the living happily ever after appears to be dependent upon the fact that the frequency with which they say to one another 'You and I could take over the world' decreases in inverse proportion to their increasing age (nineteen years and three months to nineteen years and four months in Olga's case and nineteen years and eleven months to twenty years and zero months in Rachel's case) and in direct proportion to the likeliness of them actually taking over the world. Olga and Rachel know from the beginning that they cannot be together forever – *forever? forever? forever ever?* – those repeated lines from the Outkast song, which is then played everyfucking-where the following year (the grey and newboned millennium from which grey and newboned millennial youths will hatch and spawn and spring and multiply *like snowflakes*) haunt their subsequent breakup from the non-named l.o.v.e. affair of the foreverness of one summer, as the times in which Rachel and Olga take to the clubs and ingest whatever nasty white powder they can procure from the usual sources masquerading as cocaine or MDMA and they dance like wildcats, stalk their way through afterparties in flats and garages and sheds and gardens feeling like they are creating mythology there and then but also knowing that there is no difference between creating mythology and just living your fucking life, but then when everydayness seeps back in Olga retreats to Safe Mode which involves chasing and obtaining and shagging boys and turning her back on Rachel who does not have Safe Mode and instead grows a sizeable ball of heartaching resentment which lodges itself inside her next to the sizeable ball of world-weary cynicism and the ball of undigested chewing gum until one day the ball inside Rachel that is Rachel erupts (as much as Rachel ever erupts, which is Very Little) and asks Olga what she actually wants, to which Olga replies that she wants boys, and that is the way it will always be, an utterance that in fact provokes the opposite reactions in the teller and the telt as might be expected in that Rachel is liberated and Olga is enchained.

But we digress. Look:

is standing there holding the form that says a big NO to story one and faces story two, in which Olga Adessi, wild and wayward, plump and pockmarked, maligned and misunderstood, applies for sixth-form college again, retakes her A-Levels, gets straight As, is awarded a full scholarship to study Politics with History at Liverpool University but becomes instantly disillusioned with the manifestations of class division amongst the first-year students as well as finding the Americanised 'freshers' mentality with its posters and its fairs and its societies and its desperate virginal eighteen-year-old boys chugging beer through plastic funnels all extremely nauseating, so drops out after the first term and comes back to Blackpool and moves back in with her mum for a bit, working as a receptionist at CONNECT, which is a centre providing a range of services around family planning and support for teenage mums, where she sometimes sees Treesa, who occasionally helps out there now that Lulu has started school. Sex mad/party mad/book mad/mad mad Olga continues to smoke like a bastard and her already raspy vocal cords drop a few quartertones lower; Rachel stops cutting herself regularly after someone points out to her that it hurts the people around her more than it hurts her, which she has not really considered before.

But we digress. We're at the arse end of the millennium.

Rachel

sees a doctor, who tells her she needs to run like a bastard to keep the evil depression at bay. Outraged at such an oversimplification of the problem Rachel nevertheless gives it a go and sometimes it helps. So now Rachel sits perched on a wall. Perched between one thing and another. Rachel who when writes the self hates the self. Rachel holds hands with Olga whom she could psychoanalyse as the big Other as the one she cannot access as the tool she uses to mutilate herself but Rachel then sometimes learns to see Olga as an Actual Person rather than an Evil Muse, which feels like a big step.

Olga, an actual person

Olga misunderstood. Olga bullied. Olga weird accented weird haired weird brained undiagnosed weird kid. Olga smart. Olga at some point was fucked up, fucked up, was fucked up, fucked up again, was fucked up again. Olga learned wiles. Olga at heart a very straightforward soul desiring marriage and kids and a big loving family. Olga fiercely aware of injustices and reading newspapers. Olga who thinks big but not small. Olga a real revolutionary. Olga gives in the envelope and enrols to resit her A-Levels but does not turn up for the exams because she starts taking a lot of acid which takes her on 48-hour trips and the rest of the world is cancelled and nullified, and when the world returns she is tired and needs to rest. Someone tells her that each time you take acid you go a little further down a road and there is no turning back on that road;

no retracing your steps. But – and she stops, and pulls at a strand of hair, and tied into the hair is a shell, not from the beaches round here but perhaps from a European shore somewhere, and she thinks that each time she feels herself going further down that road she will tie a shell in her hair and it will ground her at that particular point in the road so she doesn't float off altogether. Olga puts on her Jefferson Airplane album. *Remember. What the dormouse said. Feed your head.* Olga wants to fuck up the idea that that road, the acid road, the road we go down and from which we cannot return, is the wrong road. What if it's the right road? And she also finds the concept of irreversibility a strange one. If she were a fictional character in a novel, let's say, then the author hypothetically has the power to reverse time and take her back a few steps on that road. In fact Olga never set foot down that road. The road never existed. Metaphorical roads are not to be trusted or given the weight of material existence. Material existence is not where it's at. Olga had a breakdown aged twenty-five and found God. After finding God, Olga thanked Him that she never went too far down the metaphorical road of deliberate brainbefuddling.
She still has her wits about her.

In the Future,

the sea levels have risen to such an extent that the Piers are completely submerged. The top of the Tower is still visible. Olga's great-great-great-great-granddaughter can be seen, rowing boldly from one floating shack to another. Each of the floating shacks visible is replicating some aspect of Blackpool's nightlife or shopping centre using the floating bits from large dismantled structures. When the Sandcastle's glass building and plastic tubular slides were all variously repurposed, one roaring success had been to chop the tubes into slices about half a metre long and then pile ten of them on top of one another in a pyramid formation and secure them with rope. These variously coloured triangles worked well as cheap and colourful shopfronts for miscellaneous supplies, with clear plastic-covered products stacked up in each circular space and the seller sitting in the cushioned ring of another short slide of the tube upended on the water the other way, attached to the pyramid shopfront with another rope. We look around and we hear birdsong: not the usual crying of the gulls, though of course that can be heard – the birds were here long before we were and will be here long after we have gone – but also the song of tree birds pumped through a speaker, coming from a floating shop somewhere fifty metres across the water. Look, there is a car driving-swimming over there, and look, there are some dogs swimming over there. Someone has made a floating shack and painted a sign on the side that says AID STATION. There is music coming from a tinny radio and there are drinks for sale: bottles of Fanta, Coke, water and beer. Fanta capitalises on its former sponsorship of the Tower by proudly displaying an image of the half-submerged Tower on the front of its labels. There are plastic lei flowers decorating every surface. Jerry, who currently runs the Aid Station, is similarly clad in a Hawaiian shirt. His skin is brown and very wrinkled, and no one has ever seen him without sunglasses. Jerry also runs the FLOATING PARTY BUS, where people can visit at night. But the Water Police only allow these parties once a month because of the sound pollution and its effect on the surrounding floating neighbourhood. Sound carries an unbelievable distance over water. Taxi boats still come and visit from higher inland spots, towns still intact, not yet climatically affected. There is a Wild West feeling to the floating world, which is obviously immediately commodified, but with a more globalised palette. This is evident in the signs adorning the shacks selling fast food for the waterways, such as Buffalo Bill's Smokin' Ribs, Irie Vegan Jerk Boathouse and Ahoy! Bubble Sea Tea. The drinking spots also do a roaring trade in the summer months: the 90s Retro Boat Bar is one of the most popular and long-standing and now sells its own merchandise, such as Global Hypercolor bucket hats and special swimming 'beer goggles' with a holder for your beer and a straw, so you can swim and sip simultaneously. The underwater visits to the Sunken Palace Nightclub are exciting and spooky: the Art Deco squares of the club's original frontispiece lie broken at the bottom of the seabed, and Sheryl and Paul lead scuba tours with a retro trance soundtrack pumped through headphones, and punters can stand in their weighted neon-flashing diving suits and dance on the different concrete levels. Several dance moves have become popular when wearing the full scuba-diving kit: the 'seabed shuffle' is a complicated kind of flossing developed from the dance craze of the 2010s. The tourism industry is still booming.

Treesa

The older I get, the older the age of the people I relate to. By the time I'm forty I'll have to go and hang out in the nursing homes. I have lived more life, more lives, than other people my age. What's the point in regretting, what's the point in wishing things were different, wishing I hadn't had Lulu, that Lulu didn't exist? What's the point? We only get a certain amount of energy in this life, and it's needed for other things. Other fights. Choose your battles. Liam has a dream to work for the council, in the parks and gardens. He doesn't want to stay stuck in the kitchen, chucking dried oregano over everything, microwaving pasta ribbons in beige sauce in plastic boxes, shoving pizzas in and out of ovens. He doesn't want to forever carry that kitchen smell around with him, in his clothes, in his hair, in his skin. He wants to be outside. He wants to look after the trees. He's got a dream of being a tree surgeon. He went and looked it up in the library, what he would need to study to get there. To see Liam get to the stage of being able to say that he wants that, to hear him say it, is magic. Things don't stay the same. Things change. One day I will visit Liam in Stanley Park and when his work mates are off in the van he will snip off a rose and give it to me. We learned romance the wrong way round. We did the kid first. But at the moment we are learning it, and it's not perfect, but there are moments when it kind of works.

And what do I want? I want to get to a stage where I know what I want. The problem is I don't know what I want. I know what Lulu needs, so I do it and it stops there. But did I ever know what I wanted? Yes, I wanted to go to the Olympics and represent Great Britain on the beam. I was fuckin ace on the beam. But it's not gonna happen. So I need to work out what's next.

Going back to that moment on the beach, with Olga and Rachel, the feeling that I was feeling what they were feeling, only I was only watching, and then the panic of thinking that I should forget the feeling, delete it, never think about it, and then later in the bar when I ran away, ran home, found Liam, kissed Liam, knew that feeling wasn't there with Liam, the feeling that I felt just from seeing what I saw. And maybe feelings like that only happen on the beach at sunset when everything looks romantic and sexy and magic and maybe if I had seen it happen in the fruit and veg section of Tesco's then everything would be different. How can you find something amazing and disgusting at the same time. How is that possible. Why did I run away?

Going back to that other moment. September 1996. The biggest moment of my life. The moment of my life where I was the biggest, and then the moment of my life where I had to be the biggest. Biggest strength, biggest soul. I was not human in that moment. Pure animal being. In the amniotic fluid inside me, this little child creature swims around, glides around, apparently wants to get out. I am the sea. The sea inside.

I am going to give birth to this fucking thing if it kills me. I am going to turn myself inside out if I have to. Past the point of caring about tearing myself in two. I am going to do this. There is no choice. Either I do this or I die. I refused drugs. Liam takes drugs. I do not take drugs. Not even ones to stop me feeling the pain of another human being tearing itself out of me. It is not pain like breaking a leg or cutting your finger or even not landing properly on the beam and bashing all the tender parts of your body. It is pain that makes me feel like I am going to pass out or lose myself. I am not really in my body. I am somewhere over there, a fly on the wall, watching myself.

She's been here since the beginning. Mrs Wilson. In the waiting room, sitting with Carol from CAMHS with her beige mac and Thora Hird glasses and dangly parrot earrings. For some reason it helps to know that Mrs Wilson's there, in her pinafore dress and demin jacket and soft permed hair. There's something I can learn from her, I just don't know what it is yet. She really cares. On this day, the weirdest day of my life by a million miles, when a whole new little *person* is coming out of me, Mrs Wilson and Carol from CAMHS have taken time out of their days to come to the Vic and sit in the waiting room while Dad paces around smoking outside, Mum sits in the corner and Liam holds my hand. Think about flipping on the beam. What is it that stops you from landing on your head. Nothing but pure magic. I am learning. I can push through all of it because the only thing I am pushing through is myself. It is okay to need to feel pain. I am alive. I am going to live.

All of us

Intimacy. Although we wouldn't say that word yet, because it's older than us. And yet we are older than we are. And every time we write of intimacy we write as a we. Best collected in moments. Stubbled leg: razed field of burnt black sticks. Each stick has a thickness, it could be a leg itself, or the blackened stump of a felled tree. And the sounds, inside this moment right here now. The tiny sound of a solitary chewing gum chew, inside a dry mouth, inside a silence. The jaw begins to get tired. The gum forgets that it's there. And when we kiss we sometimes hear the gum, collecting any drops of moisture it can find, working against our jaws, our jaws still working. Kissing with gum. Kissing as floating. Only the slightest touch is possible. Softest slightest touch. Skin becomes membrane. Touching as osmosis, floating inside layers to become. Never have I ever. What rough magick. I sigh and become thespian. Belt and breeches. Whose hose are these. I think I know. Heart bursts and melts, a million glass needles shivering down your back. The temperature zooms up and down. Are we gnomes in a cave or inside the world of pure imagination. Cowls upon our backs. Imagined as exoskeletons. Imagining evolution on fast-forward. Or rewind. Accelerevolving. These things return. The shape you always see. The key to everything. It's the curlicue carved into the top of the wooden bannister in the house from your childhood, which then transforms into a kind of whorl which is also an ear which is of course also a shell. And a treble clef. Cochlearical. And it is the deepest most intimate thing, connected to birth, death, fertility, engendering, vertiginous exposure reminding you that one second is enough to show that one second is enough. A cycle, a whorl, awhirl, awave, awash, adrift, for sure, forsooth. Lyrical not lyrical. It comes in waves. Everything.

Afterword

SOME POINTS FOR REFERENCE

There are some familiarities to be found between the structure of *Pleasure Beach* and two rather daunting canonical works of literature: Homer's *Odyssey* (set in mythological ancient Greece) and James Joyce's *Ulysses* (set in Dublin, 1904) – especially in the order and themes of the chapters. It is important to assert, however, that *Pleasure Beach* can be enjoyed without any knowledge of nor reference to these older texts at all. Nevertheless, the following explanations could be useful and/or enjoyable for readers, to give a sense of continuity with the worlds of the other two texts.

What follows are some brief notes explaining a few of the connections and inspirations within these chapters, particularly where the content or style overlaps with something from *Ulysses* or the *Odyssey*. *Pleasure Beach* is its own story first and foremost, but in terms of structure, theme and myth, these figures and forms are there to be found. In addition to this, I provide a brief explanation of the formulae that are listed in the schema for each chapter, and their relation to the story.

Chapter 1

Telemachus is the son of Odysseus, the great adventurer from Homer's *Odyssey*. Telemachus waits at home for his absent father to return. This is depicted in Joyce's *Ulysses* as the young man Stephen Dedalus, who has left his father's house after the death of his mother. In Chapter 1 of *Pleasure Beach* we meet all three main characters, beginning with

Olga, who is the one who resonates the most with Telemachus. Olga's father has also abandoned her, although we do not learn this until later in the novel, when she daydreams about her Italian papa living a stereotypical Italian life, even though she has no knowledge of Italy or Italian people to base this on apart from what she has seen on the TV: in total, the Dolmio advert and season one of *The Sopranos*. The mathematical formula for this chapter is $P = 3a$, which calculates the perimeter of an equilateral triangle. This represents the journey of the chapter, with the three points of the triangle as the three characters: Olga, Rachel and Treesa.

Chapter 2

Calypso is the witch who keeps Odysseus imprisoned on her island for seven years. In Joyce's *Ulysses*, this is the episode (episode 4) where we are introduced to the other main character, Leopold Bloom, who is making breakfast in bed and running errands for his wife, Molly, who is having an affair, which Bloom also secretly knows about. Calypso is, perhaps, reincarnated in *Pleasure Beach* as the customer Carlotta, who comes into the chippy at 10:36 and is served a Cinzano and lemonade by Olga. Carlotta is a benign figure with a mysterious past. The spirit of Calypso also manifests within Olga, who demonstrates within this chapter that she has the power of stopping time, psychonautical journeying and creating filmscapes and soundtracks in her head. The chemical formula is C_2H_5OH, ethanol, to represent the alcohol in Olga's bloodstream.

Chapter 3

Proteus is the god of the sea in Homer's *Odyssey*. Like the water that he embodies, Proteus is a shapeshifter. In *Ulysses* the reader witnesses the troubled young intellectual Stephen striding along the beach while considering a huge range of questions to do with sensory perception, the nature of vision, of knowing, of experience, of life and death. This action of internal journeying through thought is precisely what we see the equally troubled young intellectual Rachel doing in Chapter 3 of *Pleasure Beach*. While Stephen is walking along the beach, Rachel is stationary, hiding out in her bedroom and trying to piece together her brain after the events of the night before. The shapeshifting is no less present, though, as she considers some of the concepts that she learned at university before she ran away. It is the concepts themselves that are shifting, and through her confused and altered mindset Rachel also considers the nature of knowing, of thinking, and of philosophical and theoretical concepts, all of which lead her straight back to her new obsession with Olga. The chemical formulae are vWF and GP1b alpha, the Von Willebrand factor and the composition of platelets in the blood, denoting the process of coagulation or blood clotting.

Chapter 4

Hades is the land of the dead in Greek mythology. Odysseus travels to Hades in order to speak to Tiresias, the blind prophet, to learn about his fate. In *Ulysses* the theme of death is also explicit in this episode as we observe

Leopold Bloom attending the funeral of his friend Paddy Dignam. In Chapter 4 of *Pleasure Beach*, Olga visits her friend Terry Tiresia (Cash Converters employee by day, drag queen by night) to ask her advice about what happened with Rachel. Terry shares several similar qualities with Tiresias in addition to a name. Tiresias is also a gendershifter, having been turned into a woman as a punishment and then turned back into a man again. The blindness of Tiresias manifests in Terry only as a specific kind of blue–yellow colour blindness called tritanopia. According to some disputed sources, in the *Odyssey* the colour blue is never mentioned throughout the entire text, leading to my own playful speculation that Homer also suffered from this blue-blindness. The chemical formula here is also related to the colour blue, as it is $C_{37}H_{34}N_2Na_2O_9S_3$, or brilliant blue FCF, a synthetic blue colour.

Chapter 5

Aeolus is the 'keeper of the winds' in Homer's *Odyssey*, and he gives Odysseus a bag containing strong winds to help him on his way home. The 'winds' are interpreted in Joyce's *Ulysses* as the hot breath of journalistic communication, and Joyce's Aeolus episode is full of newspaper headlines and the language of advertisements (Leopold Bloom's profession). Chapter 5 of *Pleasure Beach* mimics the format of newspaper headlines, and the subtitles are imagined headlines as Olga daydreams of stardom throughout her journey on the number 14 bus to Blackpool Sixth Form College, where she has an appointment at 2 p.m. At this point in the twentieth century, mobile phones were just being introduced into some people's lives, but the texting function was rudimentary. The chapter provides a brief snapshot of the state of telecommunications at this place and time. Olga walks along the Mowbray Drive industrial estate, home to local station Radio Wave, the local paper the *Evening Gazette* and the digital signage manufacturer Scanlite. Olga uses her phone to text Rachel, and the pixelated winged envelope of the text message is the symbol for this chapter. The chemical formula $C_{18}H_{19}N$ is 4-Cyano-4'-pentylbiphenyl, a liquid crystal used for digital displays.

Chapter 6

Scylla and Charybdis are two sea monsters who guard a passage of water that Odysseus must get past in the *Odyssey*. In the corresponding episode of Joyce's *Ulysses*, Stephen Dedalus is giving a lecture at Dublin's National Library in which he sets out his theories about Shakespeare and his play *Hamlet* in particular. The 'monsters' he navigates are more conceptual ones, and have been interpreted by some as various oppositional forces within philosophy. In *Pleasure Beach* the 'monsters' are less scary and dangerous; they are two of Olga's former teachers, whom she meets when she goes back to Blackpool Sixth Form College to get advice about putting her play on the stage. Stephen and Olga both desire literary recognition for their talent but do not receive it, perhaps for reasons more linked to their social background. The ratio 3:2 sums up this chapter because it is related to Mr Thornton's discussion of the music of the spheres, which comes from the ancient musical-mathematical theory of Pythagoras. The ratio 3:2 is the 'pure' perfect fifth in Pythagorean musical theory.

Chapter 7

Nestor in Homer's *Odyssey* is a wise old man whom Telemachus visits on the search for his father. In Joyce's *Ulysses* the Nestor section is episode 2, whereas in *Pleasure Beach* it comes at Chapter 7. Stephen Dedalus is teaching during this episode and encounters the unsavoury Mr Deasy, who gives him his meagre salary. In *Pleasure Beach* this chapter takes place at the Sandcastle Waterpark and is the first one to take place from the perspective of Treesa. Treesa, her daughter Lulu and her mum Lou are at the Sandcastle with its assorted pools and slides. They encounter a different figure associated with Treesa's schooldays, the secretary Mrs Wilson. Mrs Wilson is a much more kindly and sympathetic figure than Stephen's Mr Deasy, and we learn how Mrs Wilson had supported Treesa when she discovered she was pregnant while still at school. The chapter is entirely set within and amongst the pools and slides of Sandcastle Waterpark and is flavoured by the chemical HClO, hypochlorous acid, which forms when chlorine dissolves in water.

Chapter 8

Lestrygonians are the cannibalistic giants who appear in Book 10 of Homer's *Odyssey*. The theme of eating and consumption is at the centre of the Lestrygonians episode in Joyce's *Ulysses*, where it is lunchtime and Leopold Bloom goes to Davy Byrne's pub for a cheese sandwich and a glass of red wine. Consumption in various forms also frames this chapter in *Pleasure Beach* – not just of food but also alcohol, drugs and music. Rachel discusses her bulimic episodes, Olga gets doughnuts from the pier, and later Rachel recalls her experience in the two different rooms of the Heaven & Hell nightclub, fuelled by two different substances that she consumes and the associated music: alcohol in Heaven, where they play pop and R&B, and ecstasy in Hell, where they play hard trance and techno. The chemical substance in this chapter is 3α,7α,12α-trihydroxy-5β-cholan-24-oic acid, which is cholic acid, a primary bile acid found in the stomach.

Chapter 9

Lotus-Eaters in Homer's *Odyssey* are a race of people found on an island by Odysseus and his crew. The crew spend their days eating lotus flowers, which clearly produce a kind of soporific or psychoactive effect because Odysseus' men lose the desire to go home or even to move at all. Conversely, this episode in Joyce's *Ulysses* charts Leopold Bloom as he is constantly on the move: running errands, visiting a church, putting money on a horse. Conversely again, *Pleasure Beach* returns to experiences of intoxication and psychedelia as we go on a journey through the Alice's Wonderland fairground ride and witness fragments of Rachel and Olga's conversations from the early hours of the morning. The chemical compound flavouring this chapter is $C_{20}H_{25}N_3O$, lysergic acid diethylamide, or LSD.

Chapter 10

Wandering Rocks are a group of rocks in the sea featured in Homer's *Odyssey*, through which it was notoriously difficult to cross safely, just as with the monsters Scylla and Charybdis. In this episode of *Ulysses* there are eighteen complex and interweaving subsections matching the eighteen episodes of the novel overall, introducing multiple micronarratives and fragmentary characters. To a certain degree this also takes place in *Pleasure Beach*, although there are not exactly eighteen sections. The sections dated 16 June 1999 are interspersed with paragraphs of notes depicting the history of the North West of England, from prehistoric times up to the end of the twentieth century. The chapter becomes more fragmented towards the end, with miscellaneous sections giving a variety of perspectives and voices to the town. The formula is C_3S (Ca_3SiO_5), which is the formula for cement, from which concrete forms the town as it is perceived in modern times.

Chapter 11

Sirens in Greek mythology are bird-women whose hypnotic voices could lure sailors off their course and to their deaths. In Homer's *Odyssey*, Odysseus manages to escape the Sirens by tying himself to the mast of his ship so he cannot react to their song, and by plugging all the ears of his crew with wax. In Joyce's *Ulysses* the entire Sirens episode performs and enacts not just music but sound in general, stretching and bending the language so that the sound leads the movement of the narrative, rather than plot, character or action. In the Sirens chapter of *Pleasure Beach* we also see Rachel considering both music and sound, especially the sounds of words, but she also considers timbre and her own continually frustrated attempts to perceive synaesthetically (a phenomenon whereby stimulation of one sense, for example hearing, causes a certain perception in another, for example colour). Rachel does not have synaesthesia, but Olga may well do. The 'AHA' moment shows Rachel believing (falsely) that she has actually constructed a synaesthetic connection in her head. The words 'Claritas is quidditas' refer to a moment of 'epiphany' that Joyce describes in *A Portrait of the Artist as a Young Man* when the young artist finds radiant beauty in the soul of the commonest object. This idea is also discussed and jokingly referred to by Rachel as 'epiffanny' in Chapter 3. The equation for this chapter is $vw = f\lambda$, which expresses the relationship between the speed of sound, its frequency and its wavelength.

Chapter 12

Cyclops or Polyphemos is a giant who eats some of Odysseus' men and who is then blinded as punishment. In Joyce's *Ulysses* the Cyclops is reincarnated as the Citizen, a bigoted man whom Bloom encounters in the pub and who insults him with antisemitic slurs. In *Pleasure Beach*, Olga also faces an adversary, in the figure of her arch enemy Nikki Rawlings, who has had it in for her since schooldays. It is not clear why Nikki hates Olga so much, but it is suggested that it is something to do with the fact that Olga is a bit different, with her multinational parentage (her mum is Polish and her absent dad is Italian) and her obsession with reading Shakespeare on the school bus. Olga might also have mocked Nikki's eyes at some point during school (the blindness of the Cyclops is translated into nystagmus, the condition that Nikki suffers from, which manifests in an involuntary shaking of the eyes). Olga could very possibly also have had sex with one of Nikki's many boyfriends when they were both still at school, although this is not directly referred to in the novel. The chapter splinters into many different fragments of text, just as the glass of Nikki's drink shatters into shards when it hits the floor after she has thrown her vodka and Coke in Olga's face. The formula is H_3PO_4, phosphoric acid, which is the acid contained in Coca-Cola.

Chapter 13

Nausicaa is a young nymph in Homer's *Odyssey* who encounters a naked Odysseus and helps him to find his way home via her mother, Arete, and her father, Alcinous, to whom he recounts the story of his adventures so far. In *Ulysses* this episode introduces the character of young Gerty MacDowell, who sits on the beach and daydreams sentimentally about romance while simultaneously being aware of Bloom watching her from afar and masturbating. In this chapter in *Pleasure Beach*, Olga and Rachel are both recounting some fragments of their meeting earlier that day, while Treesa also recounts observing Olga and Rachel on the beach, getting closer and eventually kissing, and she notices momentarily and with surprise that this sight turns her on. The mathematical formula for this chapter is A = $\sqrt{3}/4\ (a^2)$, which calculates the area of an equilateral triangle. Rather than the distance between the three points of the characters as in Chapter 1's perimeter formula, this chapter focuses on the area of the triangle: the space between the three characters as they are now all together.

Chapter 14

Ithaca is the homeland of Odysseus, which he finally reaches in the last books of the *Odyssey*. In Joyce's *Ulysses*, Bloom and Dedalus are walking together towards Bloom's home, where Bloom will offer Dedalus, who is drunk, a bed for the night. This episode is written in the style of a catechism or interrogation, entirely in the format of questions and answers, sometimes to the point of a deliberately absurd or annoying compulsiveness. The Q&A format is also present in this chapter of *Pleasure Beach*, the difference being that towards the end Olga begins to respond to the questions a bit, showing some reluctance and even resentment towards the questions posed by the nonspecific questioner. The mathematical formulae for this chapter are $x(t) = (2+\cos(3t))\cos(2t)$, $y = (2+\cos(3t))\sin(2t)$, $z = -\sin(3t)$ for $t\in[-\pi,\pi]$, formulae used to calculate the figure of the trefoil knot depicted at the end of the chapter and expressing the interrelations between Olga, Rachel and Treesa.

Chapter 15

The Oxen of the Sun in Homer's *Odyssey* are sacred animals on the island of Thrinacia, symbols of fertility that Odysseus and his crew are instructed by the gods not to harm. In Joyce's *Ulysses* the episode takes place in the maternity ward of a hospital while a friend of Bloom's gives birth, and Joyce parodies the 'gestation' of the English language in 32 chapters in chronological order of the developing English language. In *Pleasure Beach* a similar journey is undertaken, with one significant difference: the voices inhabited in this chapter of *Pleasure Beach* are female, whereas all the voices of Joyce's chapter are male. The 'journey' taken is understood here literally as the journey taken by the tram that runs along Blackpool Promenade, from Starr Gate in Blackpool's South Shore up the coast to Fleetwood Ferry. The mathematical formula for this chapter is $Ax^2 + Bxy + Cy^2 + Dx + Ey + F = 0$, which is a formula for calculating conic sections. This is a reference to the ancient Greek mathematician and philosopher Hypatia, who was famous for developing these geometrical theorems and discusses them in this chapter with the aid of an ice cream cone.

Chapter 16

Circe is an enchantress in Homer's *Odyssey* who puts Odysseus under a spell so that he is trapped on her island, and who then turns his men into pigs. In *Ulysses* the episode takes place in the red-light district of Dublin, where Bloom and the drunken Stephen are wandering. The narrative in this very long section goes through many different voices, characters, fantasies and transformations, sexual and otherwise. In *Pleasure Beach* this chapter recalls several scenes from the early hours of the morning, which are some of the hours that Olga and Rachel have been trying to remember. We witness Olga and Rachel playing Torture (a card game) with two boys they have met; we see them having a kind of telepathic conversation through their eyes while tripping; we watch them entering fantasy worlds together. Reality is the thing being transformed, as we are led to the point where Olga abandons Rachel and thus the reason for her shame at the beginning of the novel. The formula for this chapter is $E = PF/R$, a simple calculation for a sorceress: energy/effect of the spell = (power used × focus) divided by resistance.

Chapter 17

Eumaeus is a swineherd in Homer's *Odyssey* who has remained faithful to Odysseus while he was away and when others were attacking his home. He is the first person whom Odysseus visits when he arrives back in Ithaca. In *Ulysses* we watch while the drunken Stephen is taken by Bloom to a cabman's shelter for a coffee and a bun, where they encounter an old sailor and his stories. In *Pleasure Beach* this chapter recalls more scenes from the blurry early hours of the morning and also from the night before, such as the moment when Olga sees Rachel for the first time, and later when Rachel and Olga kiss for the first time. The chemical formula is $H_2O\ (s) \rightarrow H_2O\ (l)$, the simplest way of showing the process of ice melting into water.

Chapter 18

Penelope is the wife of Odysseus, who suffers and waits for him at home while he is away on his epic voyage and while many suitors are invading her home. In this final episode of Joyce's *Ulysses* we hear the voice of Bloom's wife, Molly, in the form of a long, unpunctuated stream of consciousness, flitting between memory and the present. In the final chapter of *Pleasure Beach* the voices are multiple and sometimes intertwined, and we switch between the voices of Olga, Rachel, Treesa and various combinations of these, as the narrative considers the multiple, potential, unsettled futures of each character beyond the constraints of the twenty-four hours of the novel. The formula is $t = t_0/\sqrt{(1-v^2/c^2)}$, a formula for calculating time dilation.

There are many people in many places whom I would like to thank for their inspiration and encouragement during the long gestation of this book.

In Vienna: Birgit Pestal, for cochlearical & more: thank you :). Cris Argüelles, who suggested I contact Prototype: thank you so much! I am also very grateful to the crew of friends who came along to early readings and patiently listened to a Northern English accent, and to everyone at Vienna's amazing Shakespeare & Company Booksellers for their generosity in hosting readings.

In London: thank you to the wonderful humans at Prototype, particularly Jess Chandler and Aimee Selby. I'm grateful for such an insightful and nourishing editing process. For encouragement with early writings and readings, thank you to colleagues and friends Éadaoin Agnew, Matthew Birchwood, Fred Botting, Tina Chanter, Felicity Colman, Martin Dines, Jenny Kuper, Patricia Phillippy, Stella Sandford, Selene Scarsi and Isabella van Elferen. Discussions about the KLF and ley lines with the one and only Charlie Blake inspired the mythical trippy beginning to Chapter 9. My brother Neil Palmer suggested the title of *Pleasure Beach* when I was still unsure about what to call this project – ta chuck!

In Blackpool and the North West: my pal from younger days, Rick Thompson, helped me out by suggesting more up-to-date Blackpool-related info, dating from after I left the area in 2002. Rick also suggested that I consult Blackpool historian Nick Moore's wonderfully thorough *History of Blackpool*, an impressive resource that gave me the details I needed to build the historical notes in Chapter 10. Sam Skinner and Nathan Jones for inviting me to their 2017 event at Blackpool's Grundy Art Gallery, where I was able to do a reading in Blackpool for the first time.

Thank you to my parents, Pat and Chris, for all their encouragement and enthusiasm throughout this project.

Thanks to Edinburgh University Press for permitting a reprint of the poem 'Hymn to Sol', which also appears at the end of my book *Queer Defamiliarisation: Writing, Mattering, Making Strange* (2020).

Big fun and big love to the all the party people in Blackpool, Glasgow and beyond: you know who you are, and without you I could not have written this book.

And finally, this book is dedicated to one of the kindest humans Blackpool has ever seen: piano teacher and all-round extravagance extraordinaire Howard Morgan, who didn't get to see this book finished, but knew that it was being written, and was actually there in 1955 watching Marlene Dietrich at the Opera House and told me the story of how she lost an earring on the Big Dipper.

( ) (   ) p   prototype

poetry / prose / interdisciplinary projects / anthologies

Creating new possibilities in the publishing of fiction and poetry through a flexible, interdisciplinary approach and the production of unique and beautiful books.

Prototype is an independent publisher working across genres and disciplines, committed to discovering and sharing work that exists outside the mainstream.

Each publication is unique in its form and presentation, and the aesthetic of each object is considered critical to its production.

Prototype strives to increase audiences for experimental writing, as the home for writers and artists whose work requires a creative vision not offered by mainstream literary publishers.

In its current, evolving form, Prototype consists of 4 strands of publications:

(type 1 – poetry)
(type 2 – prose)
(type 3 – interdisciplinary projects)
(type 4 – anthologies) including an annual anthology of new work, *PROTOTYPE*.

Forthcoming

(type 2 – prose)
Book of Mutter by Kate Zambreno (2025)
Appendix Project by Kate Zambreno (2025)
Fair by Jen Calleja (2025)
Happiness by Yuri Felsen, trans. Bryan Karetnyk (2025)

Back Catalogue

(type 1 – poetry)
Plainspeak by Astrid Alben (2019)
Safe Metamorphosis by Otis Mensah (2020)
Republic Of Dogs/Republic Of Birds by Stephen Watts (2016/2020)
Home by Emily Critchley (2021)
Away From Me by Caleb Klaces (2021)
Path Through Wood by Sam Buchan-Watts (2021)
Two Twin Pipes Sprout Water by Lila Matsumoto (2021)
Deltas by Leonie Rushforth (2022)
Island mountain glacier by Anne Vegter, trans. Astrid Alben (2022)
Little Dead Rabbit by Astrid Alben (2022)
Emblem by Lucy Mercer (2022)
A History by Dan Burt (2022)
Journeys Across Breath by Stephen Watts (2022)
Artifice by Lavinia Singer (2023)
Incubation: a space for monsters by Bhanu Kapil (2023)
Virgula by Sasja Janssen, trans. Michele Hutchison (2024)

(type 2 – prose)
Fatherhood by Caleb Klaces (2019)
I'm Afraid That's All We've Got Time For by Jen Calleja (2020)
The Boiled in Between by Helen Marten (2020)
Along the River Run by Paul Buck (2020)
Lorem Ipsum by Oli Hazzard (2021)
The Weak Spot by Lucie Elven (2021)
Deceit by Yuri Felsen, trans. Bryan Karetnyk (2022)
Our Last Year by Alan Rossi (2022)
Vehicle by Jen Calleja (2023)
Lori & Joe by Amy Arnold (2023)

The Earth is Falling by Carmen Pellegrino, trans. Shaun Whiteside (2024)
Prairie, Dresses, Art, Other by Danielle Dutton (2024)
The Seers by Sulaiman Addonia (2024)

(type 3 – interdisciplinary projects)
alphabet poem: for kids! by Emily Critchley, Michael Kindellan & Alison Honey Woods (2020)
The sea is spread and cleaved and furled by Ahren Warner (2020)
Songs for Ireland by Robert Herbert McClean (2020)
microbursts by Elizabeth Reeder & Amanda Thomson (2021)
Monochords by Yannis Ritsos (trans. Paul Merchant), with Chiara Ambrosio (2023)
Sorcerer by Ed Atkins & Steven Zultanski (2024)

(type 4 – anthologies)
Try To Be Better ed. Sam Buchan-Watts & Lavinia Singer (2019)
PROTOTYPE 1 (2019)
PROTOTYPE 2 (2020)
Intertitles: An anthology at the intersection of writing & visual art ed. Jess Chandler, Aimee Selby, Hana Noorali & Lynton Talbot (2021)
PROTOTYPE 3 (2021)
PROTOTYPE 4 (2022)
Strangers Within: Documentary as Encounter ed. Therese Hennigsen & Juliette Joffé (2022)
PROTOTYPE 5 (2023)
Seven Rooms ed. Dominic J. Jaeckle & Jess Chandler (2023)

(House Sparrow Press)
A Sparrow's Journey: John Berger reads Andrey Platonov (2016)
Infinite Gradation by Anne Michaels (2017)
Doorways: Women, Homelessness, Trauma and Resistance, ed. Bekki Perriman (2019)
Dialogue with a Somnambulist: Stories, Essays & a Portrait Gallery by Chloe Aridjis (2021)
Through the Billboard Promised Land Without Ever Stopping by Derek Jarman (2022)

Pleasure Beach by Helen Palmer
Published by Prototype in 2023

(third printing)

 A CIP record for this book is available from the British Library.

Design by Matthew Stuart & Andrew Walsh-Lister
(Traven T. Croves)
Typeset in Marist by Seb McLauchlan and guest typefaces Akzidenz-Grotesk, Helvetica Neue, John Baskerville, Garamond Premier Pro, Sign Painter and Times New Roman
Printed in the UK by TJ Books

ISBN 978-1-913513-44-3

(type 2 – prose)
www.prototypepublishing.co.uk
@prototypepubs

prototype publishing
71 oriel road
london e9 5sg
uk

LOTTERY FUNDED
Supported using public funding by
ARTS COUNCIL ENGLAND

( )